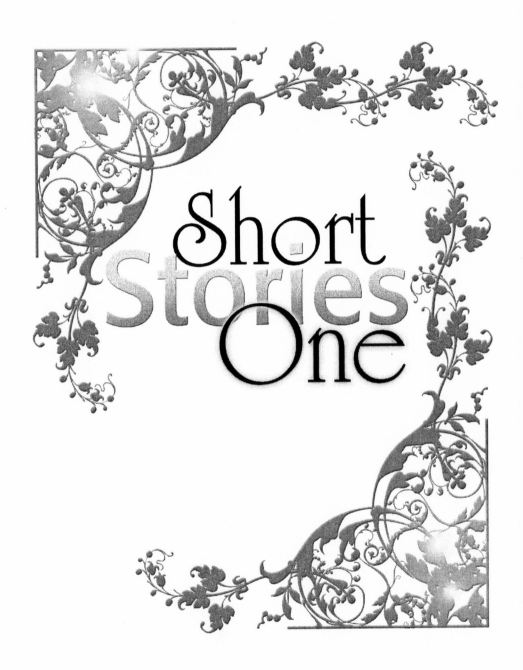

# Short Stories One

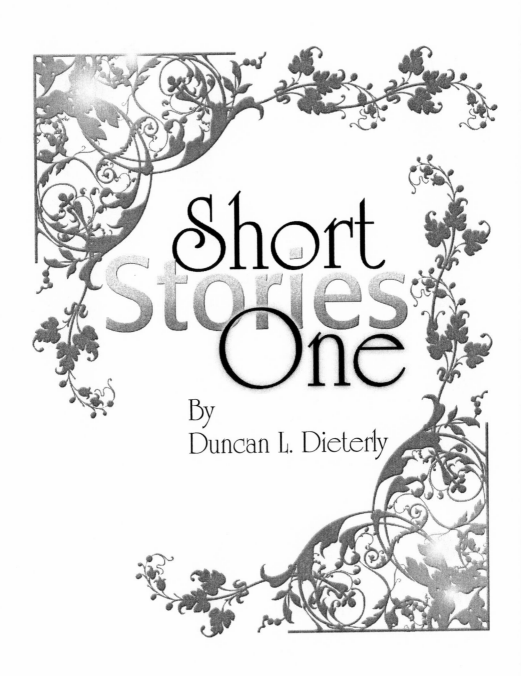

# Short Stories One

By
Duncan L. Dieterly

**To order additional copies of this book, contact:**
Xlibris Corporation
1-888-795-4274
www.Xlibris.com
Orders@Xlibris.com
43580

# Contents

# The Flame

The sharp toe of a shiny black shoe sliced into the snoring man's neck.

"You scumbag bastard!" a voice from on high vomited venomously. Startled from his stupor, the man uncoiled from his comfortable fetal position, rolling away from the stabbing pain. He tried to get up but blundered into the hovering arms of the rosebush under which he had fallen asleep. In its embrace, pins of pain shot through his hand, neck, and cheek. He shrieked, "Oh oh shit! Goddamnit!" He rapidly rolled back again. Trying to get away from the pain, he lurched backward to rip free from its thorny embrace. The relentless shiny black shoe toe caught him in the lower back and then the side. The furious, flaying man was wildly kicking out at him with his foot and raging obscenities at him.

"You fucking son of a bitch!"

The victim managed to stagger to his feet. Chunks of his coat were ripped away by the roses' clutching thorns. He slipped on the freshly sprinkler-dampened-and-drenched grass, falling painfully to one knee. He scrambled away from the incessant pendulum leg whose foot kept hammering and striking, swinging and striking at him.

Cold water smacked him hard in the side of his unshaven face. It knifed into his eye. He cried out in pain.

"Christ – what the hell!" Grabbing his face, he crawled and hopped away from the stream of icy water. It hit him in the ass and poured down his back and legs. He stumbled away from the flood of angry water, words, and waves of fear. Half falling, rolling, and staggering down the sloping green hill, he landed on his butt in the wide clean gutter.

Lurching to his feet, he ran. He ran away from the fading wave of verbal vindictiveness. He rounded a hedge and grabbed at it for support, clutching and wrenching handfuls of green leaves. He fell to both his knees, gasping for breath.

"UH – Uh oh – OHH!" His hands let the leaves fall to the ground. He didn't have the energy to run anymore. He was gulping loudly for air desperately attempting to regain his breath.

Sitting upright, his hands surveyed and rubbed his aching eye. It was throbbing. He straightened the many layers of filthy clothing, picked off the broken clinging rosebush branches, and tried to lick the blood off his hands. He wiped his neck and chin with the end of one of his many shirts. Pale red bloodstains emerged among the other rich stains of life to mix and blend. He looked down at his lucky red alligator shoes. They were both still tied with greasy twine. He shined them by rubbing them against his pants leg, first his right foot, then his left. Satisfied with himself, he smiled. He knew that the shoes, which he found last week, would bring him luck. He just knew it!

Shading his eyes with both hands, he looked at the rising sun. Guessing it must be about seven thirty in the morning, he shakily stood. He attempted to smooth his multilayered clothes, repeatedly patting the torn spots as flat as possible and thinking, *I really didn't remember leaving a wake-up call.* His sense of humor was awakened and he smiled to himself. He limped merrily on his way, heading for the "church." With a little luck, he could get there in time to help serve. His effort would earn extra pancakes for his breakfast.

The angry man watched the staggering scraggly rag pile escape around the bush. His wrath was becoming cold and cruel.

*That bum was in my yard! That bum running down my street,* he thought. He returned to his house wall and turned off the hose. He dropped the hose on the ground, without even thinking about which one of his employees would pick it up for him, and wind it neatly onto its heavy metal holder. He stomped toward his three-car garage, flicking the automatic door opener he had taken from his pocket. He walked briskly into the opening cavern. Once inside, he removed his jacket and hung it in the backseat of his car.

Slamming the heavy door shut, he noticed water drops on his freshly polished Italian loafers. He rubbed each shoe behind the calf of his leg to bring back the warm deep shine, first his right foot, then his left foot.

Settling himself in his groove in the luxurious large Mercedes-Benz, he started the car. Tramping on the gas pedal, he sped backward out of the garage. Hooking to his left, he half turned the car. Shifting into drive, he accelerated down the long driveway and hung a wheel squealing left. The silver car streaked on its way.

"Call the mayor!" he bellowed. The automatic car cell phone dialed the mayor's office. He picked up the receiver and was holding it to his ear as he turned onto the freeway entrance ramp.

By the time he hit the first traffic jam, a voice stated, "His Honor the mayor's office. How may I help you?"

"I want Cleveland, NOW!"

"Of course, Mr. Franklin, I will tell His Honor you are calling." Her syrupy voice was designed to soothe like a cheap cough medicine.

There was a brief pause and a very warm voice said, "Hi, Martin! What are you doing up so early?"

"Can the PR crap. Do you know what was on my lawn this morning?"

"Nooo, I'm sorry, I don't. Your paper?" A weak thrust of humor.

"A goddamn vagrant! In the middle of my prized roses! I thought you had agreed to do something. Take care of the homeless riffraff that have invaded our town!"

"Well, yes, but these things take time," the mayor mildly parried.

"Time? Hell, let's kick ass. Is there a council meeting today?"

"Yes, but we aren't scheduled to get into the homeless issue."

"Issue? Hell, I want an ordinance. And I want it now! I will have Clark of my law department deliver the necessary papers to you at lunch. You take it from there."

"We should go slowly on this issue. There are many people who sympathize with the plight of the homeless."

"Sympathy, sympath-shee. Let them sleep at their houses then, but I want them off my lawn. You got that!"

"Well, yes, I can understand your concern." Reluctantly, he continues, "I will get the ball rolling."

"That's better. See you at the club tomorrow."

He hung up. Then he demanded the phone to connect him to his executive assistant. She wouldn't be at work yet, but he could leave a message on her phone mail. The phone rang three times, then the canned message said sweetly, "This is Marline Airs, Mr. Franklin's executive assistant. I am not here right now. Please leave a message at the tone."

He impatiently waited for the phone to quit prattling and, at the tone, snapped, "Get Clark in law! I want a draft of an ordinance banning homeless vagrants from our city limits. He is to deliver it the mayor's office by noon today. Contact Sally Crothers, the council member; Bob Hughs, the chief of police; and Jimmy Brand, the city manager. Tell them I expect their support on the ordinance, today!" He hung up, smiling as he pulled off the freeway heading for his private parking garage.

Later, Jake silently slipped through the back door of the "church." Jake stood swaying for a few moments while his eyes adjusted to the darkness of the windowless back room. He idly stroked his dirty hair using his stained, knotted fingers as a comb. He straightened his clothes and pulled at his crotch, adjusting his underwear. Inching toward the half-opened inner door to the kitchen, he peeked inside. The pulse of human sound surged in from the large room. Sticking his head around the door, he blinked and spotted Harvey. Harvey was talking loudly with Frank. Harvey's hands waved and moved with the rhythm of his speech. The man in the red shoes slid up to Harvey's elbow. Harvey stopped in midsentence, turning to confront Jake, "Jake!" he cried. "Where you been? Get an apron on! Get cooking, man! The doors will be open in ten minutes, and we are shorthanded today, very shorthanded."

Jake grinned, grabbed a graying apron off the rack, and tied it on. He immediately went to his station. He smartly busied himself pouring the mixed batter on the preheated griddle.

*Hiss!* cried the mixture as it started to cook.

Jake was now a man with a mission. He was making pancakes. He could flip them onto a plate on the old table to his left side with his left hand as he poured out the golden spots of pancake batter with his right. Using a small grimy clock hanging above the stove as his guide, he waited exactly three minutes to flip them on their back sides. After another two minutes, he flipped them from the griddle and started pouring again. He could cook up twenty-eight pancakes in five minutes.

He could keep up that pace for hours if someone brought him fresh batter. He therefore produced 336 cakes an hour. That was enough for approximately 112 people.

On a good day, he would keep ahead of the crowd, shoving into the small storefront kitchen for the needy. This was a good day, but there was no one to bring him the batter. He took almost eight minutes to mix it himself. He usually spilled generous portions on his clothes.

Today, he worked hard. His face was glistening with perspiration, and for several minutes in the middle of the rush, he almost lost his tempo. He was feeling dizzy from hunger. He managed to get through it, and when all were served and the door locked shut, he sat down to eat his big stack of pancakes. He hunched over his plate and shoveled the food into his gaping mouth with his fork in his right hand. His left arm and hand circled the plate, protecting it from any surprise attacks. As he ate, the phone rang. Harvey got on the line. Jake finished his breakfast and listened to Harvey's conversation while he pretended to be busy cleaning his red shoes with a paper napkin.

Harvey was upset and asking rapid-fire questions. "Why? Who started all this? That son of a bitch! Well, sure it's important, but I will have to close down tonight then! Yeah, I guess you are right. It is better to close one night and not permanently. Do you think we can stop it? Well, sure, you know it is silly. I will be there at six, and when they bring up the homeless ordinance, I will be ready to fight all night. You know, Ted Baker did a lot of legal research on this for us last year. I still don't see how they can move so fast. It usually takes them a couple of months to schedule a meeting, much less introduce and pass an ordinance. Yeah, Bret, thanks. See you tonight."

He slammed the phone down and sat there for a minute. His shoulders started to droop. He sighed deeply three times then quickly regrouped his spirits. He stood up and turned to the three people in the back and yelled, "Let's get this mess cleaned up and get ready for tomorrow."

Three voices sang out in unison, "What about dinner?"

Harvey wearily shook his head and told them, "Some big shot righteous citizen is up in arms because some drifter pissed on his roses or something. He is having an ordinance presented tonight at the city council meeting to make it a criminal offense to be homeless. It will never pass, but I have to be there to speak on your behalf, so there will be no dinner served tonight."

Their faces fell so, low he hurried to add, "But tomorrow, we will have an extra big breakfast. Ah, with some bacon even."

This cheered them up, but tomorrow morning was a long way off. It took them a while to clean up the dishes and the griddle. When the kitchen looked good, he shooed them out and locked up the shelter. Grabbing his hat, he left through the back door and headed for his home.

Jake was full and happy. The rest of the day flew by for Jake. He spent most of the morning on a sunny street corner panhandling. When he had gathered $12.62, he lost interest, drifting off to other more interesting things. He stole some damaged fruit from behind the grocery store for his lunch. He bummed a ride to the park from a nice old man in a beat-up truck. He spent the afternoon playing cards with a couple of people. The deck was missing a few cards, but they managed to work it out. He was even able to locate some extra newspaper in the trash can to ward off the late-afternoon chill. The sky clouded up and got darker in the late afternoon. The wind started to blow, swirling the trash and debris about the streets.

*It is going to be cold tonight*, he thought. *Yes, real cold*. He thought of the shelter, which was always warm, but remembered it was going to be closed. He quickly tried to remember where he might find a cozy corner but realized he would be on the outside tonight. He went into McDonald's and bought a large cup of coffee and four burgers for dinner. He slipped several dozen blue sugar packets into his coat pocket and emptied four into his steaming mug of coffee. He lingered in McDonald's to keep warm and watched all the people eat and talk as long as he could. He really liked to watch the kids jump around in the balls. He often dreamed that, one day, he could do that and just jump and fall and jump again – he just knew that would be great fun.

He noticed that the manager, a short red-faced Mexican, was eyeing him closely. He knew he had no rights, so he slyly slipped out the side door. He was able to snatch a handful of cold fries from a deserted tray as he passed on his way out. He jammed the greasy treasure in his breast shirt pocket for later.

The wind was now crying mournfully through the trees. He cut up an alley, pulling his layers of clothes closer to him. He slipped down a side street and located the overpass on the main road to the park. He looked over his shoulder as he climbed the low guardrail then slid down the hill. Barely keeping his footing, he stopped at the bottom of the ravine. There was no water, just lots of trash. He moved slowly up the ravine, toward the North he believed, searching for useful objects. It was steep and difficult going. *People toss so much stuff down here*, he thought. If it had been brighter, he would search for some of the better stuff to sell to the thrift stores in town. He had to stop and rest several times. It was now dark; the moon was shrouded by clouds.

The wind whistled across the top of the ravine, not reaching the bottom. For that, he was grateful. He tried to find some boxes or wooden crates, but there was nothing to be had. He finally stopped at a small flat area. It had been carved out by others' numbed fingers and packed down by their homeless back sides. He sat down and tried to keep warm. It was cold. He constantly rearranged his clothes and the newspaper layers to get the maximum of warmth. He lay on his side and pressed against the side of the ravine. It was cold. It is hard to sleep when you are cold. But thinking of the bright side, it was harder when you were wet too. He was at least dry. He had several layers of clothes and newspapers wrapped around his body.

And best of all, he had on his lucky red shoes. He was busy trying to condense his body into the smallest possible size when he realized he needed some heat. He unwound his body and started to search the ravine for sticks. He had to feel blindly about in the dark; but he gathered some sticks, a few pieces of paper, and some dry grass. He guessed it was about nine thirty. It was a long time until dawn. He piled his small fuel supply on the lip of the ledge, away from the wind. It was now poking its icy fingers down into the ravine. Fishing in his pockets, he located more fuel – some greasy napkins, some pencil stubs, and a few pieces of cloth he used for a handkerchief.

*Boy, he wished Harvey hadn't closed the shelter's kitchen tonight.* He was always warm and cozy at the "church." He wasn't supposed to stay there at night. But he hid in the closet until everyone left and turned out the lights. Then he would come out and sleep on one of the tables. He was sure Harvey knew about this, but neither one said anything about it.

Jake knew better than to ask, and Harvey was too polite to accuse him. His numb fingers finally located a matchstick. He carefully struck it against a rock. He set some bits of twine on fire. He added some scraps of paper and then the pencil stubs. The fire was the size of large cigarette lighter flame. He bent close to it and warmed his hands, nose, and checks. It felt wonderful! He slowly built it higher to the size of a Coke cup. He was running out of fuel.

"Jesus!" he cried as he frantically searched his pockets. He sacrificed a precious layer of newspapers. He tore it up and fed small bits of it into the hungry flame. The heat increased. The insatiable flame demanded more fuel. He ran his hands along the rough ground and rocks. He found a small broken board and several large tree roots, which he pulled up frantically. He broke his kindling into small fragments, cutting his hands in several places. He fed the flame.

It gave the warmth of life, but it wanted more fuel to keep up the heat. He foraged farther from the dwindling flame and then rushed back to feed it when he found something. He had used most of the fuel he could locate in a radius of ten feet. When he left the flame, the cold returned. He was only warm if he found fuel. He started to move up the ravine in search of more fuel. A gust of cold wind rushed past him and scattered his precious fire off the ledge onto the ravine floor.

As he turned and watched, the hungry flame found its own fuel. It started to writhe higher and dance seductively. He laughed and rushed back to the flame. It was knee high now. He wasn't sure as to what to do now. He wished to stay warm. He kicked at the ground around the flames to encircle it and tame its searing tongues. The ground was rocky and unyielding. He fell to his knees and tried to scrape a trench around the fire. His cold fingers clawed wildly. He had no tools. As he scratched at the earth, the tongues licked higher in search of fuel. They found an overhanging bush limb.

He fell exhausted on his side and rolled away from the searching flames. The flames clawed quickly up the embankment and into the trees and surrounding bushes. He jumped up. Things were happening too fast for him. There was heat! Smoke! Exploding sap crackled. The fire was not just warm but hot – very, very hot. Gripped by fear now – running, staggering, and falling – he tried to scamper up the side of the ravine. His hands found tree roots, rocks, and bushes. He frantically dragged and pushed, twisting and jerking to get away from the fire's cries and the increasing heat. He pulled himself out of the ravine and crouched on all fours on the dark edge.

Panting and sucking the cool air, he gasped, "Uuho, uuho, uuho!" He slowly regained his breath. The flames were flashing higher. Their searing fingers were searching for him. They wanted to hug him in a wonderful warmth. The stark moon had broken free and high. The wind was strong and cold. The fire was climbing wildly toward him. The flames' arms were outstretched offering to embrace him. He stood up quickly and ran. He ran across the finely pedicured backyard lawns, ran from the fire's crackling siren song. Ran, ran – lungs bursting and eyes popping – ran for safety.

The police found him later that hour skulking around in an alley. They were laughing about their desk-sergeant foolishness as they approached him. They didn't bother to read him his rights or tell him what he was charged with. They didn't even speak to him, just motioned at him. They all knew the routine. They continued to chat and motioned him to turn around. They cuffed him and pointed him toward the police car parked at the head of the alley. He walked ahead of them. When they arrived, the smaller officer opened the back door. The taller, gingerly guiding his head, placed him inside the warm police cruiser. Jake sat motionless. His head was down, and his hands were clutched uncomfortably behind him. He smiled softly to himself as the policeman climbed in front and continued to talk, "Let's bag the vag and take our break."

"Sure, this cold makes me hungry. We can stop at Sara's and have some conversation with our doughnuts."

"Sure, conversation. Are you still trying to poke that broad?"

There was no reply. He knew it would be for vag, and he knew they would sentence him to thirty days. This made him shiver with the anticipation of a warm cell. Thirty days during the coldest month.

*What luck!* he thought. *Thirty days with three meals a day. Thirty days with my other homeless friends.* He looked down at his lucky red shoes and clicked the heels together three times. Life was good. The police cruiser moved slowly. The radio crackled.

"We got trouble. Fire in the Carson ravine. Firemen on-site calling for crowd control. Get civilians and looky-loues out of area. Get moving!"

They hit the siren, accelerating as it shrieked its warning. They reached the intersection in seconds, swung the cruiser to block it, and jumped out. Waves of flames were just past the road. People trudging and struggling with strange dark objects were intent on escape. People carrying their possessions were on the road. The policeman blowing shrieking whistles directed and hurried the people away from the barricaded fire area. The fire trucks were up farther, and you could see the arcs of water crashing down on the ravine and two houses that were smoldering. Jake was watching all the activity from inside the warm cruiser.

A silver Mercedes-Benz pulled up, braking sharply to avoid hitting a fleeing family. A well-dressed man got out. He approached the two policemen, talking at them excitedly. He wanted to go past the rope into the fire area. He talked faster and louder. He was waving his arms. He threatened them with clenched fists. Jake twisted around and cracked the window with his cuffed hands. He caught the following, "You must let me by! You don't understand! I live in that big house. That's my home! I have to save it! I live there. I must get to my house! Damn it! Do you know who I am?"

The blank-faced policeman held him at bay with blocking gestures. He was gently forced back toward his car. The tongues of flames were leaping higher. Their eerie glow cast strange shadows on the people and the man's polished car. Jake rolled the window down farther to listen and watch. The man was screaming profanities and shaking his fists at the policemen but fell back quickly when they raised their menacing black clubs. The red of the fire flickered above the nightsticks and made them look like burning clubs. As the man slammed the door to his large car closed in frustration, he shouted through his open window, "Goddamnit! The major will hear about this! That's my property!" Then, dazed by the situation, he pleaded plaintively, "Where can I go?"

One of the perspiring policemen hissed lowly, "Go sleep with the mayor, you asshole."

The large silver car squealed away through the smoke, back toward the heart of town. The policeman, working hard, moved the barricade back in time to let him pass. They scrambled out of the way of the car. The roar of a collapsing home signaled the success of the advancing fire. More fire engines were approaching, clogging the road with banshee sirens shrieking. Jake had rolled the window closed and was warm and comfortable. He was enjoying the show.

## The End

# Where the West Wind Blows

Jo-Jo opened his eyes. He pulled the tattered blanket that covered his head down very slowly below his cold nose. He blinked and peeked out at his world. He could see the deep, scarred, and darkened bottom of the table above his head. The surrounding black was gone. There now were grays and shadows. It was another day. He looked out from under the table, pushing out on the ragged sheet that covered the table and created his sleeping boundaries to see the familiar. There was the cold, stained sink, the sagging stove, and the groaning refrigerator. He crawled off his small naked, dirty mattress. His ragged blanket folded, he put it in the center of the mattress. He put his stuffed monkey on top. He removed the sheet on the table and did the same with it, carefully covering his monkey. It was cold. He had on two pairs of paints, two pairs of underwear, three shirts, and lots of different colored socks. He was still cold! His skin was 'goose bumpily' and bluish.

His mother's bedroom door was closed. He tiptoed around the room, looking in the box of a few clean clothes and then in the huge pile of dirty clothes in the corner for something else to put on. Both baskets were empty of little boy clothes. He went to the refrigerator. With the back of his hands, he rubbed his eyes open. He then opened the door in anticipation and saw the bleak light blink on. **Several cans of beer were there and an old bowl of something half covered with foil that had changed to a deep brownish purple, no milk and eggs, nothing else.**

He shrugged his narrow shoulders sadly. Pulling the chair over to the sink, he climbed up. Standing on tiptoes, he was able to reach the cabinet above the sink. He opened it wide and saw a couple of cans of corn and his box of Coco Pops. He pulled it down and poured it into a bowl he dredged up from the variety of dirty ones filling the sink. He rubbed it clean with his hand before filling it. Even though he emptied the entire box of cereal, the bowl was only a quarter full. He added some water from the tap. Sitting down at the table, he ate his breakfast with a plastic spoon he picked out of the sink. Hopeful, he looked into the kitchen table drawer for a stray packet of restaurant sugar. It was empty.

He silently stared at his mom's door as he crunched down his Coco Pops. His thoughts wandered outward toward the future, toward this day.

*What should I do?* he thought. His mother was asleep. She would not get up till dinner. They no longer had a TV or a radio. He shrugged his little shoulders and figured he would do his usual "chores." His chores consisted of making the rounds of all his friends and then coming home to have dinner with his mom.

The small empty apartment was bleak and lonely. He rummaged around in a large pile of ragged newspapers in the corner. He discovered his shoes. He slipped them on and tied the left one. When he tried to tie the right one, the worn shoestring broke with a tiny snap. He licked his fingers and made a point with the remaining stub of shoestring. Carefully, he pushed it through the eye. He made a small tight knot on the side of the shoe. He looked down to admire his work and went to the sink. Climbing up on the chair again, he filled a jar with some water. He swallowed the water and rubbed his teeth with an old sink rag. He was ready now. He went to his mother's door and listened for a noise but heard none. He went to the apartment door and unlocked the four bolts and went outside, pulling the door closed behind him with a snap.

The hall was dark and dank with strange, fearful smells. He carefully picked his way through the trash down two flights of rickety stairs and went to Mrs. Martin's door. He knocked boldly. There was no answer. He knocked again. He waited, staring at the peeling white paint, the peeling yellow paint, and the peeling brown paint – all subsequent layers on the old door. Finally, he pushed hard at the door, and it swung open with a slight cry. The room was dark, but the TV was crackling and flashing. The garish screen was dancing with light dots.

He went in carefully and shut the door as his eyes became adjusted to the dark. He saw Mrs. Martin. She was sprawled on the couch, snoring slightly. Her cup of coffee had fallen from her hand, dropped to the floor, spilling its contents on the tired yellow carpet. The liquid stain was there, but the liquid was long gone into the recesses of the old building.

Mrs. Martin always drank a lot of coffee. Her coffee came from a flat bottle, and she drank it cold.

She always said, "No sense in heating it up. Just wastes electricity."

Jo-Jo's grandmother used to make coffee, but hers was always steaming hot and had a wonderful smell to it. Sometimes, when it was really cold, she gave Jo-Jo a sip. It was bitter, but it sure made his tummy warm and toasty. Jo-Jo liked Mrs. Martin since she usually always fell asleep in the morning after her coffee. Jo-Jo could then change the TV station to the cartoons and sit and watch them all morning. That is just what he did. He found an old blanket in the corner and pulled it directly in front of the TV. He turned on the cartoons and turned the sound down low. The upper part of the picture was streaked with lines, but most of the action happens in the bottom anyway.

The apartment was empty and silent except for the humming voices of the cartoon characters. About eleven, when the news suddenly came on, Jo-Jo awoke. He had fallen asleep on the blanket. He stretched and scratched his armpit. He got up. Mrs. Martin was still fast asleep. He went over to the stove and saw several empty coffee bottles. He searched her cupboard for food but only found a package of crackers, a can of tomato paste, and some macaroni in a torn bag. He put the crackers in his pocket and visited her refrigerator. Hers was as empty as his. There was some jelly, a half-eaten yogurt, and two shriveled hot dogs. He opened the jelly and pushed his finger into the jar. He was able to scrape up three big fingers and then one small finger of jelly, which he sucked into his mouth with great relish. He put the empty jelly jar back. He closed the refrigerator door. He then left the apartment, saying in a low voice, "Goodbye, Mrs. Martin."

When he got on the street, the wind was blowing up from the waterfront. He pulled his over sized shirts down to his knees moving up the street toward the alley. There were people asleep in the doorways. Chunks of paper were floating on the wind. Cars were moving, crawling slowly in the street followed by large clouds of smoke pushed out of the exhaust pipes. Jo-Jo wished it was summer again. He wished his grandmother still came to take care of him. He slipped up the alley and behind the tenement building.

There was a low rumble of voices as he approached the cardboard box town that had sprung up behind the house. His grandmother had warned him to stay away from "box town," but she was no longer around, and it was too tempting for a seven-year-old boy to avoid. There were several people standing under the telephone pole arguing about something. He easily slipped by them unnoticed. Their loud voices faded, but their anger continued as he moved away. He headed for the largest box in the middle of the others. Here is where his friend Mr. Sneedy lived.

Mr. Sneedy was the founder and mayor of "box town." Everyone liked and respected him. Now on this day, he had gone out early to "pick up" some stuff. Mr. Sneedy was always "picking up stuff" and bringing it back to his cardboard home. The box was covered with a frazzled rug that hung down to the ground on two sides. When you walked behind the rug, you entered an enchanted land. Mr. Sneedy collected everything he could "pick up." He rejected no item that had a use.

Jo-Jo peered into this amazing castle. His eyes scanned all the familiar objects and judiciously noted Mr. Sneedy's new stuff. Jo-Jo let the rug fall behind him and entered the warm box. He sat down on a green pillow and picked up a broken coffeepot to play with while he waited. He snapped the lid on the pot several times and thought how nice it would be to go to the park. He liked Mr. Sneedy best of all because he always had some candy hidden among his many layers of clothes.

Mr. Sneedy would tell him wonderful stories about the ocean. Mr. Sneedy had been a captain of a huge ocean liner a long time ago. Jo-Jo liked to close his eyes and fall asleep in the corner of the box while Mr. Sneedy told him sea stories. Mr. Sneedy never seemed to mind him sleeping there. He usually woke up in time to hear the end of the story. All Mr. Sneedy's stories had very happy endings with a party, fun, and lots of delicious food for everyone to eat.

Mr. Sneedy helped Jo-Jo understand things. He also protected Jo-Jo when children chased him to steal his pennies, books, or clothes. Mr.

Sneedy knew everything, and he even gave Jo-Jo a broken watch and his one-eyed stuffed monkey. The stuffed monkey had no other features. Jo-Jo called the monkey Ringo. Jo-Jo kept him safe in his blankets on the old mattress at home. Jo-Jo would tell Ringo sea stories at night like Mr. Sneedy until Ringo fell asleep.

Jo-Jo fell asleep, his little body sliding off the pillow down to the hard, cold pavement. He dreamed of the time his grandmother had taken him to a place she called the park. He had been able to play on the swings and go up and down on a teeter-totter. He even was able to dig in the sand with a stick. The park smelled of grass and sand. He saw animals in the trees at the park. He liked the park. He had fallen asleep on the bus going to the park and also coming home. So he could not find the park without his grandmother. He once tried and ended getting lost. Two boys in some gang "found him" and took his book bag and old baseball hat before chasing him down the street.

He awoke when something crashed against the box. Mr. Sneedy's small voice rose in anger.

"Get out of here, you varmint!" His cane crashed down on the rat that was scurrying along the front edge of the box. Jo-Jo peaked out in time to see him scoop up the dead rat with his cane tip and toss it disgustedly toward the wall.

Mr. Sneedy turned and said after a long cough ending in a laugh, "Hello, Jo-Jo. Long time no see, me hearty." Mr. Sneedy always said that to all the people he met. Jo-Jo smiled back and, pulling at his shirt, held up the package of crackers. Mr. Sneedy thanked him, and rummaging in his massive array of clothing, he pulled out and handed him a half stick of gum.

Jo-Jo gratefully popped it in his mouth and chewed vigorously. It was sweet and tasty. Mr. Sneedy bent down and entered the box, and they both sat down. Mr. Sneedy leaned from one side to the other, unburdening himself of stuff. Mr. Sneedy wore about a thousand assorted items of clothing: paints, shirts, jackets, and jumpsuits. He waddled around in this attire to the amusement of all those people he encountered during his travels far and wide. He was able to store many things among the variety of folds, tucks, pockets, and layers. After a trip, he would sit down and begin to unload.

He would reach in and under or over, and with much effort, out would emerge one of the many things he had picked up. There was no telling what he had picked up. It was like Christmas every time Mr. Sneedy unburdened himself. He pulled out several shoes of different sizes, two empty Pepsi bottles, several dozen magazines, a saucepan missing a handle, three broken mirrors, a thermos that rattled sadly, a small yellow ball that he handed to Jo-Jo, and a belt with large metal studs.

After he unburdened himself, he sat back and slowly verified his finds. Jo-Jo waited, his eyes reviewing everything Mr. Sneedy had magically produced.

"You look blue, Jo-Jo," Mr. Sneedy observed.

"I'm not sad," Jo-Jo replied.

"No no, I mean blue like in cold blue."

"Well, it is a little colder than I expected."

"Where is your jacket? You shouldn't be out without your jacket!"

Jo-Jo looked down and mumbled, "Lost it."

"Lost it! You mean someone stole it!" Sneedy burst out indignantly. "Did your mother steal it for medicine again?" he inquired sarcastically.

"No no! It was the Stallions. They got it off me."

"Oh, that is bad, bad, bad – bad!" Mr. Sneedy replied with his eyes turning sadder. "Well, that won't do. You need to keep those little bones warm, and you need a good jacket!" declared Mr. Sneedy as he crawled deeper into the back of his box and spent several minutes digging through piles of items and clothes. He returned, holding up a black jacket with one sleeve missing. He motioned for to Jo-Jo stand up and try it on. It was so big that it covered Jo-Jo from neck to toe.

"There, now you will be warm."

Jo-Jo looked at and smoothed the jacket and felt the warmth returning and thanked Mr. Sneedy.

The big church bell rang out five times.

*How did it get so late?* thought Jo-Jo. It was time to move on. He said goodbye to Mr. Sneedy who was cleaning something. Then he ran down toward the waterfront. The waterfront had a small beach, which was a muddy area full of rocks and sticks between a looming dark dock and a burned hulk of a falling-down warehouse. It allowed the children their only access to the river. The river was always full of interesting things and strange floating colors.

Jo-Jo was looking for Smarty. They called Smarty that because he wasn't. Boys are very clever when it comes to hurting someone.

Smarty was twelve and a very big twelve. Most of the boys didn't mess with Smarty. When he was younger, they had; but after they had hurt him by throwing rocks at him, he turned in a rage and beat them all with his fists and tossed all three of them into the river. No one messed with Smarty after that.

Smarty was building a boat. He was going to be a pirate. He had tied several garbage cans together, but he could not get them to balance. They always tilted to one side or another. He had been working on that problem for over a year. When Jo-Jo arrived, there were several boys playing in the dirt; and Smarty was sitting, staring at the lopsided boat. At last, he stood up and picked up an old can and filled it with mud. He then filled each garbage can with a can of mud. They sank deeper in the water but slowly became upright.

"Yassss!" yelled Smarty as he had discovered ballast. He was very excited and picked up Jo-Jo and put him in one of the garbage cans. The craft lurched a little but stayed almost upright. "How much you weigh?"

"About sixty pounds I think," Jo-Jo guessed.

"Hmm, I weigh over hundnert. Hmm," Smarty thought out loud. He carefully added another can to the empty garbage can, and the boat tipped slightly in that direction.

"I will be ready to sail tomorrow. Are you going with me?"

"Huh?"

"You going pirating with me?"

"Well, I will ask my mom."

"Sure!" Smarty said with a laugh. "You do just that."

"If she lets ya, be here at dawn tomorrow." With that, he ran off for home.

Jo-Jo stayed and played at the water's edge until he heard the church clock strike six. Then he ran for home. His mom would be awake, and she would fix them dinner. He had some trouble running with the large jacket and, every once in while, stepped on the edge that flapped around his feet as he dashed along.

*Hmm, maybe she would even fix me a sandwich with lettuce,* Jo-Jo thought. He especially liked ham sandwiches with lettuce.

When he got home, he peeked in on Mrs. Martin. She was fussing around in the kitchen, mumbling to herself, so he quietly closed the door and hurried on up the stairs.

When he used his key and opened the apartment door, he was met by a cold black space. No lights were on. No fire was in the stove, no dinner was being made, and no one had stirred since he left. He turned on the one bare overhead light in the apartment. He heard the scampering of rat's feet and the scurrying of cockroaches' legs as the lights stark glare drove them back into their dark recesses. He looked into the refrigerator, but it had remained unchanged. He looked at his mom's door. It was still shut. He sat in the only chair and stared at the door, hoping it would suddenly open. Maybe his mom had been stung by bees again. He sure hoped not. They made her so sick.

She was the only person Jo-Jo knew who was stung by so many bees. This happened to her very often. Her arms would be covered with little bee bite puncture marks. When it did happen, she would lie in her bed and just sing little songs, then she would cry and finally fall asleep. Jo-Jo could never understand how the bees got into the apartment, why he never saw them and where they went after stinging her.

But there was no doubt about it. His mom would show him the sting marks on her arm. They seemed to like her arms. They were red and swollen and all streaked blue. Jo-Jo had never once seen the bees though. He had never even heard them buzzing. He was lucky. His mom said, "Jo-Jo, youse lucky, the bees jus don't like little boys." He had tried to watch for them and then trap them in a jar he had gotten out of the garbage can in the back of the building. It would be wonderful if he could do that! Then they would have honey to eat, and his mom would not be stung anymore. Why he could even sell the honey and buy some food, some lettuce!

As he waited, he dug around in the pockets of his new coat. Lo and behold, he found a small stick of candy stuck in the bottom of one. He pulled it loose and popped it in his mouth. It was hard and sweet. He sucked on it a long time. When it was gone, he walked to the door and listened. Not a sound. He pushed on the door. It was locked. He knocked on the door. There was no answer. He knocked harder. Then he knocked as hard as he could until he was tired and his small fists hurt.

He went back to the chair and sat down. He knew it was getting late, and his mom had to get to work.

*Should I wake her?* he thought about it for a while and then decided he better wake her. She was a wonderful dancer, and whenever she went to work, she would bring home some strange and wonderful food. He was hungry. He was very hungry. His mother was a beautiful woman when she got dressed up to dance. She seemed like a queen to Jo-Jo.

Jo-Jo knocked again. Still, there was no sound, no answer. He went to the broken stove and reached behind it to find the extra key his mom hid there. She was always losing her keys. Jo-Jo frequently had to let her into the apartment in the morning and also help her unlock her bedroom door. That was why they kept the extra key.

Jo-Jo opened the door, peered into the dark, and called, "Mom, Mom, it's time to get up."

He pushed the door open enough to slip into the room. He stood still for a moment; and as his eyes adjusted to the darkness, he called, louder this time. "Mom, it's time to go to work. You don't want to be late!" he scolded.

His eyes scanned the familiar objects – a one-arm chair covered with a pile of worn clothes, the bed heaped with a knot of frayed blankets, the boxes around the edges bulging and overflowing with his mother's colorful costumes. Then he saw the pile of clothes next to the bed. It was large and silent. He approached it and saw it was his mother, curled up on her side. She was hugging her stomach. He touched her covered shoulder and shook her gently, "Mom, are you OK? Mom, get up. Please, Mom, you're gonna be late."

The blanket covering his mother's shoulder slipped down; and when he reached out and touched her bare shoulder, it was very cold, icy cold. He drew back, and the light from the open door that had been blocked by his body flowed over his mother, and she looked up at him with strange blank staring eyes – and she was blue!

He jumped into the corner and cried, "Mom, Mom, oh, Mommy . . ."

The sobs surged through his small body, and the tears started to streak down his cheeks, and all he could do was yell, "OOOOOOoooo!" He hugged his legs tightly to his chest.

Mrs. Martin, who had listened to the strange wailing for several minutes before venturing out of the safety of her apartment, found Jo-Jo in the corner. He was crying and moaning loudly. She drew him to her and enfolded him in her large body, hugging him close. He could smell her body and the accumulated odors of smoke, coffee, and tea. He pushed into her to hide. She gently pulled him over toward his mother until she saw the side of her cold blue face. His jacket, which had been falling off, dropped onto the floor. Then clucking like an old mother hen, she quickly clutched Jo-Jo into her grasp, immediately pushing him from the room.

As they left the room, she gently said, "Jo-Jo honey, your mom is gone. I mean she has gone to heaven, to be with your daddy."

Jo-Jo was sparked by these words and cried, "My daddy ain't dead!"

The woman pulled him with her as they went downstairs to her room. She did not reply to his remark. She knew that there would be a better time to explain it all than now. She just said, "We will go to my apartment, and you can watch TV. OK, Jo-Jo? OK, Jo-Jo honey?"

He was sitting, watching a strange show with lots of noise and music. She had wrapped him in an old blanket. Mrs. Martin had then gone to "make arrangements."

Suddenly, he started to cry, quietly at first then louder. He stayed like this until the program ended.

He then stood up, allowing the blanket to fall on the floor, turned away from the TV, and hurried up the stairs to his apartment. He slipped in and got his one-sleeved coat; he went to his bed and got his monkey. He put the coat on and wrapped it around him. He was afraid and did not go back to see his mother. He turned off the light and shut the door.

He was alone on the dark deserted street now. He just started to run and ran until his lungs ached from the cold. He turned the corner and found the right building. He ran up the steps and inside and, using his finger, found the number 487 linked with the name McGuire. Smarty, whose last was name was Damon, lived with his uncle and aunt, Mr. and Mrs. John McGuire. Climbing the four flights of stairs, Jo-Jo knocked loudly, and the door opened only a few inches. The warmth and odors of this home reached out to Jo-Jo. He called, "Smarty, Smarty. I want to go!"

Smarty's voice called from somewhere inside the apartment, "Where?"

"To the sea, pirating! I want to sail tonight!"

Smarty said in hushed tones, "I can't come out." Then in a small embarrassed whisper, he said, "Not allowed out after dark."

"But we have to sail now. I must leave now!"

After a pause, Smarty, who had been thinking about this request, replied, "I can't go, but you take the boat ifin it so important."

Jo-Jo wheeled around, leaving the door behind, running again down the stairs. The door snapped closed with a click. He ran through the night toward the dock. He could see his breath, spewing out and disappearing in wisps of fine smoke. He dodged people and jumped over empty containers. No one paid any attention to the small ragged boy with the full-length jacket missing an arm as he ran on.

When he got there, he stopped to catch his breath. After a few minutes, he dropped Ringo into one side of the boat. He climbed in with him and untied the ropes that were holding the bobbing garbage cans snug and close to the pier. They were cold and wet, and his fingers became cold and wet. The ropes finally came open and slipped into the water with little splashes. He held on tight to the garbage can's edge with both hands and peered over it into the dark night.

At first, the boat just sat there, bobbing slowly up and down. Then it began to move and sway. The wind was strong and cold. Jo-Jo picked up Ringo and hugged him close, hunkered down so only his eyes barely showed above the rim of the cans. The cans started to sway and jump in the dark water. The wind pushed, and the river's relentless current caught the craft and carried it swiftly away toward the river's deep center.

It seemed to happen fast. The lights from the shore faded quickly into dancing stars. He tried to steer the craft with the wooden plank Smarty had stuck in one of the garbage cans. But he didn't know how or where to steer, so he just gave up. He was tired of struggling with the board and dropped it back wet and cold into the other can. He squatted in the garbage can hugging Ringo tightly. *Maybe this was not such a good idea*, he thought to himself, cold, frightened, and all alone.

In a way, it was pleasant to be moving swiftly and not having to do anything about it. *It must be like riding in a car*, he thought. He had heard the "box town" people talk about driving cars. It started to rain lightly, and he peeked out over the edge of the can. The river was rising and falling with occasional white teeth showing on the crests. There suddenly was lighting and terrible rolling thunder! The garbage cans whirled and twisted, bobbed and tilted as the rain now poured down. Jagged light flashes filled the sky. It must be like the teacup ride Mr. Sneedy had told him about at the carnival. Mr. Sneedy had promised to take him to the carnival someday to ride the teacup.

Jo-Jo looked into the dark with large widening eyes. He didn't think sailing should be like this. He slid down into the bottom of garbage can and started to sob.

The garbage cans took a big jump and landed half on their sides, scooping the river into them. Jo-Jo was soaking wet and a numbing cold seized him. He peered over the lip of the garbage can and saw a huge ship shadow crashing toward him. It rushed by with a whoosh, barely missing the bobbing craft! The river seemed to jump and climb higher around him. The bottom of the garbage cans hit something and tipped over. He was almost tossed out.

The raging river was tossing his craft about wildly and, finally, casually threw it toward an embankment. The garbage cans scraped the length of the concrete, swung free, and were bouncing and rolling. Now they were approaching a mud bank that reached into the water. Just then, Jo-Jo saw a large tree, branches reaching and clawing at the craft. He ducked down. He was again thrown high in the cans, which struck something on his side and then dropped to strike hard on the bottom. Jo-Jo closed his eyes tight and was wishing he was back in "box town."

Without warning, a strong hand grasped his coat at the base of his neck, and he was out of the garbage cans flying through the air. He clutched Ringo and closed his eyes as tight as could be. He came to rest in the arms of a huge dark man. The huge face and large eyes peered down at the boy. A big grin filled the face with teeth, and a deep voice laughed, "Hello, Moses, what you doing in this here river? This damn night? No, never mind. Ima taken you home to my Bessie. She will get you warm enough. Then you can tell Jacob your tale." The man wrapped a blanket so tight around him he couldn't move, but he carried him so snuggly he didn't even want to move. He felt Ringo in his arms, and he felt warm

He was getting cozy and warm. He felt safe and comfortable. The man moved effortlessly with large wide strides toward a light in a house in front of them. It loomed larger and brighter as they closed in on it rapidly.

With eyes closed tight, he had a wonderful thought, *Maybe it is breakfast time!*

## The End

# Father

*A father takes care of his own the best he can. After all,*
*he is all they have between them and the angry world.*

## San Jose, California
## January 15, 2007

L arry rolled out of the driver side's wide-opened car door, shoving the heavy door closed behind him with a heavy kick from his boot. It crashed closed solidly. The car shuddered in response. He walked slowly toward the light. The light was cast through the dusty plate glass windows of the Circle K. It clawed into the parking lot, throwing odd shadows across the debris and trash. Reaching the glass door, he hesitated momentarily to quickly pull up the rear of his dirty Levi's with his left hand while straight-arming the door hard with his right. The door flew open. Striding boldly inside, the stale, warm air rushed to hug him. He stood still eagerly embracing the stale, warm air. He moved his head slowly to the right then to the left, his narrow pale eyes scanning the store.

He saw several customers milling around the checkout counter. He slipped silently down the front aisle away from them. Skirting the dry goods, he headed for the magazine rack against the back wall. His shirt was stained with various alcohol blends, and his nose was running a little from the blow he scored when he closed the bar. He grabbed up the latest *Hustler* magazine. He tried to slide the magazine around inside the plastic cover to see what it was hiding. He tried hard to spot some "T and As." No dice. The protective covering designed to avoid offending solid citizens and protecting innocent children did its job with prudence and pride. They were there, he knew it, and he would just have to wait to get it home to see them.

He turned left and approached the large upright refrigerator. He opened the heavy door and felt its cold breath as the wave of frost hit him. He pulled out a six-pack of Millers. His hand had become cold and icy. His arm tensed, and the large bicep flexed slightly, distorting his faded tiger tattoo. He meandered back to the front of the store past the cheese products, crackers, and cookies.

He stopped in front of the candy racks. Facing them squarely, with the beer pack on his hip, he rubbed his free hand on the leg of his Levi's and looked carefully for his one and only favorite. He spotted it. He grabbed three extra large Snickers bars and moved on.

*Nothing like a cool one and a Snickers,* he thought. Now there was only one old woman ahead of him. He looked at the dirty coffee machine on the counter and thought, *Fuck, someone's not doing their job! What a mess. Punk wet back help, no damn good greasers.*

The old woman was arguing quietly with the cashier about something. Finally, she gave up with a weak shrug and, grabbing her small brown paper bag, left in disgust.

"Some people!" the cashier sighed, shaking his head. Quickly snapping out of it, he returned to his appropriate customer-service-robot role. Turning on a broad smile, he said, "How kin I yelp ya? Did you find everything?"

Larry made his best positive grunt to both questions and pushed his stuff over the counter toward the stocky man. The cashier had a lopsided smile. It made him look funny. Larry figured he didn't know how silly he looked because he continued to flash his lopsided smile.

*Someone should tell him,* he thought. Larry dropped a damp crumpled twenty on the counter when the man finally said "Thirteen seventy-nine" after his nimble fingers had scanned all five items.

The grinning clerk swept the twenty-dollar bill into his small pudgy hand. He then held it in both his hands, snapping it flat several times, and then held it up critically to the light. Satisfied, he hit the cash register buttons, and the drawer popped open with a dull jingle.

"Thirteen seventy-nine, eighty, ninety, fourteen, fifteen, twenty dollars." He systematically counted the penny, two dimes, one dollar bill and five dollar bill out on the counter. He pulled out a paper bag from under the counter, snapped it open smartly, and put the items in the bag. Peering down into the bag, he rearranged them several times. When he was finally satisfied, he pushed it toward Larry, giving him his best biggest lopsided grin.

"Ugh-huh," Larry grunted with a sly return smile. He scooped up the change and stuffed it into his pocket. Lifting the bag at the top with one hand, he quickly put his other under it for support. The bag was thin, and the beer was heavy. He turned about-face, walking quickly forward and straight out of the door. He looked back quickly to check out the woman's ass that just passed him going in. It moved with a nice rhythm. He smiled to himself and laughed lowly.

*What a splendid ass*, he thought wistfully.

Unlocking the car, he wrenched open the door and tossed the bag over onto the passenger seat. He collapsed heavily into the driver's seat. It grasped his body and cried softly in greeting. The car was old. It was filthy. The inside of his car was covered with trash – fast-food wrappers from a wide variety of "gourmet" drive-throughs, bags, crushed beer cans, a sea of cellophane wrappers, napkins, and broken straws. The smell was that of old sweet and stale beer. He was comfortable with it all. He fired her up, popped the headlights on, shifted into reverse, and backed out fast.

He turned left when he hit the street and ran for home. He was tired from working a double shift at the bar. It was three in the morning, and he was ready to get some sleep. He glanced at the bag and thought about having a cool one right now but decided to save them for breakfast. He would only keep himself awake belching if he downed one now.

He thought, *It hadn't been a bad night. About seventy bucks in tips!* He had at least eight free shots when no one was watching; and Alice, the late-night barmaid, had shared her homemade egg salad sandwich with him. If she only would share her hair pie – now that would be something! Maybe he ought to just grab her ass? *Yeah, grab her ass and show her what a real man is all about. Nah, Hank, the boss, wouldn't like that at all. Not a good idea. No siree, not a good idea.*

He rubbed each of his eyes with his left fist and tried to stay alert. He pulled into his driveway a few minutes later. The small house, which was dark in the shadows, had a tired, sagging outline.

He turned off the engine and listened to it misfire a few times. He grabbed the bag, jumped out, and stretched. Then he strode up the dark steps. He fumbled in his pocket for the keys, located the door key, jammed it home, and twisted hard. The door lock opened. He swung the door open, and he entered, reaching out his arm for the light switch on his right.

His head exploded! Pain, stars, and blackness! He fell hard into the house. The bag went flying. The six-pack bounced hard and loud on the floor. Several cans tore loose and rolled across the floor, caroming off the wall. One ruptured and began to spray foam. It spun helplessly around on the floor.

*Hiss.*

It came to an abrupt halt between two old tennis shoes and died. The Snicker bars flopped out, and only the magazine held its own, staying modestly hidden within the bag.

A cascade of cold water soaked him awake. He was in a chair. The room was dark. It was just gray shadows and blackness. He jerked forward and tried to move, but his arms and legs were not working. His mouth, his mouth refused to open, so he could not shout. His head pounded! It was pounding all across his back and down his left arm. In the dark, he could barely recognize his own living room.

*What in the hell!* he thought, shaking his head. He sensed a slight rustling behind him and tensed.

He felt a warm breeze tickle his neck. A voice near his ear said sadly, "You shouldn't have hurt my girl."

He tried to wildly wriggle and whimper a defense, any defense. He tried to speak. God, he wanted to speak. He wanted to explain. He could only mumble through the wide cloth gag.

"Muumm." It was weak. It was pitiful.

He was frightened and tried to scoot the chair around to escape. A hard hand grasped his shoulder and held him in place. He struggled hard but was held tight. He was sweating. But neither he nor the chair moved under the firm pressure of the hand.

The warm breeze returned. "You and I and God know what you did, even if justice is blind."

A hardening voice whispered, "You shouldn't have hurt her, my girl."

In spite of the cold water soaking his clothes and his hot perspiration rolling down his back, he tried to gain control. His mind was whirling, trying to figure the scam, trying to get the edge. He thought, *I could always get an edge.* He needed to get the edge. He knew this guy was serious. *Christ, how could I explain I'm innocent? Whatever this guy thought I did, I didn't do it! I didn't do anything,* he thought wildly.

The hand held him tight and pressed him down. His arms and legs were taped to the chair, and his mouth was gagged and taped. The warm breath returned. "You shouldn't have hurt my girl." It was a harsh angry voice now.

He really wanted to explain. *Oh, if he would just give me a chance, I would explain it all,* he thought as he felt the warm sweat in his crotch now.

The warm breath said, "Jenny was a nice girl. She was a good girl. She was a loving daughter."

It all suddenly crashed into him in a flash now! Jenny was the girl he smacked around in some motel room when they were both drunk. He thought, *Christ Jesus! I didn't mean to really hurt her. She was such a nasty bitch. She tried to run way. She screamed. I hate it most when they scream.* He was frantically trying to figure a way out. *Fuck! Where is my edge? Gots to get the edge on this sick dude!*

Suddenly, a cold line was pulled hard across his throat.

Warmth, he felt warmth spilling down his chest. It was pouring onto the top of his fat stomach. A comfortable warmth! Before he understood, his head dropped forward. His mind blurred, fading to gray, dark gray, then black. The warmth flowed down the front of his body onto his thighs as he sank in the engulfing blackness. He smelled something, something familiar.

*Blood!* this last thought screamed through his mind.

Larry died quietly. The man behind him wiped the blade of the hunting knife slowly on Larry's dirty left shirtsleeve. There was not much blood on the knife, and it blended in with all the other bar stains. Just one more dirty streak.

He carefully placed the knife in a small box. The box was the size of a ream of paper. It was partially full of sand taken from a nearby construction site. Bending over a small table by the door, he used the duct tape to seal the box. The silver backed tape glinted in the light, arcing through the window from a waning moon. It covered the box he held. When he finished, he tucked the box under his arm. He listened for a while in the dark. The faint dripping, splashing sound of tiny drops of blood hitting a puddle was all he heard.

Bending down, he picked up the paper bag. The magazine settled down. He dropped the tape into the bag. Backing up slowly, he let himself out of the house, closing the door behind him. He removed the key ring and keys still dangling in the lock. He pulled the door shut but didn't bother to lock it. He walked briskly down the sidewalk, turned left for three houses until he reached his rental car.

He opened the door and got in. It was a late-model car, clean and cold. He started it up and drove away slowly at first. Several minutes later, he pulled slowly up onto a bridge. Rolling down his window by hand, he threw the box over the low fence barrier. It hit the edge and tumbled over. He had just begun to accelerate when he heard the light splash. He looked down at his hands. He peeled off each of the thin driving gloves with the help of his mouth. First, one hand was on the wheel and then switched. He put them in the bag from the Circle K store.

It now contained the magazine, receipt, gloves, and tape. He drove to a Denny's restaurant on the corner of Market and Dogwood. Parking his car in the empty lot next to the restaurant, he got out with the bag. Walking past the dumpster, on the side of the building, he casually dropped the bag into the dark hole. He heard the faint thud as it landed on something soft.

He crossed over into the parking lot of the restaurant. He relaxed as he entered the warm restaurant. He stood waiting for someone to notice him. The old waitress did and sat him in the middle of the room at a clean, shining table. A tired younger waitress approached him from behind with a coffeepot in one hand. He smiled at her and ordered, "Coffee and pie, apple pie, please."

She nodded and didn't bother writing it down but just returned to the counter. As she went back into the kitchen, he slid out of the seat and went into the bathroom. He washed his hands several times. He really had to pump the old soap container to get anything out of it. It had certainly seen better days. He dried his hands with three paper towels he tore from the roller. He tossed the towels into the waste can.

He tore off another. He pushed opened the stall door with his foot. He used the towel to grasp and pick Larry's keys out of his pocket. He dropped Larry's keys into the stained porcelain john. He flushed it twice using the towel. While the water swirled and danced, he dropped the towel into the bowl and watched the whirling patterns, thinking, *I should have hurt him more. I should have made it hurt more. It had been too easy and too smooth.*

He returned to the table now. It was laid out with steaming coffee in a white mug and a piece of worn-looking apple pie. He sat. He moved the pie around on the plate; it didn't improve its appearance with relocation. He picked up the fork and ate it slowly.

## Dayton, Ohio
## January 17, 2007

"Come in, Blake," a cordial voice called from inside the office.

Blake Mannering shut the outer door behind him, crossed through the waiting room, and walked into the office of Dr. Mark Ogelbe, PhD. Mark smiled broadly at Blake and motioned with his arm for him to sit on the leather chair directly across from him. He was sitting behind a low coffee table that was almost bare. It contained a slim black phone and a black leather notebook. On top of the notebook was a silver cell phone. Next to the notebook were three sharpened pencils.

Blake sank deeply into the chair, throwing open his suit coat and loosening his tie. He relaxed and offered his best submissive smile.

"Well, how are we today?" inquired Mark as usual.

"Fine, just fine, Doctor."

"Well, you let me be the judge of that," Mark scolded, laughing slightly at his warm humor.

Mark moved the cell next to the black phone and picked up the leather notebook, opened it, positioning it on his knee, and picked up the first pencil.

"Let me see. You just got back from vacation? That right?"

"Yes, as you suggested. I went away for two full weeks."

"You look good, fit, alert, and ah – even tanned?"

"Yes, I spent a lot of time around the hotel pool."

"Well, good for you. What else did you do?"

"Well, I took some books along, but I have to confess I never read more than three pages. I did just as you suggested. Relaxed, went swimming, tried new foods, tasted some wines, and walked on the beach."

"I see." There was a painfully long pause.

"Did you drink much?"

"No, not really. Just a glass of wine or two with my meals. I never got a bottle."

"You have been back three days now. How is work going?"

"Just great actually. When I got back, they had several new assignments for me. I just dove in and am really enjoying them. I also have an opportunity for a promotion if I can successfully complete one of them quickly."

"Sounds great." Another painful pause, then the doctor asked, "How about Jenny?"

Blake looked down quickly but raised his gaze back to Mark's commercially concerned face.

"Well, I think . . ." Short pause. "I hope. What I mean is, I feel I have finally adjusted to her" – another short pause for effect, with shallow breathing – "departure." He finished quickly. He sighed heavily and then continued, "I have put away all her things and do not look at the scrapbook as much as I used to." He paused again, looking down and sidewise and then slowly back at the psychiatrist.

"She was a wonderful daughter, but she is now only a . . . a memory." He stretched out his last word with a slight sob.

"And the anger?"

"Well, I am doing the relaxation exercises you taught me. I have taken up yoga, and that helps. I think I am in control."

"You don't seem convinced. Convince me," Mark demanded sharply.

"Well, you know how much anger and confusion I had when we started. I am – I'm still a little afraid it may come back." Then he quickly added, "I really think it is under control. I haven't even had an argument at work. Not even a small one. I used to argue all the time, even before Jenny – ah, Jenny died. It was only after her death that I started to really lose it and strike out at everyone. I have been calmer than ever, and I just don't allow the old demon to take control."

"Good. Let's review." This was Blake's cue to relax. The way Mark reviewed was to prattle on and on with his own idea of the world and his exalted place within it.

"You came here over a year ago because you were disruptive and threatening at work. You had been arrested in a drunken bar fight at lunch, and your boss gave you one last chance to straighten up. At first, you fought therapy and me. Then you finally started to understand the impact of your anger on your life in the past, present, and future. Although you had been separated from your daughter, over the years, you still loved her. And her vicious death was a tremendous shock to you. How do you feel about McBont now?"

Blake couldn't help looking away. He bit his lip and rearranged himself in the chair. Then he cried out loudly.

"Well . . . eh," he started slowly, "I have been putting him out of my mind. I just think of all the good things I can about my daughter. I remember the happy times and try and accept the fact" – he paused – "I have lost her, and nothing is going to change that – not even, not even – " He started getting agitated but forced himself back down toward control. "If they find her killer," he finished.

"I see." Mark waited and waited, eyeing Blake. Blake didn't know what he wanted at this point; so rather than chance a failure, he just looked pitiful, sad, and tragic. He didn't say anything.

After several minutes, the therapist began again, "You no longer think Larry McBont killed your daughter?"

This hit him hard and directly. This was the hardest one of all; he had rehearsed it many times and thought he had it locked. He edged forward in the chair leaning toward Mark and replied earnestly, "What happened in that room that night is known only by God, and he will take care of it. McBont was there, and he was acquitted so" – he paused – "what happens is in the Lord's hands."

*Just the right mixture of avoidance and religious cover-up to show I'm past the idea of revenge*, he thought.

"Hmm, I assume you feel you're cured, and we can end our treatment sessions?"

"I, well, feel that I am in control. I don't think, I don't think I will ever be 'cured.'" This seemed like a good humble direction. He had gotten the idea from some Alcoholics Anonymous materials, which he was now parroting.

"I would like to think I can function without any more therapy. However – ah, however, I am afraid something might happen. So if it would, OK. I would like to continue a little longer until I feel more sure of myself," he said with reverent humility.

"Ah, I see. That is a good, sound idea. I think you have made tremendous progress, Blake. Let's review."

Blake's thoughts drifted as the therapist did another one of his endless reviews. He responded throughout the monologue for the next thirty minutes with the right mixture of sincerity, humility, and pandering that he had been practicing. The doctor's monotone and droning review was concluded. Mark was smiling like the Cheshire cat. The wheels of his mind were whirring around with his grandiose thought, *I have cured this poor accursed man. I have healed his emotional rupture. What a preeminent therapist I am. What a formidable mind I have.*

Finally, Blake rose and shook Mark's hand as they ended the session. He averted his eyes and thanked him over and over again.

Mark smacked him soundly on the back then pushed him through the door. As the outer door close behind him, Blake moved quickly to the elevator, stifling a laugh. When he was in the elevator, he laughed out loud. He thought proudly, *Lies, all lies, but that damn fool can't tell. I guess reading all those therapy books helped. I just figured out what he wanted and fed it to him. I loved my wife and daughter so much, even after she broke my heart when she took Jenny and left for California. I tried to keep in touch, but I was not good at getting past my ex-wife. She hated me for some reason and wouldn't let me talk to Jenny. I loved Jenny and was so very proud of her all those years she worked so hard. The only way I knew what was happening in her life was though my ex-sister-in-law who kept me updated every week. Jenny was a wonderful young woman, and I was just not a good dad.*

He hadn't gone on any damn vacation! He went to San Jose via San Diego and did what every father does when someone hurts his daughter. He killed the miserable son of a bitch that had taken her away from him. He only hoped that the revenge he took for her would, in some way, link her closer to him. He began to cry.

## San Jose, California
## January 29, 2007

He wearily snapped the file cover closed and tossed the overflowing folder on top of his desk. He had only been working the case for six days, but it looked like a dead-end one. Some of the papers slipped out crookedly. He had gone over all the information the file offered and couldn't tease out anything worth a damn. Leaning back in the old wooden chair, he reached into his left-hand jacket pocket and pulled out a Snickers bar. He wore an old wrinkled blue blazer and an open-necked polo shirt. His desk was strewn with paper coffee cups guarded by a fort of files piled up along the outer edges.

Peeling the wrapper slowly, he took a large bite and savored the taste. The chief of detectives, Steve McClain, walked in briskly and stood over his desk, glaring across the top of the file fortress. He waited while the detective swallowed. His tired eyes stared down at the large man disdainfully.

"Well?" he demanded.

"Well what?" Mason replied defensively.

"What about our suicide?" he asked sarcastically.

"Oh, that," he replied.

"Well, I need to do a couple of more interviews, but this is the nature of the beast."

He sat forward in the chair and started to explain in a rolling voice, "Larry McBont, a small-time street hustler and doper was found at approximately four fifteen early Tuesday morning the 16th of January by his boss. The boss, Hank Shore, accompanied by a female companion, had gone looking for him. He had closed his Pussy Willow Bar at two on Monday night or, rather, Tuesday morning. The bar is located on Twenty-fourth Street in the Woodside area. Larry had neglected to show that night for his usual evening bartender shift."

"This caused some consternation on the owner's part. He had called McBont repeatedly during the evening and got no answer. They found

Larry 'packaged' in his living room with his throat cut. Blood was all over and around him. They managed to stumble in it and make a mess. They called the police at 4:25 a.m. on Mr. Shore's cell phone. A black and tan was dispatched, and Officer Milton Tepits and his partner Charlie Merit arrived at the scene at 5:01 a.m. The found the boss and his companion, one of his barmaids, one Mildred Wilson, on the front steps. By this time, she had puked into a porch chair and was crying.

"The coroner later confirmed that the neck was cut with a sharp blade with such force it almost severed the head. The victim was unconscious almost immediately and died within two to four minutes – give or take, a few seconds. He bled to death. He was taped into a porch chair – a match for the other one on the porch. He also had a bruise on his left shoulder and a large contusion on the back of his head. Other than that, there was discoloration on his legs and arms from where he was taped. Time of death was estimated at between 2 and 4 a.m. sometime Monday morning the 15th of January. That's it! No witnesses and no close neighbors."

"How they get in?" asked the chief, going back to square one as always.

"It was the boss's house. He allowed Larry to rent it as part of his pay for working at the bar. They had a key but said the door was unlocked, and they just walked in." Detective Mason shifted in his chair, which cried out in distress, and continued his narrative report.

"Larry has a rap sheet that is mostly small-time drug dealing and woman beating. He had several aggravated rape charges over the years that were dropped before trial or settled out of court. Last year, he spent three months in the county jail for a drunk and disorderly and attacking the arresting officer. His latest jail jaunt was six months ago when he was charged with the rape and murder of some young thing. He was again under lock and key for 127 days, courtesy of the county. The trail was only into the fourth day when the charge was dismissed due to mishandling of evidence by one of the district attorney's bright boys."

The detective was now sitting upright, reciting all the details. He had pushed the remainder of the candy bar under a handy folder.

"Chief, my snitches tell me that while he was in county awaiting trial, he got crossways with a local gang member. The gentleman in question is Stony White, head of the Raven Ramblers. That is about it."

"Fingerprints?"

"Only Larry's, the victim. Hank's, the boss. And Mildred's, the bar girl with the queasy stomach."

"Murder weapon?"

"No, none turned up. We searched the house, the yard, his car, and the general vicinity – nothing. We did find a couple of knives in his car and some in the kitchen, but they didn't check out. No human blood. However, get this; one had animal blood on it, probably a dog's. The crime lab was unable to even suggest the type of knife other than it was very sharp."

"Anything missing?"

Detective Mason slowly rose his bulk from the chair and stalked about the room slowly. "That is hard to say. All indications were nothing had been removed, searched through, or damaged except the porch chair that was inside the house. There was a six-pack on the floor with one empty can. The place was a pigpen, but no signs of anything missing were detected. It didn't look like he had much beyond a TV, an old boom box, and boxes of old CDs. His boss and bar girl verified nothing was missing so far as they could tell. But who knows? He could have had something stashed they didn't know about – jewelry or some money. His wallet, a large pocketknife, and rumpled fifty-two dollars in small denominations were in his pants pocket. However, he had no keys."

"Neighbors hear anything, anything at all?"

"No one was outside. The house is an old one that sits back from the street with the drive in the front yard. There is a vacant lot on one side, and the other side is a house for sale that has been empty for several months. The house backs up on a steep embankment that drops into an open drainage ditch. Across the street is a rental, and on either side are small run-down apartments. All the bedrooms are in the back. One has six units, the other four. No one heard a squeak."

"So what's the story?" he asked flatly.

"Well, the way I see it, he was murdered by someone or 'someones' who had an attitude for him. The most likely player is Stony or one of his goons up for a gang initiation. He locked up the bar on Sunday night or Monday morning and came home. He was jumped, wrapped, and murdered."

"Who had the beer?"

"Best guess is the killer who may have been celebrating. It was probably the Vic's beer, and that is why they left the rest – wrong brand."

"Who identified the body?"

"His boss."

"Any family?"

"No one seems to think so. No mail, personal phone book, or photos. The files indicate he is from the East Coast, apparently New Jersey, and has been in California for over fifteen years. No answering machine or PC around."

"Who was the girl he raped?" The chief jumped in another direction. They both presumed he was probably guilty and got off on a stupid technicality.

"Jenny L. Mannering, an analyst with McCormick and Company in Palo Alto."

"What about her family? They couldn't be happy about him raping and killing their daughter and him walking away from it?

"Well, her father lives in Dayton, Ohio. She hadn't seen him since her mother left him and moved to Santa Cruz over eight years ago. The homicide guy working the case told me he was contacted over the phone and didn't take the information very well. He got all upset and started crying. Then he got a real hard-on and started screaming and yelling at the officer. Someone pulled him away from the phone and ended the conversation by getting the address of the station house. However, he was never heard from again and didn't show at the funeral. No one spotted him at the trail. The mother said he never gave a damn about either of them."

"The mother?"

"Well, she is the real case – seems to be more interested in reaping a legal and public personal harvest than as to what happened to her daughter. She was outspoken in the courtroom and later really blasted the district attorney in a TV interview. She is currently suing everyone involved. She is a sort of 1970s 'hippy hat' that still practices Zen and likes to get media coverage."

"The girl have any friends? A boyfriend, brother, etc.?"

"Nah, she was a loner. Only child who played by herself, worked her way through college, worked hard apparently according to her college advisor, didn't drink or do drugs. She had a good job, lived by herself in a nice apartment. A nice plain kid I guess, just in the wrong place at the wrong time. Her employer liked her, and she was apparently well liked by the other employees. I hate to see it happen, but she had a real victim's profile. It's a shame someone didn't give a damn about her."

"Yeah, like about half of the cases we see. Too bad she didn't have a father to watch over her or a mother to care."

"You are right about that, a tootsie roll mom and a crybaby absentee dad doesn't give you much of an edge these days. Yeah, just a brief visitor on our grim globe." Mason got eloquent occasionally.

"How did she get involved with that prick in the first place?"

"They met in a yuppie singles' bar in the downtown area. Larry apparently swept her off her feet or doped her and got her to a nearby motel. About one in the morning, there was noise, screaming and shouting. The night deskman called the police. When they located the room and got in, she was there – raped and beaten to death. Larry ran for it, but they had him on videotape, so he was picked up later that week. His story was they had a good time. She passed out, and he left. She was fine when he left her."

"They couldn't make it stick?"

"DA office lost and contaminated evidence." This was a dismally familiar story anymore with the DA office.

"Well, check out the gang angle. I have two more stiffs coming in from Los Gatos, so we don't have a lot of time to get the culprit. Frankly, it is no big loss one way or the other. However, if it was a gang member, I would just like to get him locked up before we have another murder. If we don't get him on this one, we will on the next I suppose."

"OK."

The chief laid down another two file cases on his desk and, turning away, ambled out of the room. *So much for the suicidal bartender case. Sleep well, Larry,* thought Mason as he reached slowly under the folder and located his Snickers. He slipped it out and began to eat it slowly. He really was getting tired of all his cases piling up and all the dead ends he and his fellow detectives continuously ran into. *This guy, Larry, was human but what a scumbag!* Well, Mason was only going to be around another three years, so it was not his job to change the precinct. He had to catch the bad guys, and that was it. He crumpled up the wrapper and tossed it into the waste can under his desk. He pulled the two new folders off the top of his fortress and placed them front and center. He leaned back. His chair groaned as he started to open the top folder.

## The End

# Preemptive Strike

Paul Waterman sat in his worn padded porch chair on his patio behind his home. It was yet another warm California evening. There was a slight breeze swaying the big wind chime hanging at the end of the roof eve of the patio cover. The slight tinkling was always a pleasant sound to him. He watched its swaying and strained to hear its sound, but only once in many minutes did it chime, oh so very lightly. Paul usually sat outside on the patio every evening at dusk. He was gong to be fifty-eight next month. He had worked for many years at the Downtown Auto Store and was a little tubby from not doing much but sitting in a chair and checking accounts.

Every evening after dinner, his wife, Patty, would clear the table and load the dishes into the dishwasher. She stabbed the On button and then plunked herself down on their old green couch. She would kick off her flip-flops, put her feet up on the coffee table, and squiggle around in the cushions until she was comfortable enough to watch her evening TV programs.

As he sat there, he suddenly recalled, surprisingly, that when they were first married, he would watch TV with her. They would laugh and talk about the programs and hold hands. But after eighteen years of marriage, he no longer cared for them. Although the programs' names changed, they all still seemed to be the same tired stories but now heavily laced with sex, potty mouths, homosexuals, and ridiculous commercials for uninteresting and unimportant things.

Now his wife's friend, Carey, always dropped and in and watched the programs with her. This intrusion used to be just on a special occasions until Carey got divorced and was living alone again. She now came by every night at the same time, like clockwork, every single night!

Of course, Paul also remembered when they were first married, they usually ended up roughhousing on the couch, then on the floor, and then making love before the programs were finished. It was when they grew older and watched them all the way to the end that he lost interest and began spending the early evening alone on the patio. His wife went to bed by nine o'clock every night; so after she turned off the TV, Paul would prowl around the downstairs, doing odd chores and reading the newspaper or watching the ten o'clock news. He didn't go to bed until after eleven. Patty was sound asleep by then, snoring lightly.

As he sat quietly, the darkness slowly embraced him. He tried to remember when he had decided. He thought, *It is hard to recall actually.* He had been angry with Roger Braxton, his neighbor, now for years. The oleander bushes were just the last straw! But he decided – he defiantly decided – that he would make a preemptive strike. Maybe it was after President Bush's speech or just after he read a newspaper article about preemptive strikes or maybe it was something on the news. Oh, what difference did it make? Now was the time to strike!

Somewhere back in time, he had determined that was his answer, a preemptive strike against Braxton. That would successfully open the war with one decisive battle and close the war to his satisfaction all at once.

Once he had made that decision, he became calmer and more relaxed. He even started to talk to Braxton over the fence or out in the front of the house when he saw him. No raised voices, no angry incriminations, just the usual stupid things neighbors say to each other regarding the weather, mail, the commute, Friday's ball game, or whatever. Braxton was a little more open and talked to him about his life to some extent, but Paul was not really interested. That was just his preparation phase. It was the softening-up phase. Now he was almost ready. He was waiting for Thursday. It was now only Monday.

*Not long now!* he thought.

On the first Thursday of the month, Braxton's gardener cut the oleanders that ran the length of the dividing fence between the two houses. They grew about two feet above the fence before being trimmed every month. Most of the cuttings fell into Paul's yard. He then had to rake them up and toss them out. That was the transgression! That was the unforgivable travesty he would end – and end soon! He would walk out into his side yard, and there, they were waiting for him to finish the job! Besides being a total bad neighbor, he was also filling Paul's yard with poison. Yes, poison! Paul remembered the case of a woman who attempted to poison her husband with oleander juice from their yard plants. He lived, however, and she was caught and convicted. Served her right.

*What kind of a neighbor fills your yard with poison?* he raged inwardly to himself. His anger made him squirm and shift in his chair. The old webbing sighed as he shifted his weight around.

His battle plan was now fully formed. He would come home early on Thursday and rake the oleander cuttings up and pile them near the fence line. His side yard sloped down in a terraced fashion from Braxton's higher yard. It was a little hard to climb up to the fence line on Paul's side since it was steep and eroded by years of Braxton's excess sprinkler watering pouring under the fence and down his slope.

The plan was just to wait until about nine o'clock in the evening when Braxton would be watching TV and drinking his wine. Paul had spotted all the bottles he threw out every week in his trash barrel! The man was a lush! Then Paul would righteously hurl all the cuttings over the fence back into Braxton's yard. In the morning, when Braxton would find them and realize he had been struck by Paul, Braxton would further recognize what a bad neighbor he had been and make amends in the future. He mulled this over and over and began to try and figure out what Braxton might do.

*Toss them back? Possibly. Rake them up and learn his lesson and make sure to instruct his gardener to be more careful? Hopefully, that was the expected outcome. What if the stupid son of a bitch didn't even notice? Wouldn't that be something?* Well, he will probably come storming over to Paul's house, pounding on the door and then start screaming at him. In that case, Paul would have considered himself very successful in his preemptive attack.

Yes sir, preemptive strike, that is the ticket. Now he heard the TV click off and the two women's voices trail off as Patty walked with Carey to the front door. He stood up and yawned and stretched. He heard one last tinkle. He turned and entered the darkened house through the sliding glass door.

Thursday, he drove down the street slowly and slipped into his garage silently. His wife had gone to her friend Carey's house for dinner, and he was on his own. He shut the garage door, went into the house, and briefly checked the mail. There was nothing of interest there. Walking into the kitchen, he slowly went over to the refrigerator and took out a cold beer and popped the can top. He took a full gulp and climbed the stairs to the bedroom to change into his preemptive striking uniform. There were, he knew, certain precise professional rules to this preemptive strike business.

He had his old dark pants and shoes ready in a corner of his closet. However, the tennis shoes he had selected had some white stripes on the side, but he cleverly had blackened them with shoe polish. He put on his old torn black sweatshirt and had found a dark blue ski mask in the closet, which would cover his face. He put it on and then peeled it up so he could breathe and went downstairs to locate his dinner. Patty had left a nice tuna sandwich on the table covered in foil.

He sat down at the kitchen table and ate it slowly. He finished the remaining beer but wisely refrained from having a second one. He had to be a lean, mean fighting machine. He was enjoying the anticipation of the approaching preemptive strike moment. He got up and peeked out the dining room window. Sure enough, there were the cuttings all over his hill! He checked his watch and went outside. He patiently raked them into small piles about an armful in size. When he was finished, he counted them. He was very precise and careful not to make a lot of noise while raking. Twelve piles were all ready to go at the bottom of the slope.

He was perspiring and a little out of breath. He stealthily retreated, hardly breathing. He was now waiting for the cover of darkness to protect his preemptive strike. He was too excited to sit on the patio, so he went into the house and turned on the TV news. They were talking about another gang murder. He relaxed and almost fell asleep in the chair watching TV when he snapped alert, realizing it was time!

Checking his watch, it was ten past nine. He was late. He rushed into the backyard toward the fence and tripped over the rake he had carelessly left on the ground. He was able to check his fall with a lightning like reaction, grasping at several tree limbs, but lost his ski mask, which was perched on the top of his head. After rummaging around on the ground like a dog searching for a bone, he finally located it and put it on, pulling it all the way down. He could smell his breath that it partially retained. It was all tuna and beer odors.

He was ready now! Then in the dark below the shadow of the fence, he had trouble finding the piles. He stumbled over one, kicking it apart in the dark. Grumbling, he had to reluctantly return to the house and get a small flashlight. He came back, shining its small beam on the ground. Holding the light low to the ground, he located the messed-up pile and all the other piles.

He hurriedly raked the scattered pile together while balancing the light with his left hand. On his last stroke, the flashlight twisted and jumped out of his hand, landing under a large dark bush. Swearing quietly, he had to get down on his knees and feel around for the flashlight. It was so dark under the bush, he didn't even see its beam. After several minutes, his hand finally touched the metal case of the flashlight. He grabbed for it. However, when he pulled it out from under the bush, he raised his arm too quickly and the stickers of the old rosebush bit into his arm in several places. He cried out, "Ouch!"

He quickly clamped his hand over his mouth to stifle his cry. He sat back and checked his arm for remaining stickers. He pulled several out and rubbed his arm. He got up awkwardly.

His plan was so simple and direct. What was the problem? He was to scoop each pile up one at a time and climb up to the fence and toss them over.

He swept the area with the flashlight one more time to locate them all. At the closest pile, he stooped over to pick it up and dropped the flashlight again. He heard it rolling away down the hill and then down the grade of the sidewalk that ran parallel to the fence. He stumbled after it and finally picked it up after it got lodged against a rock. He turned it off and stuffed it angrily into his back pocket.

He trudged back to the waiting piles. He filled his arms with the cuttings of the first pile and struggled up the hill. He had some trouble because his shoes slipped on the steep slop and damp grass. He had to stop frequently and ensure he had a good balance before taking another step. Several times, he stopped, and his body weaved back and forth and then to the side before he was sure he had good traction and balance

It was like a balancing dance each time his foot slipped. When he was finally at the top, he stopped to catch his breath. He huffed and puffed away heavily for a few minutes. When he had his breath back, he counted to three, "One, two, and three." He lifted the pile high and hurled it over. Well, not quite! He hurled them into air all right, but the short strands of oleanders guarding the fence top blocked them.

They all silently fluttered back to the ground, hitting him in the face and shoulders, ultimately resting around his feet and covering his dark strike uniform. He angrily knocked them off his shoulders and head and scratched around in the dark with his fingers to gather them up again. Clutching them hard, this time, he hurled them higher and harder with all his might. Once again, most of them did not clear the upright oleanders and showered back down on him. They landed all around his feet.

He stood there with the oleander cuttings on his shoulders, on his head, and leaning against his pants legs. Slowly counting to three, now he was mad and almost blind with salty perspiration. He was perspiring so hard he had to pull the ski mask off. He stuffed it angrily into his back pocket. Once again, he carefully gathered up the cuttings and stood as close to the fence as he could and counted "One, two, three!" and hurled them with every ounce of energy he could muster.

He frowned as they once again fluttered down around his feet. He was now beaten and discouraged. He was tired and mad. He returned to the house in a darkening mood. He went into the dark kitchen and got another beer. Popping it open, he went outside and sat down heavily in his patio chair. He needed a better plan.

*How could I get the damn oleanders into my neighbor's yard?* he thought and thought. *Maybe a catapult like they used in the Middle Ages? Where do you find one of those?* he wondered. He struggled and struggled, and no good ideas loomed up in the turbulent but empty ocean of his mind. Then, out of nowhere, he thought about bundling them and pitching them over with a pitchfork like he saw them do with hay in the old Western movies. He allowed that idea to percolate around within his mind and take shape as he finished off the beer.

Tossing the empty can in the garbage container near the house, he finally slapped his knee and said lowly, "That's the ticket! That is the new preemptive strike plan!"

He rushed into the garage and found some twine and his shovel. He didn't have a pitchfork. He turned on the outside light and bundled each pile and tied them tight. Then he turned off the light and rested. It was later than planned, and he was tired from all his efforts. His breath was heavy, and he was perspiring. His face was wet even after he wiped it several times with his sleeve. He dragged each bundle up to the fence and then had to rest again.

*My god, it is forty-five minutes past nine o'clock. Patty may be home any minute,* he thought.

He rushed down the hill into the yard toward the patio. He sat down on his chair and impatiently waited, straining for a sound. In a few minutes, at about ten after nine, the front door opened and closed. Patty came in. She did something in the hall and then came back to the kitchen and opened the sliding door.

"I'm back, hon. Are you OK?"

"Sure, dear. Did you have a good time tonight?"

"Oh, so-so. Carey is a little sad these days."

"Oh well, that' s too bad," he added, trying to sound sympathetic.

"Yes, it is! She needs to get out more and do more things. We all have been telling her that! Well, I am going to bed. Did you eat your sandwich?"

"Yes, thanks, dear."

She closed the door, turned off the kitchen light, and went upstairs. He was alone in the dark again. Not even the wind chime was talking to him.

He waited a good fifteen minutes. Then he rose up slowly and stealthily approached the neighbor's fence. He was determined to strike and strike now! He took the shovel he had retrieved from the garage. He started on the pile he had been trying to toss over. He lifted the pile into the shovel and had to step forward quickly. It was heavier than he thought on the end of the shovel. The shovel wobbled around no matter how he held it. His feet slipped, and he danced about to establish a secure footing. He was trying to keep his balance, keep the bundle balanced, and get a good solid footing as first one foot and then the other slipped and twisted on the slope.

Finally, when everything was just right, he swung the shovel in a large arc. When the top of the handle struck the fence with a dull thud, he felt the weight of the oleanders spring forward and fly into his neighbor's yard.

He repeated this maneuver eleven more times, first dancing around on the slope until his weight and the bundle were balanced. Then with all his strength, he hurled it into his neighbor's yard.

He was getting very tired, wet, and disgruntled. Finally, with the last pile on its way, he heard a strange metallic clank and the neighbor's dog barking. He stood still, and he heard the dog's feet padding over to the fence. He heard it sniffing near the fence and pushing its weight against it. Paul held his breath to almost bursting. The dog sneezed loudly and wandered away back to its bed. Paul took a deep breath and staggered back down the hill, almost slipping several times.

Arriving at the bottom, Paul rejoiced, "The strike had been successful! All piles had been locked, loaded, and launched."

Letting the shovel drop on the ground, he staggered back to the patio. He sat down heavily in his padded chair. Exhausted, he sucked in several big breaths of night air.

*Oh oh, he would have to notice the oleanders if they are tied up. He will know! My god, he will know! Don't panic!* he advised himself. *That is OK. The message is just stronger and clearer that way.*

He smiled to himself in the dark and pulled himself upright. He went inside and had a big glass of tap water.

*We will see what happens tomorrow,* he thought. He thought about a shower and then felt he was too tired. He used the excellent excuse that he might wake his wife. She needed her rest.

He had been asleep about three hours when a lot of noise outside woke him. There was, it seemed like, a siren and people moving about. Then he heard an indistinct brief cry. He sleepily got up and pulled on his robe and went to the front door to peek out. He looked out the small window and didn't see much but lots of shadows moving around quickly and some light flashes. He cracked the door open enough to stick his head out and immediately jerked it back inside, shutting the door quickly.

"My god! There are several fire trucks in front with firemen and hoses all over the street."

He opened the door again slightly and heard them talking as they worked. His neighbor Braxton with his wife was near the closest fire truck with blankets wrapped around them and a fireman handing them big steaming mugs of coffee. Although other neighbors were emerging from their homes and coming over to check the wild scene, he decided it was best not to join the party. He tiptoed back upstairs and slowly took off his robe and slipped back into bed. Patty was a very sound sleeper. She frequently took sleeping pills.

He lay there for a long time until the noise subsided and wondered what it was all about. Finally, he slipped into a restless slumber. The next morning, he was up early. Eagerly, he went downstairs and put on a pot of coffee as usual. He had dressed in an old running suit. He went out into the backyard.

It was going to be a nice day. He glanced over toward the neighbor's fence, and he saw nothing! No fence, no oleanders, just a scarred muddy dirt hill!

*What happened? It must have been a fire, but how? Who?* All questions he wanted answered. He walked over for a closer look. The fence had vanished except for the two corners that held the other fence lines at a ninety-degree angle. He was surprised to step into slippery mud. The slope was soaked, and there was a lot of water pooled at the foot of the hill in his yard. There was not an oleander in sight. There were charred bits of the fence on the edge of the hill. The house had strange black streaks all over its side.

He went back into his house and poured some coffee. He finally got up the nerve to go outside to get the morning paper. He innocently walked out into his front yard. He acted casual as he bent over and picked up the paper. As he stood there, he allowed his gaze to fall on the neighbor's house. It took his breath away as he realized there had been a fire over there. The front of the house was also streaked with the black marks, and the fence on their joint side was wiped out!

A voice behind him surprised him.

"Some mess, Paul? You should have seen it last night when the flames were leaping sky high. By the way, where were you last night? Most of us came out to, ah, help."

"Eh, I was asleep last night. I didn't hear a thing. Well now I do remember I had a strange dream about fire engines, but I don't know anything about it. What happened?"

Carl Balm from across the street was a real gossip and pain in the ass; he had plenty to say and filled Paul in on everything. According to him, "Their neighbor had too much to drink, as usual, and set his house on fire. He had come close to setting the whole street on fire! The fireman told him it started in the backyard, and it looked like it was the charcoal grill."

"Either it was knocked over by the dog, or it fell over. The half-cooled briquettes caught the fence on fire. The fire had not caught the house on fire but scarred the entire side, trying to gobble it up. The fireman had put it out before it got into the house itself. They were lucky that the house was only damaged on the outside, but the fence was sure a total loss on that side as well as the plants and some in expensive patio furniture."

Carl continued confidentially, "Braxton was awakened by the burning sound and called the fire department, and he got his wife and dog out of there fast. He was still a little plowed and kept giggling about the whole thing."

"For once, the fire department was on its toes and got here quick, and they put it out in about an hour."

"Oh wow!" exclaimed Paul.

He went quickly back into his house and tried to think it through. He sat there at the kitchen table, sorting through the newspaper and thought about what had happened.

*Maybe I had somehow done it? No, how could that be? Well, I heard that noise. Maybe I knocked the grill over? No, it must have been the dog, not me. Yes, the stupid dog did it.*

Anyway, all of the oleander bushes were gone, so that was a big improvement! When Patty got up, she was upset when she heard about the fire and immediately made some cookies and within the hour was on the Braxton's doorstep with her healing food. Patty had a long talk with Bertha, Braxton's wife, and came back full of additional information. Patty told him what Bertha said, "It was Bertha that heard the fire and called the fire department. Roger was passed out on the couch. He probably knocked over the grill when he was looking for more beer in the outside ice chest. Bertha was very upset about his drinking. This was the last straw. She was talking about getting a divorce."

Paul listened quietly but said nothing. No one had told him how hard it was to deal with the unexpected fall out of a preemptive strike.

He was very upset about any role he might have had in causing a fire. Paul felt depressed and went to the lodge in the afternoon, driving away from both houses. The talk there was of the fire, but no one knew much more than what he had already heard. He headed for home stopping at the grocery to get some milk and chocolate chip cookies.

He got home, and there was a note from Patty that Roger had called several times, and she had gone to her mother's and would not be back until nine o'clock that evening. There was yet another tuna sandwich in the refrigerator for him. Paul tried to watch TV and got very restless. He looked at the note several times and then decided he better finally call Roger. He dialed the phone and waited while it rang, once, twice, three times, hoping he would get the innocuous answering service voice. Then a slurred male voice answered, "Hi, he, aha, hello." A small burp could be heard.

"Roger, it's Paul. How are you doing?"

"Fine! Considering, I mean, I have lost my house and now my wife. And the insurance company says I missed my payment, so they do not have to pay me anything. Other than that, OK."

"Oh my gosh! That is terrible."

"Yeah, and I can't let the dog out because of the fence, so I have to walk it every other hour."

"Well, I am sorry. Is there anything I can do?"

"No no, I will be OK. Thanks for calling. You want a beer?" Braxton slurred.

"No, not tonight."

Paul hung up the phone and sat there for a while, feeling tired and sad. "Perhaps preemptive strikes were not all they were cracked up to be," he declared to himself. He finally found a baseball game to watch on TV and had several beers before eating the sandwich Patty had left him. It wasn't tuna but baloney on rye with swiss cheese and mustard – his favorite.

When Patty came home and let herself into the house, she found him asleep on the couch. She woke him up, and they both went silently upstairs to bed. It had been a long day. The next morning, Patty was up early and was having coffee with Paul. He had sort of forgotten about the trouble and was reading the newspaper about the never-ending war in Iraq. The phone rang. It was early for them to get a call. Patty answered it, and Paul looked at her inquiringly.

She waved it at him and said, "It's for you."

"Me?"

"Yes, Paul. The man said he wanted you," she spoke with some irritation.

Paul reached out and, taking the phone, answered the call by saying, "Hello."

The voice at the other end said, "Is this Paul Waterman?"

"Yes," he replied.

"Are you Mr. Roger and Bertha Braxton's next-door neighbor?"

"Well, yes."

"I am Jenkins Harken of the Imperial Insurance Company. I would like to drop by today and ask you a few questions. Would noon today be OK?"

"Well, yes, I guess. What is this about?"

"Just a formality regarding the Braxtons' fire insurance claim."

Paul hung up the phone and was worried. He thought, *They know. Someone had seen him, and they know!* The morning dragged on for Paul. Finally, at noon sharp, the doorbell rang. When he opened it, there stood Mr. Jenkins Harken. He introduced himself and pushed into the house while handing Paul his card. "Can I look at your neighbor's house from your backyard?"

Paul took him through the kitchen. He opened the sliding door and ushered him into the backyard. Harken had a small camera and immediately took some pictures toward the Braxton place. He ambled over to the base of the hill and poked around but finally returned to the house. He picked up the shovel and placed it against the house wall. He returned and then entered the kitchen. Paul offered him a chair at the kitchen table, and they both sat down. Harken was writing in a notebook and finally said while finishing up, "Well, it looks like the whole damage to the house, fence, and yard is about $6,800."

"Oh," said Paul. *Why is he telling me this?* he thought to himself.

"Yes."

"I thought Roger had forgotten to pay his premium?" Paul inquired.

"Well, I don't know anything about that, Mr. Waterman. It is apparently paid, or I would not be sitting here. We will settle with them for the fire damages. It looks like an unfortunate accident, but I need to advise you, you will have to pay for your half of the cost to replace the fence since it is a joint ownership item."

"Me? Why me?"

"Well, it is a joint property line, and you both own the fence in accordance with the deed Mr. Braxton provided me. I estimate the replacement of the fence and painting will run about $3,000. So you will have to pay $1,500, or, of course, your insurance company will." He smiled reassuringly. "Of course, you can work out the details out with Mr. Braxton as good neighbors always do," he said, giving Paul a small but happy smile.

"Let me get this straight." Paul started getting angry. "I have to pay for half the fence that drunk burned down?"

"Well, you are responsible for your portion of the repair if it is repaired. I do not think anyone has claimed he burned it down nor do I expect they will. It is not really that complicated. Just inform your insurance company and give them my information from the card I provided you, and we will work out the details with them. There will be no problem I am confident of that." Again, there appeared the reassuring smile.

Harken snapped his notebook closed and rose to depart. After the man left, Paul was furious. They had saved all year and had barely $2,000 dollars in their bank account. Now he had to cough up $1,500 for a fence replacement.

"What is happening in this world?" Paul was very agitated and finally found his insurance agent's phone number in the telephone book and dialed him. When a male voice answered, her said abruptly, "Ross, this is Paul, Paul Waterman."

"Yes, Paul, what can I do for you today?"

"Well, my neighbor has had a fire, and our joint property fence burned down. His insurance company said I had to pay for half the repair."

"Well, that sounds correct on a joint ownership item like a fence."

"Well, OK, here is the agent's name and – "

"Just a minute, Paul, let me check your policy."

After about thirty seconds, he was back. "Oh, Paul, you cancelled the fire clause for external structures several years ago, remember? Your policy would no longer cover the fence."

Paul sighed and looked down at his feet and asked in a small voice, "Are you sure?"

"Well, yes, I am looking at your policy online. So in this case, we will not get involved. You should work it out with your neighbor's insurance company, and maybe next year, you will want to add that clause back?"

Paul mumbled "Yeah, OK, thanks" and hung up.

He lay down on the old green couch and tried very hard to understand what was happening to him. He now would have to come up with the $1,500! Talk about unfair. He remained there until his wife came home. He told her about the agent's visit and the insurance situation. She listened quietly, and she looked sad.

"Well, I guess we will have to wait another year for that vacation," was her only comment as she went slowly upstairs.

"Yes, Patty, I am sorry," he called out from behind her.

"Oh, Paul, you are not to blame. Who would have guessed that fool would set his fence on fire?" Her voice trailed back down the stairs.

Paul got up and went outside to sit on the patio. He heard the phone ring, and Patty answered it and talked for a while. After hanging it up, she joined him. She plopped down in a chair next to his and started in, "That was Bertha. She had made the insurance payment for Roger. She has forgiven him, and they are going to take a short trip while the house and fence are being repaired. The cleanup crew will be here on Monday to start, and she asked me to let them into the house if they have to get inside. She will give us a key later today. She is so excited they are going to San Diego and will not be back until late Tuesday. Oh, and then the gardener will be here on Tuesday early to replace the plants."

"Plants? What plants? I'm not paying for any plants!"

"Oh no, of course not, dear. She said their insurance payment included an amount for that repair. She also said that they were so lucky to find out that the gardener's brother specializes in inexpensive large lot plant orders. He is going to do it all for just 10 percent above his cost. So they will even have an extra amount of money left from the insurance payment. Isn't that great?"

"Yes, great. Did she mention what kind of plants they were putting in?" he asked hesitantly.

"Well now, let me think. Whatever they had before I think she said. Whatever they were, they grew like mad."

"Oleanders?" The question hung in the air.

"Oleanders, why, yes. That is what she said. Right. How did you know? You don't pay any attention to the yard."

"Just a lucky guess," he said in a growling tone. Then to himself, he thought, *Oh no, here we go again!*

Patty jumped up and went into the house. The sliding door clicked shut behind her. Paul sat quietly, looking into the backyard.

He had to reluctantly admit to himself that his father was right. "There is no free lunch." And he added his own corollary, "Preemptive strikes suck. They are risky games at best that will always cost you in the long run."

After some time thinking about the past few days' events, he felt like crying but bit his lip and toughed it out. However, he cried out in anguish to no one in particular, "Damn those bushes! Damn that Bush!"

## The End

# The Uninvited Guest

It was almost December. It was late in the afternoon on Saturday. The blue sky was fading into a deeper gray. The wind was picking up outside his comfortable small cabin. The trees were starting to sway and sigh. Morgan Stark had been living there, almost like a hermit for over three years now. His wife had died five years ago, and he had just lost interest in their old life and his environmental protection efforts in Los Angeles. He had resigned himself to leaving the California crush and glitter for a quiet change of pace, his retirement to the mountains.

He had submitted a two-week resignation letter for his director's position with the Native Indian Save the Earth (NISE) group. None of the board members had protested very much actually. They could get a younger less-opinionated man for a lot less money. He had sold his home of twenty-five years in Montebello, an affluent Los Angeles suburb. He had sold or given away all their accumulated belongings and moved here to Idaho with as little as possible to remind him of the past. Unfortunately, although all the material things were scattered behind him, he still remembered.

Morgan was a five-feet-eight-inches-tall man who walked with a slight limp caused by mild arthritis. He was graying rapidly but still had a full head of hair. He had crooked teeth that showed when he smiled, which was seldom. His quiet gray eyes were always alert and observing his world intently. Over the past three years, he had developed a definite lifestyle routine. Every day, he got up at dawn and hiked around the forest area that surrounded his cabin for several miles. He would return in an hour and fix a bowl of dry cereal and have two pieces of whole wheat toast without butter.

He then put on a big pot of coffee. While the old tarnished pot was percolating sluggishly away, he strolled down to the mailbox. It was about a mile away at the end of his long snaking gravel driveway. He would get his mail and, most importantly, the daily morning newspapers. He then returned to the small kitchen and poured a big mug of dark coffee. He would sit down at the old white kitchen table and sort the mail. He read the mail quickly since it mostly was dull and boring advertisements. The mail was all advertisements anymore sprinkled with an occasional monthly bill. He, however, enjoyed working methodically through the pages of his three daily newspapers.

He had no phone, not even a cell phone. His generation's communication style had not been seduced into the insidious constant dependence on a cell phone to reach out and touch someone at all times of the day or night.

When he completed that chore, he would read a book until noon. He had been trying to read only fiction books so he would not get too excited or involved. He then fixed himself a sandwich. He stocked packages of deli ham, roast beef, or turkey. Morgan alternated his choice of sandwich meat each day unless he was very hungry then he used several together. He used both mustard and mayonnaise and only a token amount of shredded lettuce to satisfy the veggie gods. He walked in his small garden behind the cabin while eating it with his trusty big endlessly refilled mug of coffee. He would check all the bird feeders and refill those that needed bird seed. When that task was complete, his day was half over.

At one o'clock sharp, he sat down at his computer and answered the e-mails that still came pouring in at him from all over the world. Depending on the questions asked, he could spend several hours responding to them. Occasionally, he would even have to research something to provide the questioner with a comprehensive answer. He had his well-worn library of source books and a large set of personal files and reports in several old file cabinets. They generally wanted to know about some environmental problem or issue that he had been associated with in the past. Sometimes, it was a reporter. He didn't answer the reporters, just trashed their e-mails without bothering to read them.

When he was finished, he played solitaire on the computer until six o'clock sharp. His grandmother had taught him to play the game as a child to keep him busy. They used an old worn deck of cards back then, not a fancy electronic gadget. She had to frequently slap his hand or admonish him with a clucking "tish tish' when she noticed he was cheating. It was his cheating when she wasn't looking that killed his interest in the game. However, when he got a computer version bundled in his software on his PC, he found he could not cheat and, once again, was intrigued enough to again take up the activity in earnest. After all, if it was good enough for Napoleon, then it was good enough for him. Of course, Napoleon, who was a European, played patience, which was the English term for the Americans' solitaire.

Then, he fixed a light dinner. Generally, he depended upon a large stock of frozen dinners that he heated in the microwave oven. He finished the evening watching TV for several hours. He had indulged himself with a satellite dish, so he got an ungodly number of channels. He especially liked old movies then any history program or current events program. He successfully suppressed any feelings that might compel him to do more productive work. He would watch the late news. He actually relished wasting away his entire evening. It was his one really bad habit. He would then get ready for bed and, propped up with several pillows, read his book until midnight. Turning off the light, snuggling down into his blankets, he would drop off to sleep. He always slept soundly. However, he didn't sleep long. He knew he dreamed but seldom remembered about what or why.

The only day he interrupted this schedule was on Saturday. On Saturday, he didn't take a hike but drove his aging 1999 Ford truck into the little town of Braxton about twenty-five miles away. It was another thirty miles farther south to Boise. Braxton only had three eating places, and two were more bars than diners. So he frequented the Gibraltar Dinner and Sandwich Shop. That is where he indulged himself with his weekly big Saturday morning breakfast.

He liked to have two sunny-side up eggs and a rare steak with lots of heavily buttered rye toast. He skipped the side of fried potatoes in deference to his doctor's dire warnings. He also had several cups of steaming hot coffee. He would flirt with the young waitresses and leave them a big tip. Funny though, they seemed to change so frequently, he had trouble remembering their names. He just called them all "darling." He was old enough to get away with that. He wondered if the turnover was because the owner was such a foulmouthed person or that the girls, once they got trained, could find better jobs in the larger more interesting cities.

The owner of the Gibraltar Dinner and Sandwich Shop was Calvin Mitrand. He was fifty years old and had lived in the town all his life. He was not a good cook but had worked in the restaurant until his father died just before Morgan had moved into the area. Calvin inherited the restaurant from his father. He recognized his own shortcomings as a cook and immediately hired a suitable cook. Things got much better at the shop after that. The business boomed, and local people came more often to the shop to eat and talk to their friends.

Calvin was not well liked by the townspeople, but his new cook's ability certainly was. When things picked up, he was able to stay away from the shop and liked to sit at home and drink beer all day. Since the shop made him money, he had all the beer he wanted; and the more he stayed away, the more money it seemed to make for him. He was not an intelligent man, but even he finally got the connection. He was loud man. He swore a lot, so most of his customers unfortunate enough to encounter him avoided extended conversations with him. The few hours Calvin now spent at the shop during the week were the ones that his customers avoided being there if at all possible.

Since all the young waitresses spoke of going off to Boise, Chicago, or someplace else, he guessed they just worked here long enough to save the money to move on. After his meal, he would do any shopping he needed to at the local stores. He usually would be home by noon sharp to follow his usual afternoon schedule. Life was not all that bad. The days drifted past, and he even got interested in something every now and then. He was just turning sixty, and surprisingly, it looked like he would see sixty-five. While he did feel lonely on occasion, he really didn't miss the intensity of environmental causes and certainly felt relieved not to have to be begging for money all the time at the inevitable endless fund-raising events.

When the weather held warm, he liked going to town. When it got rainy, he disliked the ride and wet, but he sure enjoyed the hot coffee and the smells and sounds of the busy sandwich shop. He had been given a dog as a going-away gift by his staff, and the dog was a good one, but he disappeared several weeks after they got settled into the cabin. The local veterinarian advised him it was probably eaten by a wild creature since a lot of people in the area lost pets that way, especially the tourists who didn't understand the concept of a wilderness area. He hated to think that is what happened to his dog. He preferred to think that he got wanderlust and escaped on a great adventure crossing rivers, mountains, and deserts – living off the land until he found a place where he preferred to reside rather than with Morgan at the little cabin.

*Oh well, he is gone. Good old Barrel is off somewhere else,* he thought.

He called him Barrel since he seemed to roll around the cabin all the time in rushes of excitement brought on by every new noise and smell.

Morgan definitely decided not to replace him. He really hadn't planned on a pet anyway, and that was that. It was a little lonelier, but he didn't need to worry about something depending upon him, which had its advantages. It was the last Saturday in November, and Morgan had been home several hours after his trip to town. He was getting tired of the same questions flowing to him on the computer. He no longer had old friends, just these youngsters who liked to pester him with questions. He decided to leave the dozen or so remaining messages for tomorrow and keyed in the solitaire game early. He was unable to complete three hands and was about ready to give up but was now on one that seemed to be working out.

The front door rattled. He then realized it was not the wind but someone knocking. He didn't want to interrupt his game since his score was time dependent, but he seldom had callers, and maybe it was an emergency. He reluctantly ended his game. He rose with an effort and slowly walked toward the door, calling out, "Hold on, I will be there in a minute."

The knock was louder, now a steady solid drumming. He opened the door and was shocked but not enough to show it. There was a large solid man standing there in a dark black three-piece suit. It was a very expensive suit. A vaguely familiar voice from the long distant past asked, "Well, aren't you going to ask me in, Morgan?"

Morgan stepped back as he mumbled "Well, of course. Come in, come on in" but none too warmly.

The man looked quickly around outside before entering and then on the inside while walking into the cabins living room. He stood there, waiting for Morgan to catch up with him and scanned and studied the room expertly. He turned and looked at Morgan with a sly grin.

"Long time no see?"

"Yes, but not long enough," replied Morgan gruffly.

"Why, Morgan, I thought we were friends," responded his uninvited guest with a feigned mock surprise.

"We may have been long ago, but we are no longer friends. Now that I think about it, we were never really friends!"

The man affected sadness but obviously didn't give a damn. He sat down on the edge of a large stuffed couch and stretched his legs out, saying, "I came a long way to see you, and now I am here. Why don't we try to enjoy my brief visit? I am sure it will be my very last one."

"I can accept that," Morgan said, and he sat in a smaller stuffed chair opposite the man. As they sat, a whole sea of memories came crashing back to Morgan. There were various private and public meetings with this man; a few meals at expensive restaurants over the past; unfriendly discussions at conferences and during government programs, and, finally, the agencies' strange demands and endless large monetary enticements. *No, this man was never a friend, not even an associate. He was a bad weed that kept growing back into his life.*

The man reached into his inside jacket pocket and pulled out a large white envelope. He handed it to Morgan, saying, "We are cleaning up our past cases and feel, in retrospect, you should have this."

Morgan was puzzled. He took the envelope and opened it. He was surprised, actually stupefied, to see a check, a check for – for, my god, $500,000! It was a certified check made out to him.

"Good lord! What is this all about?" he demanded, becoming a little frightened.

The man smiled broadly and replied smoothly, "Let's call it a settlement."

"A settlement? A settlement of what or for what? For what? Why?"

"Why, for the damages the agency may have possibly inflicted on you, your family, and your friends over the years."

"What are you talking about? What damages?"

"Well, yes, that is the issue. We were required to take incursive actions in the past to perhaps interrupt or curtail your activities, and this helps us balance the account, so to speak. It is sort of a new policy the agency is introducing to clean up our past excessive aggressiveness."

"What account? I never worked for you or your damn agency!"

"Well, no, not really. But thanks to being who you are and what you are, we were able to become very successful in neutralizing your impact and blunting the associations and odd humanitarian groups you represented while meeting our goals. In fact, in retrospect, you were very integral in many policy outcomes that we established. I will have to admit, at the time, I would certainly not have described it that way. Your obstinacy forced us to be even more creative in achieving our desired agency objectives."

"What in the hell are you talking about? Haven't you learned to speak directly yet?"

The man settled back and opened his coat, pulling his vest down, and slowly stroked the couch arm lightly with one hand and continued, "Let me recapitulate. If you remember, in 1978, we approached you to do a top secret chemical research project. And you righteously refused due to your high level of ethics. We actually had several meetings with you. But despite all our persuasion, you ultimately refused, and we politely said goodbye."

"Yes, exactly. And what you called as 'politely' was more threatening than polite as I recall. So what is this for?" He waved the envelope with its check in the air.

"Well, I am sure you thought that was the end of it, but it was not. No, definitely not. You remember the tall man that accompanied me at our last meeting concerning that matter?"

"Vaguely. He was a quiet insidious person with very mean eyes. Your trainee, I believe you said?"

Pursing his lips and looking slightly pleased, he replied, "Well, he was actually my supervisor, and I was the one in the training position at the time. His name was Stewart Pierce Jones. He always remembered you and really disliked you for not accepting our generous offer. He and I ascended the agency organization over the years with him always one position ahead of me. We worked together for over twenty years on many projects and all those that involved you. In fact, he is a big part of the reason I had to come all the way out here today."

"Anyway, back to the beginning. We were quite successful in recruiting Latimure to do the research project. You remember him, big man with very sloppy eating habits. He was certainly not as competent as you but far less ethical and a very prodigious worker. He also was very interested in wealth and prestige."

"Of course, I remember him. We went to undergraduate school together. Good heavens! Franklin Case Latimure has been dead for over ten years."

"Yes, that is true, right after accepting the Nobel Prize for medical research on synthetic poison treatments. He was a great man in his fashion. He fell far short in many ways, but he became wealthy and honored doing research for us. These, of course, were projects that grew out of the original one you refused to do."

Morgan shifted his position in the chair and was becoming agitated. "There must be some point to all this?"

"Yes, oh yes, you do know me well enough to know that. But how about some of that great coffee you are always drinking as you wander around your old homestead with mug in hand." He grinned warmly, but the insidious intent of this casual remark struck home.

Morgan had forgotten so much about these people! My god, this man was a viper. A man of no scruples, a man without a heart or soul. He was a dedicated government agency man who hid his agendas even from himself.

"Of course, let me get us some." Morgan welcomed an excuse to leave his presence. He hurried out of the room. The well-dressed man eased a large Walther P38 out of his shoulder holster and placed it under the cushion next to him. He leaned back comfortably on the couch.

While he did this, Morgan was taking his time getting the coffee ready. He needed to think. He needed to think hard. Kent always wanted something, always. What could it possibly be this time? Morgan was well out of most of the mainstream of research now. He left chemical research long years ago. Morgan remembered they always made outrageous demands, offered tons of money, and then acted offended if you dared to decline. What could he possible want of him, after all these years? Morgan reappeared in a few minutes with two hot mugs of coffee and handed his uninvited guest one.

Morgan sat down and said, "Well, here it is. But I remember you as more of hard liquor man, Kent." It was the first time he mentioned the man's name.

"Oh, that smells good." Kent inhaled loudly. "Yes. I do prefer good bourbon on the rocks but not while on duty."

"Are you on duty?"

"Well, yes and no, but I now have to limit my drinking in the evening hours. My age is catching up with me fast. I also have a long drive back to the airport tonight." As usual, he didn't really answer the question.

Morgan was really becoming more alert, alive, edgy – in fact, he hadn't been so alert since the last time he had seen Kent. He decided it was time to test the waters. "When did we meet last, Kent?"

Kent's eye brows rose in surprise at the question, and he reflected momentarily then responded, "It was in DC, I think. Yes, on Christmas Eve in 2002."

Morgan looked strange since he didn't recall that at all. He certainly remembered the date since Carl and Maria were killed late in the evening on that day in a terrible early-morning car accident.

That was when they were all in DC in preparation of the big New Year's Day Green Peace rally. Morgan cleared his throat and said, "I think you must be mistaken. That was a terrible day for me personally and a very long sad night, but I don't recall you being involved."

"Yes, it was, I guess. I suppose you are right, and I am confused as I said my age is playing tricks on me. What do you remember?"

"Why I think it was in late in 2000 when you and your associate or boss or whatever he was asked me to cease editing the *Avenger*."

"Oh yes," he said, slapping his leg. "I suppose that is it. We came by your office late that night, and you were surprised and eventually you even threatened to throw us out. You had developed such a temper for being such an ethical and professional scientist. Of course, you were under a lot of pressure from the magazine's directors and then there was the tragedy of the Oristins."

This grabbed Morgan's attention. The Oristins had been a lovely couple from Georgia, and they were heavy financial backers of the *Avenger*. They had just died the day before in a tragic skiing accident in Colorado. His friend Jacob had just called him to let him know of the sad news when the Vampire Team strode into his office. He started to respond, "Yes, I was very unclear on that. Why you cared about the magazine at all. It was just a low-visibility environmental rag trying to get people worked up about problems of toxic waste dumps in the Deep South. It was hardly an issue of any military or government concern. I suspect my anger came more from the loss of my friends than from your strange late-night visit. You two were just the last straw."

"Oh, that is why you have been so wrong over the years, environmental or climate or almost anything that has a political military shade to it is our business. Everything has a military industrial complex relationship. Your actions and ideas and the military industrial complex are all linked together as are all our citizens. As you found out later, your magazine's silly assertions triggered some bigger activities, and we almost had to take even more direct action. But of course, tragically, your office burned down three weeks later on January 19, 2000. And you were out of business anyway. You should have just taken the money and taken a long vacation." He smiled broadly.

Morgan frowned; only Kent would remember the date and stab him with it. "It was always money with you guys. You were prepared to buy everything. By the way, speaking of money, what do you want me to do with this money?"

Kent threw up his hands and opened his arms widely and then said sternly, "Why, whatever you want! Take a trip, buy a car, donate it to one of your pet pinko activism groups you love to support and have continued to support. It wasn't my idea to give it to you incidentally. No, unfortunately, we have reorganized. And the new management has come up with this settlement crap. I mean, you had the offers in the past and refused, why should we balance accounts now? Seems a little silly to me, but I am an old-fashioned agent, and it is a new day dawning. It is yours to spend as you want or save for a rainy day I suppose. But you were never much of a saver, were you?"

Morgan was sitting back and studying the smooth face. There was so much under that polished surface. He had always been frightened by Kent. He seemed to be so calm and focused and knew ten times as much as you would expect he should or would about the topic at hand. He had tried to outthink him in the past but with precious little success. Kent had appeared briefly or just popped up in several periods of Morgan's hectic life, periods that were, in retrospect, always very difficult for him.

"Why do you chide me about saving?"

"Well, old man, a small pension and less than $25,000 invested hardly seems like the results of a life of diligent frugality, now does it?"

He would have been surprised that he knew this, but he now remembered how much the agency always knew about everyone and everything before they dealt with you.

"Oh well, I never made much," he defended his financial failure weakly.

Whose fault was that? Kent pressed him, "If you played along with us just once, your poor wife would still be alive."

At the mention of his wife, Morgan flashed angrily, "What are you talking about? She died of an acute attack on the way to the hospital!"

"No, she didn't, Morgan," Kent scolded. "She died because you had an old car that crapped out on you on the way to the hospital, and by the time you called 911 from a telephone booth and they got an ambulance out to you, she had expired." He then added with what appeared to be sincerity, "She was a fine and noble wife, certainly more than you deserved."

Morgan was stunned. He loved his wife so much. He had never blamed her death on the events of that terrible evening. He certainly had not worked out this line of argument. Then he realized maybe Kent was right! He had killed his wife by being too ethical! No no, he pushed that immediately out of his mind. He had to! This was just Kent's weird way of goading him and causing him emotional pain. After he regained his composure, he said, "The money? What is the string?"

"Oh, nothing much really. We would like you to turn off your environmental propaganda blog and stop encouraging others to follow in your shallow and dangerous shadow of environmental mishmash and damage."

"What are you talking about?"

"Why, Cleanenviron.net, old man."

"That isn't a blog. That is just my e-mail address."

"Don't quibble. You always were so precise and difficult. You spend every afternoon contacting others about the environmental groups you supported in the past and training hapless youngsters in eco-terrorism by encouraging them with your endless justifications of environmental importance, correctness, and concern."

"Eco-terrorism, you are insane!" Morgan raised his voice.

"Well, not perhaps that strong, I guess, in your case. But they learn the basics of environmental activism from you and then build up to it. They adapt to their own eco-terrorist capabilities."

Morgan asked incredulously, "You are giving me $500,000 to close my Internet mailing address?"

"Well, essentially. And of course, we just wish for you to stay away from the whole area for the remainder of you life. No e-mails, no articles, no books or memoirs about you or your life. No e-mail address anymore, anywhere. After all, you are retired. Enjoy it. Act retired. Let it all go. It is all old dusty history now anyway."

"Oh, this is ridiculous. All I am doing is providing a handful of people with my ideas, approaches, and history of environmental activism. I never was an eco-terrorist nor were any of the groups I worked for or supported."

"So you say." Kent drained his mug and put it down on the end table with a loud thud. He glanced out the window. The night was beginning to turn a deep dark gray. The moon was rising, and the white clouds were being highlighted.

"Well, I haven't much time to discuss the finer points of all this with you, so let's do the bottom-line thing as the bean counters like to say, and then I can go. I will then leave you in peace and tranquility. I have a plane to catch and other appointments. I am going to leave with or without the check depending on you. It is your call." He stared blankly at Morgan, searching his face for a reaction, any kind of reaction.

Morgan was still desperately trying to outrun this certain whirlwind of disaster, this government man. Like a complex chess game, there was an endgame that was being driven by Kent. Morgan didn't know the endgame, and he had to figure it out and figure it out fast! Kent was a dangerous man in a dangerous organization who was not to be taken lightly. That much he knew. He also was now vaguely aware that maybe some of the past tragedies of his life were not accidents but something else. But then, conspiracy theories were never his strength. Besides, what in the world could he have been doing that would merit that much government attention and interference?

Morgan, in desperation, decided to go on the attack. "Well, this is lot of money, but I really only have the e-mail address to allow people to contact me since I no longer have a phone."

"With that amount of money, buy a cell phone, Morgan! Stay off the Internet. Keep a very low profile," Kent said this in a sharper tone than he intended.

"What possible concern do you or the agency have around the obtuse ecological issues I discuss on the Internet?"

"Damn it, Morgan, don't be so fucking slow! Things happen for all the wrong reasons. But they happen. The agency currently has a policy that includes eco-terrorism in its definition of terrorism. Any discussions about environmental issues that lead to tree hugging or spiking, public marches for humanity, boycotts of governments or experimental animal releases interrupt our society's delicate power structure balance and, ultimately, our global industrial relationships."

"Good lord! How can you turn the desire to save an endangered species into a global industrial complex-governmental business issue?"

"Well, in all honesty, I don't. But others do. That is who is in the driver's seat now. That is who gives me my directions. Right now, due to the government's position on several sensitive issues, we are trying to minimize environmental protests no matter how mild so we can focus on the real threeat to this country – global terrorism. Your friend's silly protests are never successful anyway, but they certainly muddy the waters for the rest of us."

Morgan stood. He began pacing a little as Kent talked faster while still observing him closely. While talking, Kent looked at his watch impatiently and regretted having bothered to come inside to do this job. But then, Stewart wanted it done up close and personal, in the open, face to face. He certainly owed Stewart that much. He had also secretly wanted to see Morgan again and find out what his last thoughts might be.

Morgan said, "Well, in that case, forget it." Waving the check in Kent's face, he continued, "Here, take the damn check and get on with your work! Whatever that might be. I really do not want a life that is any different than what I now have."

"Oh, Morgan, you dumb pain in the ass. Why couldn't you be normal and greedy like everyone else on this planet? Do you know the damage you caused in your sweet ethical life? Do you even have a vague idea of your damage?"

This shocked Morgan. He was not prepared for nor used to personal attacks. "What are you talking about?"

He sat down tiredly, trying to deal with it all. It just exploded on him out of the blue.

Kent knew he was stepping over the line, but this guy really had set him off from the first day they met – not only him, but Stewart also. He would almost froth at the mouth when his name was mentioned. They just found his homegrown ethics so damn difficult, and they both hated the man for continuously denying all their endless lucrative offers.

Kent held up his left hand and, counting on his fingers, said, "Marylyn Springer, on one finger. Todd Martin, second finger. Karen Nadinea third finger. David Twill, fourth finger. Martin Freztinger, fifth finger and then – he paused – that makes five I believe."

Morgan looked confused. These were all friends he had known and worked with years ago. They had all died early in their young lives in a variety of violent accidents. Two had died in separate car accidents and two in an avalanche while skiing and the other in a car bombing in the Middle East.

Kent looked harder and, raising his other hand, continued counting. "Six, Mary Young. Kerry Sweetwater, seven. Eight, Zero Mottinspit. Nine, Thelma Marintal. And ten, Cornish Palar, not to mention your dear wife. And last but not least, our loveable Nobel Prize winner, Latimure!"

"What about all these people? They are, were, all dear friends or colleagues of mine. What are you saying?"

"Morgan, if you had taken our offers, these people would still, very probably, be alive today. But no, you wouldn't. You didn't, and then you moved though life sharing your view of your glorious global environmental fantasy you had, enmeshing those people in your schemes. They all ended up dead due to 'untimely accidents' that shouldn't have happened and would not have happened if they were not somehow involved in your nefarious environmental causes."

Morgan was really stunned. He sat there crushed in remorse. Suddenly and shockingly he realized what Kent meant but wasn't saying directly.

"This is very depressing. I came up here to forget the past. It wasn't my fault they died. How in the world could it be?"

He became agitated and then, distractedly switching the subject, said nervously, "Coffee, I need some more coffee."

Kent held up his mug and said, smiling broadly, "Me too, I guess. It is getting cold, and you never make a fire in the evening during the week."

Morgan was angry, he was activated, he was alive! He had somehow gotten up to speed with Kent. Now he had to desperately race ahead of him. He knew what he meant, and he knew what he must do to save himself. That he needed to be saved he was now absolutely certain. He had even briefly thought how he must save himself.

He left the room quickly with the two mugs. Kent tried to call someone on his cell. After three tries and not getting a signal, he gave up in disgust. He thought to himself, *Damn, damn old man. Why did I allow him to get me so upset? Stewart always was upset when they mentioned him. Now I know why. Morgan was such an exasperation to them. He had managed to blunder repeatedly into the agency plans at least four times in the past twenty years. How could that be just random actions?*

He slowly reached under the cushion and checked for the gun. He leaned back, figuring he would be done in ten minutes at the outside. He saw the check lying on the coffee table, half out of the envelope.

Morgan returned, handing him the big mug of steaming coffee. Kent took a sip and gasped "Ooohoo, ouch!" accompanied by a waving gesture, indicating that it was hot. Morgan looked at him calmly. He had to stall for time now. He had to act a critical last role.

He inquired, "Why did you think we had seen each other in December 2002?"

Kent, a little surprised at the pointed question, just slid past it with, "Oh, I just mixed up the event of the deaths, which is in your file, with the fact I happened to be there that week."

"Oh, of course. You have my file?"

Kent looked pleased that this dumb ass didn't even know his own importance. "Yes, we have a file on you, the FBI has a file on you, and the CIA has file on you. You were known as a former PhD academician who was a respected specialist in exotic chemical poison research who became an environmental activist fighting for endangered species, energy emission suppression, and, ultimately, the end to global warming."

"You gave speeches at questionable international and national meetings. You traveled to questionable countries. You drank and dined with questionable people. You had appeared on TV and radio in forums supportive of eco-terrorism and civil disobedience. Are you seriously telling me you didn't know your subversive behaviors were noted and that you had been closely watched?" he asked incredulously, showing his agency mentality.

"Well, I hadn't thought of them as subversive," muttered Morgan.

"Man, all you do is think but, apparently, about all the wrong things. If you followed up on the opportunities we offered, you would be rich, and your wife and all those other friends of yours would be here to celebrate your next birthday with you. Sixty-one, is it not?"

"What! My wife! Why are you here trying to accuse me of causing my wife's death? My god! I loved that woman, and now I miss her so much!" This was said with a striking sadness.

"Oh, for Christ's sake, Morgan! I want you to have some decent final years, for crying out loud! Do you think we liked having to take such direct action to minimize your impact? Good lord! We had so many more important problems to deal with. Jesus, we still do!"

"Then why did you do it? Why did you hound me to help you?"

Kent looked a little off guard and replied, "We needed you at first, and then we wanted to bring you to your knees. Stewart, who died last year from pancreatic cancer, always became angry when he heard about your bumbling efforts. You must understand that he was my friend as well as boss, and he really had it in for you."

"He blamed you, you know. He blamed you for most of all the problems we had initially and for those in the last several years, especially in Macedonia! He felt if you had only just accepted the generous amounts of money offered and stayed at home, but no, you had to go and shoot off your mouth to PBS and then do a *Pravda* interview."

"Blamed me for what?

"For the few failures we had over the years. The political failures we sustained in South America, Africa, and the Middle East. He was always tracing them back to you or at least to the many cover organizations you were always involved with."

"What are you telling me? All these years, somehow your agency was controlling the organizations I was associated with?"

"We manipulated outcomes to meet our government's positions at the time. When it was of a primary concern, yes, we usually stopped them dead."

"How could that have been? They were all positive activist environmental groups hoping to save some small part of the world from its own self-destruction. You are a counterespionage agency. What would you care about them!" he was almost yelling now.

"Well, you must understand that in themselves, nothing. But sometimes, they got in the way of our national global policy positions."

"What are you talking about 'in the way'? How could the get in the way? In the way of what?"

"We required certain things to transpire. We had a long-term plan and goals, and they got in the way. That is all," he stated this matter-of-factly, with a cold finality.

Morgan was flabbergasted. This polished government man sitting in his living room made no sense to him. *What he wanted was now very clear to him, but why was he there giving him money? Morgan was veering off course. He wasn't ahead of this man only hanging onto his coattails. He needed more evidence before –*

Kent leaned forward and decided to button this all down. "Look, Morgan, I am gong to give you one example and then you better catch on, catch up, and get on board! When you were with *Green World United*, they were trying to blockade the killing of whales by the Japanese. At that time, we were working to increase the prestige of the Japanese government and link them tighter to China's growing economy. This was a way to ensure their economy did not collapse."

"Your organization brought negative press down on them, and that scared the Chinese off who were just finding their economic feet. And it killed the planned industrial support to the Japanese, provided through a neutral country – all funded by us. Now do you see? You and your dedicated friends were mucking around in matters far more complex and delicate than you could even imagine."

"That is what it is all about – international global policy and the ultimate survival of our countries and our partner's economies. We did what was necessary to stop you and your groups and also mend the holes you tore in our planned efforts."

He paused and looked deeply into Morgan's eyes to see if anything was registering. All he saw was incredulous horror. He continued, "You were within an inch of dying yourself, but unfortunately, your unique connection to the ruling party in Britain created a protective barrier we were not willing to cross at that time."

Now Morgan was really lost on all this government bullshit. However, he at last now knew exactly why Kent was there. He was there to kill him in retribution for all the past problems he had supposedly caused. Kent had come to honor his dead friend Stewart and clean the slate. He felt surprisingly calm now. He was the one who looked at his watch and surreptitiously tried to see the amount of coffee remaining in Kent's cup.

Kent tossed his head back and abruptly and dramatically drained the mug. He slammed it down on the table this time.

*Bam!*

He looked across at Morgan, a smile crossing his lips. He almost laughed at the damn fool.

"Please. This is too much for me to grasp," Morgan said imploringly while he silently counted to twenty.

"Why, I need to go."

"Just remain a bit longer and explain the enormity of what you have been saying to me."

Kent got the idea and, pushing forward on the edge of the couch, said, "Oh, OK."

He had finally gotten Morgan's attention after all these years. He slid one hand partly under the seat pillow touching his weapon.

"What else do we need to discuss?"

"Why was I such an impediment to your agency?"

"I suppose because you really cared and never, never bent nor allowed us to buy you out. I do not even know how many others we have bought out just to keep the plans running on schedule, but not you. Each time, you had a noble reason not to consider our offers acceptable.

"All your associates suffered since you became such a prominent national figure. We were trapped against the 'martyr factor.' We reduced your visibility more and more, and you shrank from sight. But you were still out there, 'scratching the itch.' Poor Stewart had been stopped so many times by upper management from eliminating you, I cannot even remember. His drinking was in a large measure due to you and your inability to bend at all and his inability to crush you."

Morgan was so surprised by all this, he could not speak. Finally thinking clearly, he composed himself and quietly asked, "Do you really think I killed my wife?

"My god, Morgan, she died because you had a ten-year-old car that failed on the highway on the way to the hospital. You had to take her part of the way in the back of pig truck until an ambulance found you, and it got there too late. If you had taken some of the money offered over the years, she would be still standing here today."

Morgan began to cry. This was all too real. He could still feel her spirit slip away while he held her in the back of the truck as it bumped along toward the hospital. When it stopped abruptly and the paramedic jumped in, it was all over – she was already gone. Gone, gone a long way off.

Kent looked across at the man with some bitter sympathy but had reached his limits. He was now ready to draw the pistol; it was time to end this nonsense. He tried to withdraw the pistol, but his fingers would not close on the grip. He looked down at it and realized with a shock he could not move his arm either, forward or back. He also realized he was not able to move any other part of this body. He was stricken! *My god, this is not the time for a stroke!* he thought. He was suddenly frozen in time.

He cried out, "What the hell!"

Morgan dried his eyes with the back of one hand and pushed Kent back gently onto the couch. Kent rolled back onto the couch, and the gun slid harmlessly onto the floor carpet with a dull thud.

Morgan was very sad. He had not intended for any of this to happen. He leaned over close to Kent and said, "Can you hear me?" The man's eyelids winked, but there was no other response. The lips did not move. There was no sound.

"Well, I don't think your file on me is as complete as it might have been, Kent. I did turn you down that first time you visited my laboratory, but the problem you posed was just too intriguing, so I did do some research even without your funds. In fact, I even borrowed some equipment from Latimure. I did find the perfect synthetic poison you wanted me to invent.

"It is undetectable, and it mimics a basic heart attack or stroke. You see, I had it but never wanted it used, so I never published anything about it. The only person who knew about it was Marylyn Springer, my assistant." He held up one finger to Kent as Kent previously had to him.

"As you are well aware, she was killed in vehicle accident later that year. I saved a small amount of the poison I invented and destroyed all the documentation of its development or existence. I saved it in case, in case I wanted to end my own life. I could no longer even replicate the study, I am afraid. When you came today, I finally realized that you were here to kill me, so I had to slip it into your coffee."

He shook the man roughly. "Kent? Kent?"

His eyelids moved, and his eyes watered.

"I'm very sorry I was so much trouble."

At this point, he put on a pair of driving gloves. He took the check, wiped it and the envelope clean with his handkerchief and put the check in the envelope and slipped it into Kent's inside jacket pocket. When he was finished, his uninvited guest was very dead.

He had some trouble dragging him to the car and putting him in the passenger seat. He started it and turned it back down the road about a mile. He turned it around and then drove it gently off the edge into a slight culvert. He turned off the lights. He slid Kent's stiffening body under the steering wheel and checked his vital signs and then gently pushed his eyes closed. He buckled his seat belt.

Shutting the door, he walked home in the dusk. Tomorrow, they would come and ask him about the man. He would only say he knew him a long time ago but had not seen him in many years. He would act surprised if they suggested he had been on his way to see him when he suffered a heart attack.

As he walked back to the cabin, he thought about all the people Kent had mentioned. However, he thought about them as laughing and joking living individuals and how vital and strong they were in their convictions. He realized now that even if he didn't know it then, they had all contributed to a better world in their very small way. People like Kent and Stewart may have been responsible for taking them from the world physically, but their spirits marched along, arm and arm, in every new protest.

He really felt very sorry for Kent. The only time he had actually forced Morgan to be unethical was when he had to murder him in his own self-defense. Had this terrible man finally converted him to the violence and horror he wallowed in all his life? Had he been reduced to a dog-eat-dog philosophy because of this man and his bosses?

Although this was the first time he had ever stepped across the line of legality, he somehow felt no guilt nor remorse. He could barely imagine what the agency had been doing all these years to innocent people who were just trying to make the world a better place with their simple nonviolent protests of the governments power. He shook his head in disbelief. Jamming his cold hands into his deep pockets, he trudged home in the dark. He needed to think this all over.

*What would my poor wife think of all this?* he wondered. He would really have liked her to be able to hug him now. If she could, he would never let her go.

## The End

# South of the Border

I t was only six thirty in the morning; but Sam was up – showered, shaved, and dressed. He wore a comfortable old blue denim shirt, dark blue Dockers pants, and slip-on shoes that were worn comfortable and familiar. The outfit, like his life, was designed to be totally familiar and totally comfortable. After all, he was sixty-nine years old, long retired, and living the "good life" in sunny Southern California. His wife, Martha, was only sixty-seven years old; but she had arthritis, bad knees, a bladder problem, and some other female problems.

Sadly, for both of them, her combination of illnesses and constantly emerging new medical symptoms kept her isolated at home more and more. She rested as much as possible, and they watched a lot of TV. She no longer could take long walks nor play shuffleboard. She had been an excellent shuffleboard player and, at one time, was the captain of the senior citizens' Sun City all-woman team. In 2004, they had won the state championship held in San Diego.

Last year, he had gotten her a wheelchair so she could get around more. He would push her on walks and take her to the shuffleboard court to watch the games. She could enjoy the play and become an active participant it the lively courtside discussions of skill, strategy and motivation. Sam thought to himself, *I love her so much. I hate seeing her health failing so rapidly. Well, at least she would not have to suffer the loneliness of outliving me. I would always be around. I would always be able to take care of her until the very end – and then? Who knows, and actually, who cares?*

Sam was in relatively good health although he had his off days when his joints ached, and he became very stiff after sitting in one place for over an hour. He no longer took any medications and had stopped going to the doctor for checkups. Now he did most of the chores around the house, including the grocery shopping and laundry. He was a short man, only five feet five inches tall and rather slim. He, thankfully, was seldom ill. His dad had lived to be over eighty years old, and he had been active to the end of his days. Today, Sam felt like he might be able to beat his old man's record. Another thirteen years would be a piece of cake for him.

He had picked up the newspaper that was tossed onto the front porch and was now sitting at the old kitchen table, waiting for the morning coffee to perk. He opened the paper full length and read the front page. He was disgusted with the wars in Afghanistan and Iraq, the death and terror, all the gangs and the shootings, and the stream of the endless corrupt politicians' faces who sheepishly peered out from the pages. When had all this come about? He had worked for thirty-five years for the same company, Ralph Patterson International, at six different plants in three different states; and he had never seen the world in such terrible shape.

It really depressed him to read the news anymore. Then, of course, the obituary page now actually scared him. He no longer read it since he was not interested in dwelling upon death and dying. He heard about that all day long anymore. Neighbors alerted the couple soon enough of those in their circle who passed away. They were running an average of almost two funerals a month now. They had stopped sending flowers due to the cost but tried to at least pay their respects by attending the funerals of those they had known well.

Martha appeared in the doorway. She was a small woman, slightly stooped over and wrapped in her big fluffy pink robe. Her small cheerful face appeared to be framed by pink cotton candy. She shuffled slowly into the kitchen. Smiling at him weakly, she moved toward the table. He said, "Hi, darling!" Half standing, he reached over the edge of the table and brushed her cheek gently with a good-morning kiss.

She grinned wider like a schoolgirl and started in, "Hi yourself, you old fool. Are you sure you will be all right today? Don't you think you should take Murphy with you like you used to? Just in case there is a car problem or something?"

"Nah, he only gets in the way when I am sweet-talking all those dark-haired senoritas." They both laughed at this. Her small hand slowly reached out and patted her husband's arm several times very softly. Then she settled into her worn kitchen chair at the table. Although a small woman, she had put on some weight over the past several years and looked a little like a basketball, especially when she dropped her head onto her chest. Sam, however, only remembered her as she was when she was young and beautiful. Even this morning, as always, he saw her that way. When he first met her, she was a vibrant young woman who had dazzled him when he was introduced to her at a mutual friend's backyard potluck dinner party.

He smiled at her reassuringly and said, "I will be fine, Martha. Just fine! You take it easy today, and when I get back in the afternoon, I am going to take you to the Claim Jumper restaurant in T for an early bird dinner." They referred to the city of Temecula as T or Big T. It was only about fifteen minutes away by car.

"Dinner!" she laughed and, clapping her frail hands together, continued, "That is not just a dinner. We always end up with a week's worth of take home leftovers when we go there. But oh, Sam, I do like their food!" Her grin was an absolute beam of happiness. This really made him feel wonderful. She continued in her enthusiasm, "Remember the salmon we had last time? Oh, Sam, but can we afford it? Our check won't be here for a couple of days, you know,"

He looked at her over the edge of both his reading glasses and his newspaper, replying, "It is just a little surprise for you, honey! I have saved my lunch money, and we can just make do if you only have two glasses of wine instead the whole bottle." They both laughed easily at the joke. It had been a long time since they had drank a bottle of wine together. Neither of them could have more than one glass of wine without falling asleep anymore. They seldom had wine actually, and she really grudgingly admitted to preferring Diet Coke when pressed hard by one of her friends.

She slowly started to stand up. Sam quickly and gently pushed her back down on her chair. "What do you need sweetheart? I will get it for you."

"Just some toast and coffee, like always," she replied demurely.

He moved quickly and put the slices of whole wheat toast into the old toaster. He pushed down the lever, and they dropped out of sight. He poured two cups of hot coffee into bright yellow sunflower covered mugs. He sat down, putting one mug in front of her and one in front of himself. They both leaned forward, looking into their steaming cups, trying perhaps to read their future. They then smiled at each other while savoring the fragrant coffee aroma wafting upwards, both lost momentarily in their private reminiscences. Each then gingerly sipped at the hot coffee.

She was pleased that he still wanted to wait on her but sorry that she could do less and less each day for either of them. She worried about Sam and especially today. He was driving all the way to Mexico and back. He was really too old to do that. She knew him well enough though not even to try and persuade him to not do it. Beside their neighbors, she as well, now depended on Sam so much. They all counted on him now. He made the trip to Mexico once a month now.

They teasingly referred to it as his "making-a-drug run." Even the neighbors now referred to it as that. It had become a neighborhood joke, and they all enjoyed teasing Sam about it. The toast popped, and Sam got up and buttered it lightly, cutting it into half slices and putting it on a plate. He served Martha and then sat down. Most of their neighbors were in the same circumstances as themselves, subsisting on social security and small retirement funds that were adequate years ago but seemed to be shrinking every year. Currently, it was still the drug costs that bothered them all the most although the recent shocking gasoline price increases and unbelievable high electric bills were definitely additional problems that they now speculated about a great deal. Unfortunately, in order to enjoy their increasingly narrowing lives, they all needed larger amounts and types of prescription drugs. It seemed like every day they needed a new or additional prescription of something. Medicines were always very expensive in the United States, and all the new ones seemed to be astronomical.

It was two years ago that Sam had initially, in desperation to get the all the necessary medicines for Martha, driven over the border into Tijuana after reading something about how cheap medicine was in Mexico and Canada in the monthly *AARP* magazine. They were very low on funds, so he just drove down there and discovered he could get their medicines for half the cost and sometimes even less. Unfortunately, this was the only way he could afford them all now. He had already stopped taking the medicine prescribed for him, and they still needed more money to cover the cost just for Martha's medications.

He had told Martha that his doctor had taken him off the few medications he had taken in the past since his health had improved so much now that he was relaxing more, one of a growing number of little white lies he had been spinning for the past couple of years.

He was unbelievably lucky on the first trip. He had met a friendly pharmacist, Javier K. Gonzales, at a local restaurant where he had stopped to ask directions and have some coffee. When Sam explained his problem to Javier, he was genuinely glad to help Sam by providing the medicine he needed for Martha. Javier had a neat small store and was very personable and professional. In fact, he was the one that had suggested Sam to tell others about his pharmacy and the excellent prices. His intent was to assist the older citizens of California to get the medications they needed, not turn Sam into a "mule." That part of the puzzle just fell into place afterward. He later agreed to guarantee Sam an average reduction of 40 percent of the U.S. cost on all the prescriptions he brought in to be filled.

Upon returning that day, he related his adventure to Martha. She was delighted in spite of her anger over him taking off like that. She loved to talk to her friends and immediately just told a few neighbors. They immediately enlisted his assistance, and he now had fifteen "customers" and a monthly prescription medicine order that was in the $4,000 range. And that was with the heavy discount they were getting.

Last year, they had high hopes for President Bush's new Medicare drug plan that was introduced; but after all was said and done, few of his neighbors or he found it to be too helpful. You had to find a plan that covered all the medicines you needed, and then the reduction in cost was offset by paying additional monthly premiums. A few of the neighbors had joined up, but most of them were too confused and tired to attempt to fill out all the required paperwork.

He was always amazed to see all the medicine each of his neighbors needed to just get through each day much less the entire month. Some of them had little plastic boxes divided into twenty different compartments, all full of colorful and strange-shaped pills and a list of times when they were to take each of them. It was usually by color and shape – ten in the morning, take two small blue squares; at noon, take large green oblong ones, and so on. He now brought back a very large box full of medications, salves, ointments, and pills every month. He also noted that each family's number of prescriptions frequently increased month after month. They were "pill poppers" on a grand scale.

He went down to the Mexican border town on approximately the twenty-fifth of each month and easily returned the same day. It was a 185-mile round-trip on excellent highways. The pharmacist was close to the border, and they were now companeros, he thought. That is what Javier called him. His neighbors really relied on him more and more – not only for filling their prescriptions, but he had to occasionally lend them money to cover the cost to buy them until their check arrived.

He never mentioned this part to Martha, but she knew about it, but she never mentioned it to him either. She also was building a file of little white lies. She was so proud of him and his support to their little community. He never refused them if he had the money, but even their money was now running out. He worried more and more that he would not be able to stretch it out until Martha passed on. Once she was gone, he could get by on less and less. If he starved, that was OK too. However, he had decided to draw the line at eating dog food.

He had discovered that several of his neighbors had resorted to doing that for their Sunday night dinner when the check came on a Monday or Tuesday. Old Otto Spinger even confided in him about it and went so far as to give him his special recipe he had personally developed to use with a can of good-quality beef dog food. It included adding chopped potatoes and carrots to it as well as a lot of paprika to make it seem like a regular Dinty Moore style beef stew. He knew Otto believed that, but he could not, no matter how hard he tried.

They lived in a nice community within the small confines of Sun City, a retirement city, and they had gotten to know all their neighbors over the years. Many unfortunately had passed on, but new ones always filled in their ranks. Some of them were a little strange perhaps but they were all good neighbors to one another. They played cards and games, visited, shared recipes and the latest pictures of grandkids and great-grandkids, had potluck dinners, walked their dogs, and worked in their gardens. If it wasn't for the rising cost of living, they would all be reasonably happy. He finished his mug of coffee and cleared away Martha's dish with the toast crusts remaining. Leaning over her shoulder, he carefully poured her another mug of coffee. Pushing it in front of her, he kissed her on the check and advised, "Have another cup, honey, and then watch the talk shows you like so much. And be sure to take a nap. Tonight is going to be our big night out!"

She smiled up at him but then pushed herself up and, moving slowly but deliberately, got him a bottle of water out of the refrigerator. She handed it to him as she sat down again slowly. He took it, picked up his old leather briefcase from the end of the table, and headed out the back door toward the separate garage. His house was the only one on the block with a separate garage. That was one of his reasons for buying it. Martha, of course, had a whole set of other reasons for liking their small but comfortable home.

In the dim light of the garage, he looked proudly over his big dark blue 2002 Caddy. He loved its sleek lines. He opened the garage door with his remote and put it under the car's sun visor. He had gassed her up yesterday at the Chevron station, and it was raring to go. He shook his head to himself when he remembered, to his shock, that the tank of gas cost him over $50! He checked his briefcase and found it full of white envelops containing the prescriptions he was to get filled and a large brown business envelope with over $4,000 in cash! He put the bottle of water on the floor, wedging it tight next to the seat so it would not roll around. He wouldn't need it – he never did – but Martha insisted he take a bottle of water. It made her happy to see him go out with it.

Martha had collected the prescriptions and money. She loaded his briefcase for him. The money was all together in one envelope, but the prescriptions were in separate envelopes with the families' names written on the outside. Each envelope held at least five or more prescriptions. She also called the pharmacist the afternoon before each run and read the prescriptions to his clerk so he and the pharmacist could get to work on them in advance. She didn't want Sam to have to wait long. They should have them ready for Sam when he got there. His dear Martha was such a big help. However, she now had to rest after making the monthly call since it usually lasted for over an hour. He fired the car up. A comfortable quiet power was heard.

He backed out of the driveway and started his drive out toward Highway 215 then to Highway 15 and straight on to Tijuana. He had driven the route many times, but now there was always more traffic each month. It was a wide highway, and he usually made good time. He would listen to a news station on the radio. The time went by fast enough. It was a clean bright day, and although he was feeling a little nervous with the butterflies in his stomach fluttering, he knew everything would be just fine.

He would get there with all the money in one piece and return with the medicine. The traffic got heavier when Highway 215 swung into Highway 15, especially around Big T at the Winchester exit. He steered into the far left lanes and stayed out of any big slowdowns or jam-ups. After about twenty minutes, he passed the Border Patrol checkpoint on the other side of the freeway. They were stopping vehicles, and the traffic was starting to back up. He hoped it would all go well today, especially on his way back.

If he was real lucky returning, the Border agents would not be stopping cars, and he could just breeze through it. If anything happened to him, he hated to think what would happen to his poor, dear Martha. But then what could happen? He would be back home in a couple of hours, and everything would be fine! As usual, he set the cruise control to the precise speed limit and expected to get there in forty-five minutes.

It was a nice Thursday morning, but there was the usual downtown traffic snarl. At this time in the morning, they took the special route into town, which he avoided. It was getting warmer as he finally made it to the border entry point, and traffic slowed down. It was backed up for about a half hour's worth, he guessed. He relaxed and looked around at all the other vehicles. There were expensive and modest ones, neat and messy ones. There were trucks and buses as well as motorcycles. This mass of vehicles was surging through three entrances into Tijuana. Each person in each vehicle had their reasons for making the trip. He doubted if there was anyone with his exact reason however. The cars moved forward quickly, and after twenty minutes, he pulled even with a sad-eyed tired Mexican police officer. He looked at Sam with narrowing eyes and a bored expression and asked, "One-day shopping trip?"

"Yes," Sam replied simply and smiled.

After appraising him for another fifteen seconds, he waved him on and said, "Have a good day."

"Thanks."

He was through that hurdle and on his last leg of the trip. The pharmacy was only a mile farther. Since he was such a special customer, his friend Javier insisted on him parking in the back of the building under the wide awning. This helped keep his car cool and avoided the street and all its potential problems. He turned onto a relatively wide paved street and saw the small yellow and brown building up ahead on the right side of the street. The dignified, tasteful sign proclaimed, Farmaceutico; and under that, there was the name of Javier K. Gonzales, Pharm D. Both of these titles were in gold letters, tastefully outlined in black. He went slowly past the store's recently cleaned front glass windows and turned right slowly into a narrow drive that led him to the back of the building.

When he pulled around the corner of the building, there was only one other car parked there. *It is a dusty brown Ford SUV*, he thought. He pulled in next to it and stopped. He took off his sunglasses and laid them on the passenger seat of the car. He opened the heavy door and got out with his briefcase. He looked at the plain adobe building with the multicolored layers of paint peeling off and the mud streaks on the lower wall areas. The front of the building was well kept, but little effort was expended on the back of the building. *It must have been beautiful in its day though*, he thought.

He skirted past several large garbage cans that were overflowing with strange materials and disgusting odors. They were lined up next to the rear door. He pushed the door open slowly and went from the stark sun into a black interior. As the door swung shut behind him, he stood, blinking his eyes repeatedly, trying to adjust to the darkness.

"Senior Sam, welcome, my friend!" a deep voice said. He could see the outline of a short wide figure approaching him. It was Leon, the guard. He always casually carried a large sawed-off shotgun at his side. During an earlier visit, Javier had explained to Sam that the pharmacy had been robbed several times by street thugs in the past; and that is why he now had employed Leon, his wife's cousin, as a guard. *Why didn't he just lock the back door?* Sam had wondered but was new to the friendship at the time, seldom asking such pointed questions.

Leon arrived at his side and took his arm, leading him forward down the hall and into the small neat shop. Javier looked up from his work counter and greeted him warmly.

"Oh, me Americano friend, Sam! Welcome!" Then he teased, "Another drug run for the wild wheelchair crowd, eh?"

They all laughed. Sam moved forward. He passed the briefcase over the counter toward Javier. He pulled it to him and said, "I have most of the orders almost filled. I am almost finished. Why don't you go over to the cantina across the street? My brother, Henry, will give you a nice breakfast burrito."

Sam, who had heard this all before, smiled and nodded in agreement. It was like acting in a play every month, pretty much the same dialogue each time he came. The store did not have many items on display and had a counter with a cage similar to a bank where people passed their prescription under the glass and waited on a narrow worn wooden bench until their name was called. Then they went to the cash register and paid the clerk what was due. They then departed with their precious medicine wrapped in brown paper.

Sam shrug in agreement, turned, and went out. He had laid down his car keys on the countertop next to the briefcase when he came in. He neglected to pick them up when he left. The day was now warm, and the street was busy and cramped since so many vendors had set up on the sidewalk, and there were cars parked at random angles all along both sides of the street.

He carefully worked his way across the street and entered the cantina. Henry was not really Javier's brother he had explained to him when he first suggested this diversion. He was only his half brother, but it made no difference. He was a very friendly person, especially to a friend of Javier's. Henry had a cold beer and warm breakfast burrito ready for him.

He pulled out an old bar chair, mounted it, and sat at the bar. The cantina was dark and full of damp smells and low murmurs. The bar was worn and stained with dark drying puddles here and there. He drank from the bottle of beer and ate the burrito slowly. While it was all very good, he enjoyed the beer most of all. It was his only beer each month, and it really was a very pleasant taste. He had never been an avid beer drinker, but this seemed to hit the spot and tended to allow him to relax a little more.

There were other men in the bar speaking quietly, eating, drinking, and laughing lowly. They were not well dressed, and they briefly looked him over carefully. However, since Henry had greeted him so warmly, they didn't take any further notice of him. He could only eat half of the burrito. It was so large. It was indeed full of wonderful tastes and textures. He hated to not eat more but knew his stomach would not allow him in the long run. He had often thought of taking several of them home to Martha but was afraid they might go bad from the heat on the drive. In addition, she was no longer very comfortable with spicy food anymore.

Oh well, his monthly snack was just another one of his many little secrets he kept from his wife and everyone else. A cold beer with a giant burrito in an authentic Mexican cantina was his very private special event. Who would have guessed that of him? He put down the empty beer bottle after fifteen minutes had passed. Henry made a motion with his arm indicating to him another was his for the asking, but he had to wave him off.

"Thanks, but I am not the drinking man I was, but I do thank you for your generous offer."

Henry nodded understandingly. Sam finally dismounted from the stool and was waving goodbye over his shoulder at Henry. Henry halted him with, "Wait a minute! I have some food for Javier. Will you take it to him?"

"Certainly!" Sam replied and stopped. He turned and waited for Henry to pass a large heavy, multicolored plate filled with several steaming wrapped items over the counter to him. Picking it up, he again turned and walked out of the cantina into the screaming sunlight. The old creaking screen door snapped shut behind him.

There were several cars going in each direction on the street. He had to wait and then move fast to get across the street. He almost fell over something as he stepped up onto the curb but didn't drop the plate. It felt warm and smelled rich and inviting. Several youngsters ran up to him, holding out their hands, begging with their eyes and mouths for money. He dropped an American quarter into each small dirty hand and then quickly ducked into the *farmaceutico* before they alerted the world of the whereabouts of a generous tourist.

"Well, that was refreshing." He smiled at Javier. Javier's clerk was busy filing a box with the white bags of medicines. Each bag had the name envelope stapled to the top with all the prescriptions behind it. Javier smiled back at Sam and, with his thumbs-up, indicated that the box with many bags on the table was almost ready.

The clerk stood back, and Javier said, "There it is, senor. I had to make two substitutions and so noted them by placing a note of explanation inside each envelope. In both cases, the medication I provided was less expensive and better. It is getting harder to stock the more popular generic versions for medicines down here."

"Was the money correct?"

"More than correct! You actually had too much. Here is some change." And he handed him $58 in American paper dollars.

"Gracious!" Sam attempted to speak Spanish, generally fumbling badly with their language.

"Medicine prices fluctuate like the stock market, you know, especially now when all the big drug companies are trying to make more and more money. Jose will put the carton on the front seat of your car as usual. Jose!" he called.

The slender clerk shuffled forward to the table and lifted the carton. It was filled with the separate white bags for each family with the prescription slips on the front so anyone could see they were from a reputable doctor. He disappeared with it down the dark hall.

"Here is your briefcase that you brought with you."

"Thank you, Javier. Until next month! Have a good day!"

"I think it will be a good day, senor, for both of us." He grinned widely.

"Don't forget to stop and get some fresh fruit for your wife at the stand at the Highway 79 exit," he reminded him as usual. "I saw some great melons going past in the trucks headed your way yesterday."

"I will stop as always. I am only sorry I cannot bring some down to you when I return."

"Don't' worry. I get all I need from the back of the trucks going north. They sell it to us before finishing the run into the U.S."

Sam felt a little light-headed but OK. He got into his car. He placed the briefcase on the seat next to him behind the box of medicine. Reaching forward, he turned the key that was in the ignition, and the Caddy started up. He waved goodbye out of the open window to Leon, framed in the doorway with his shotgun. He headed out the narrow side drive. He turned left, heading back north. Heading home! He hit the button that closed the side window and turned the air conditioner up to high. He reached the entry station quickly. There were fewer people returning so early. The same bored, sad-eyed policeman waved him through without a word this time.

The trip back was a little rough coming out of San Diego in terms of thick traffic. Once he was past the Naval Air Station, it smoothed out. He was now getting a little edgy and nervous. Maybe it was the beer? He looked into the rearview mirror frequently now but saw nothing unusual. After about thirty-five minutes, the traffic slowed and he knew the Border Patrol checkpoint was approaching. He pulled off into one of the checking station lanes and slowed down.

"Damn, it looks like they are checking today!" This concerned him a little. So many times, it was closed, and he just drove through when the sign said No Checking Today. Today, they were checking!

The line was short, only four cars long, but it seemed to crawl so slowly. He fidgeted inside his car. He repeatedly slapped the steering wheel lightly with both hands. Checking his dashboard clock every couple of minutes, he was also squirming in his seat. *What was the problem?* he wondered. At last, it was finally his turn. He hit the window button and rolled it down. The tall heavyset officer in a neatly pressed uniform bent down and looked in the car window at him.

"Anything to declare?"

"No, sir. No fruits or vegetables, Officer." He looked him in the eye and did not glance over at the box sitting there with all the bags of medication. According to a strict interpretation of the law, Sam was technically smuggling drugs into the country. But no one asked him about the box sitting in the open, and he never mentioned it. The only time an agent had asked him, he just looked at the prescriptions on one of the bags and just let it go. If he had a hidden case of something and no obvious prescription, they might have taken some action, but it was too much trouble and paperwork to take care of, considering its unimportance.

"How about illegals?" Sam was stunned by the question, and his face looked it. The officer made a big smile to show he was just joking.

Sam smiled back and weakly replied, "No."

"Ok." He took another sweep around with his eyes and stood up straight. The moment froze in time for Sam, and then the officer just waved him through. The perspiration trickled down Sam's neck onto his back. He rolled up the widow, and the air conditioner once again blasted on him. He carefully pulled away without being obvious and shot into the fast traffic, putting distance between him and the checkpoint. He watched in the rearview mirror constantly for about ten minutes and then began to relax.

He took several deep breaths to further relax and felt he was almost home free. It was another ten minutes until the turnoff for the fruit stand. It was not a stand but a small produce grocery that was very popular with all the tourists and locals. Finally, he spotted the exit and pulled over to the right and was off the freeway in a flash. He pulled down the road about a half mile and, making a quick right turn, pulled into the big parking area. It was busy with lots of cars coming and going.

He went slowly around to the left side of the building and parked in the far back under several large trees. He wheeled around and backed his car into the slot, so the back was almost resting in some spindly bushes. From the inside, he popped the trunk and got out carefully, taking the briefcase with him and locking the car doors. He stretched and glanced around.

He saw the familiar old red truck two slots down from him.

There was a thin man leaning against the side of the truck with a can of cola in his large hand. He was wearing a large dusty black cowboy hat. His head hung down, so you could not see his face in the dark shadow cast by his hat brim. Sam walked down the line of vehicles and past the man. He did not look at him nor did he look back after he went past him.

He entered the large store and strolled around, looking at all the fresh produce. He was not a vegetable man himself but certainly knew what Martha liked. He got a large bag of oranges, a pound of grapes, and several avocados just for her. He picked up some homemade apple pie for himself. There were several people in the checkout line, and he waited patiently. He was still a little jumpy. He was nervous and was rattling his car keys in his pocket. He looked around at the other people, but they were not interested in him at all. He was startled by a belligerent voice behind him asking. "Well, you think they could get better help! Why do I have to stand in line all day to get a few vegetables?"

He looked around, and there was a frumpy-faced, ugly grizzled woman standing there with her arms full of a variety of vegetables. She had on some kind of short pants, and her blue-veined legs were lumpy and discolored. He offered to hold some of her items for her, and she accepted gladly. He then had a lot of items to balance but was close enough to the checkout counter that he could put his items down and hold some of hers. He was in front of the clerk quickly. He lined up the lady's items behind his. She was busy adding to the pile. He held on to the briefcase in his left hand as the clerk checked him out.

The frumpy woman gave him a big toothy smile and thanked him warmly, touching his arm several times. He just mechanically smiled back and paid the $12 he owed with a twenty, picking up his change and the two bags. He headed for the door fast. He could hear the woman's voice whining about something to the clerk. He strode quickly to his car. The red truck was gone. He put the groceries in the backseat on the floor. He got in and started the car. No warning lights went on. He checked the traffic in the parking area carefully and pulled out.

He headed out, back to the highway and home. It took some time to make the left-hand turn through the heavy traffic onto the road, but he finally got a break. He swung easily down the freeway on-ramp. When he hit sixty-five miles per hour, he felt great. He patted the old briefcase and smiled. He was thinking about the fine dinner they would have tonight and how happy that would make Martha. She deserved to be happy after all these years.

He cruised on and only just realized it when he went past the red truck that was in the far right lane. He didn't look at it but accelerated slightly above the speed limit to get well away from it. He finally pulled off the highway for Sun City exit at Ma Call Road. He stopped at the 7-Eleven and took his briefcase to an outside telephone booth. He partially took out the large bulky envelope and dropped two quarters into the phone slot and then dialed the number written on the envelope. At the other end, the phone rang three times, and then a woman's voice said, "Yeah, what's it?"

He read the brief note under the number. "The vegetables were very plentiful, and I brought home a good load. Thanks for the tip." He then hung up without waiting for her to respond. He got back into his car and drove home. It was only a short few minutes away.

He parked in his detached garage. He sat there for a few minutes, breathing in and out and attempting to relax.

*Another successful trip!* he thought. He was tired however. The trips always took more out of him than he expected. He put the briefcase under his arm and took the groceries into the house. He put them on the kitchen table. He returned for the box of medicines and put them on the other end of the kitchen table. He called for Martha, but there was no sound. He checked around the house and found her sound asleep on the couch. *Poor dear*, he thought. She looked so peaceful. He turned down the TV and slipped out of the room.

He returned to the garage and closed the garage door. In the dim light, he opened the envelope. He counted the money it contained onto his workbench. There were forty rumbled fifty-dollar bills for a total of two thousand-dollars. He took two bills out and put them in his pocket for their dinner. Above his workbench, he located a cigar box that was under a large coffee can of nails. Removing it and opening it, he saw three fifty-dollar bills, all that was left from the last trip. He hid the remainder of the bills from the envelope in the cigar box, replacing it on the shelf and putting the can of nails back on top of it. He tore the envelope into several pieces and dropped them into the garbage can.

He looked around and located his small car vacuum in the back corner sitting on his old stereo speaker. Using the bright orange extension cord, he plugged it into the wall socket and opened the car trunk. He looked into the large empty space. However, it seemed so small and close to him. He marveled that four human beings were able to cram themselves into that space. He vacuumed the inside to remove any dirt or sand. He found an old crumpled brown bag jammed down on the inside of the car trunk. He pulled it loose and gingerly examined the contents. There was an old toothbrush, a broken comb, and a half-used tube of toothpaste. He dropped them back into the torn bag and tossed it into the garbage can by the door. He replaced the vacuum and then sprayed lemon-scented air freshener into the trunk.

He stared down into the empty trunk, his mind again trying to visualize four humans bent and twisted inside that tiny area. He closed his eyes and sighed. He knew he was doing this for Martha, but it was certainly a sad state of affairs that had driven him into a life of crime at his age. He always hoped the people he helped across the border were able to find a better life. He tried to feel like he was helping them in some small way. Although it frequently came to him, he pushed the thought that he was just making money off their misery out of his mind.

When Javier introduced him to Maxwell, he thought they were going to talk about politics. Instead, they made him an offer he couldn't refuse; and they made it sound so innocent, he convinced himself they were right. Somebody would do it, and he might as well profit from the deal. Now he was not so sure, but it was too late. Far, far too late to change his mind now. He ended all his troubling thoughts slamming the trunk lid shut.

Returning to the house, he checked the time and made a note to wake Martha in thirty minutes. They need to get there in time for the early bird special meals. There was a knock on the front door, and he quickly answered it with a "Shush, Martha is sleeping."

It was Marty Franklin. He didn't know the Franklins very well, but Martha liked Elizabeth Franklin, and he overheard them talked on the phone a lot. Marty smiled apologetically and asked, "I saw you pull in, and Elisabeth really needs her medicine. She has been having problems all day today. I know Martha usually brings it over later, but I was wondering if I can get it from you now."

"Sure." He opened the door and ushered him toward the kitchen. When they were both sanding in front of the table with the box of bags, Sam turned his back to him for a moment, putting on his reading glasses. He was scanning the white bags and finally located the one marked Franklins and pulled it out. Turning to Marty, he handed it to him saying, "Here I think this is it. Check it for me please."

Marty looked at the bottles and boxes and verified it was theirs and replied, "You know, I want to thank you again, Sam. This is a godsend for us. We would not be able to get all this medicine if we paid the U.S. prices."

Sam nodded and said, "No problem, just glad to be able to help you two out."

He half pushed and half escorted Marty back to the front door. As he was leaving, Marty turned and said, "You know, if you need someone to go with you, just let me know. I would be glad to help you out." He looked like an eager kid who wanted to go the movies.

Sam said, "I will think about it, but I am sort of a lone rider anymore."

He watched Marty hurry down the walk toward his house and then closed the door slowly and quietly. He went back into the kitchen and sat down heavily in one the chairs after pouring a cup of coffee and warming it in the microwave oven. It was only three thirty, and Martha could sleep until four maybe.

While he sipped at his coffee, his thoughts went back to the illegals he had just smuggled into the country. He wondered who they were and what would happen to them and if they would be all right. Were they young or old, male or female? What was their story? It was not his business of course; he was just one of a team that whisked them into the country and onto other locations quickly and quietly. It was an ugly business that he had been pulled into, and every day, he felt sadder about it. Stopping, however, was out of the question. It was out of the question as long as Martha was alive.

Oh well, he would read his book or maybe just watch TV to relax. Once he was finished with the run, the excitement was gone. It was always a little sad for him to be back. He was tired and glad also. Emotionally, each trip wrung more out of him each month. However, he had to admit to himself though that the trips were very exciting.

For now though, the burrito burn was rumbling in his stomach, not to mention the bitter beer bite aftertaste.

## The End

# The Favor

T he two men were sitting in an exclusive bar on the twentieth floor of a high-rise Los Angeles office building. The opulence was obvious. The glass, marble, and water-gushing fountains of this high-ceiling building were designed to silently exude wealth. The quiet, controlled atmosphere was oozing wealth into the ozone. The two men had been there for only a few minutes, each arriving from their last high-intensity business meeting at the same time. They appeared relaxed and, almost bowing, started the polite dance of "social niceties."

"Well, Mark, how is your drink?"

"Excellent, as always. Thanks. My goodness, it has really been a while, Ralph."

"Yes, you were in Spain for several weeks on the Thamson Project, and I have been tied up in Peru on my international trucking merger. Are all our joint ventures still doing well?"

"Actually, yes," Mark replied with a slight smirk. Leaning forward, he raised his crystal glass and took a deep draft of his Grey Goose on the rocks. Then leaning back in the large soft white leather chair, he was relaxed and confident. The two men – Mark Harrison, president of Harrison Venture Capital, and Ralph Tango, president of Century Investments – were enjoying a late after-work drink together. It was nine thirty in the evening on a warm Saturday in May.

They were in a semiprivate room at the glamorous Treasury Room of the recently opened Ritz Ramirez Building. The room had no table, just a side table of rich, deep walnut next to each large chair with an accompanying ottoman between them. It was partially screened so they could glance to the left and see people going by but distanced enough so they would not have to acknowledge them unless they chose to.

The walls were covered in blue azure silk, and the drinks were served in Waterford Crystal stemmed glasses. Both glasses rested upon a striking white Spanish linen napkin, and there was a square gray plate of cold caviar and small imported London crackers next to each glass. The music was a light, wafting rendition of a classical pastoral.

Both men wore expensive dark-colored tailored suits and ties. They were members of an elite corporate world of commerce. Both had fought their way into the multimillion-income arena. They have been business associates for over ten years and had maintained a certain controlled social interaction on occasions like this. While they seldom visited each other's offices or homes, they each had the private number of the other in the event they needed to establish instant communication. They were tanned, relaxed, and looked younger than their ages – the "look" that was acquired only after years of vigorous exercise, maintaining a controlled diet, and using an in office tanning booth.

"Good. I was wondering if you might be ready to pursue another venture with me. Well, actually, with me and several other silent partners. Very silent partners." He winked, and they both smiled knowingly. "It would require about a sixty-five million up-front investment from you and promises to yield a 35 percent-plus return over the next three years then a 20 percent increase and then – well, it depends on a great many other issues." Ralph shrugged offhandedly.

"Well, that sounds very promising. Why don't you have your staff forward the particulars of the arrangement to Braxton, my chief analyst, and I will get back to you after he gives me a review and update."

"Certainly, it is a lot like the Bretton venture we did six years ago, and I am certain you will recall our resounding success on that one."

"Oh yes, that was one of our best ventures so far. But then, we have both been surprisingly successful in our choices."

"That is true. It is a lot easier when you are doing million-dollar deals across continents than the old start-ups we struggled with in Silicon Valley. International business has many advantageous as long as one anticipates the variety of potential problems." They spoke the strange language of the wealthy with high technology terms and a great deal of innuendo and code. For example, the phrase "very silent partners" meant essentially they were never to be linked with the project and would always be nameless to all parties. They would provide considerable up-front money and be provided with large profits for their contributions.

"I drink to that." Mark raised his glass in salute, and the other man mirrored his actions.

"Well, what is your opinion of the Chinese venture that Warton and Sons has just announced?" Ralph switched directions politely.

"I was surprised until my Singapore contact provided me with some details of the project and the players."

"Like?"

"Well, be discrete." He smiled slightly as he began, "There is a large amount of laundered money commingled with the legal funds, and it is all processed with a double accounting procedure. In addition, the Chinese government has a big stake in its successful completion, so they are prepared to be very 'flexible' on all environmental issues as well as the potential human rights nightmare it will create. As we know from the past, they are experts in suppressing those."

"For the good of the state of course," interjected Ralph then continued with, "Yes, Bradshaw over at Lofton and Meyers indicated the same thing by e-mail recently, so I think all of us know what will carry that one off. Good for Warton. It is about time they have gotten hold of a real winner."

"Yes, it will be tough to screw that one up."

"That reminds me, Mark, I would like to ask a small favor of you," Ralph concluded the statement with his most winning smile.

"Oh, what might that be?"

"Well, it is about Sara Francisco."

"What about her? I have her under contract. She is all locked up. You need her to perform at one of your charity events?"

"No. No, good heavens, no. It is a little more serious than that I am afraid." He paused, smiled his narrow smile, and continued, "I want you to sell her contract."

"Sell her contract! Whatever for? Why would you want to buy her contract? You have never shown the least interest in the entertainment sector? Are you diversifying?"

Slowly shaking his finger negatively, Ralph leaned forward and said, "You misunderstand me. I do not want to buy her contract. I am advising you as a good friend. She is going to have a slump, and now is the time to dump her."

"My god, a slump! She just made two platinum records this year, and we have all kinds of promotional tie-ups and options in the mill."

"Remember what happened to Marcella Wise in 1999?" Ralph continued patiently.

"She went insane, I think."

"Well, of course, that was the public spin. But there is a little more to it than that. She had a prescription pill problem, an eating disorder, and was a manic-depressive. She went 'star big' and got way out of hand. Her agents attempted to control her. Then she attempted suicide. This was followed by a drunken car accident that killed several people. After that, she faded faster than water into the Sahara."

"Well, what does that have to do with Sara?

Ralph's eyes were getting hard; and his patience, never great, was fading rapidly. "I am advising you as your trusted business associate to sell her contract within the next thirty days." He looked cold, direct, and harsh now. His face was tense, and his age began to appear in the wrinkles around his eyes and temples.

"Well, damn it! We have a considerable investment there. We had great earnings projections. I stand to lose money if I sell her now."

"Well, Mark, I am sure you will recoup any loss you may experience now, very soon. If you lose several million, I will make sure you are included in yet another venture that will yield profits far in excess of that. Besides, in your company, eight or so million is just pocket change. I suspect you will only lose, at most, four to five million."

"Well, I don't know, Ralph. It is a strange and surprising request."

"Trust me on this. Sell the contract, cut your losses now, protect your firm's reputation, and forget it. At your stage in your business, your reputation is far more valuable than a few million more or less."

"I am very surprised by your request and am very curious as to why you are making it now." Mark was agitated and unsure. He was sitting on the edge of the large chair, leaning forward and stirring his drink nervously.

"I don't need to explain myself to you but to say this, it is important to our future business association for you to do this small favor for me.

After all, we are close business associates. And if something besmirches your reputation, I cannot allow it to taint my operations. Something is going to go terribly wrong in her career, and you need to be free and clear of her when it happens, that is all. I am asking you to do this as a concerned friend." He was looking cold and unyielding. He had moved into a sharp personal tone that had a lot of underlying implications and possibly even a threat.

"Well, can I have some time to think about it?" Mark pleaded to stall and gather some intel on what this might all be about.

"Certainly. If you can see fit to grant me this little favor, I will meet you on my yacht three weeks from now on the thirtieth of the month, and we can spend the weekend reviewing the proposal I mentioned earlier. If not, well, let's just say I will not be able to accommodate you on that venture. We may meet at a much later date for a cocktail, perhaps in Vienna in the early fall."

While finely coded, his meaning was crushingly clear. Do it now or forget doing business with me for at least the remainder of the year! Mark was surprised by this. Although they have had many disagreements and had argued over the endless details of their potential joint ventures in the past, he had never been threatened by Ralph in this manner. Could he continue his successes without Ralph? Probably, but they had done so well together, he would not like to risk it right now. Maybe after a few more deals, he could back away without any further involvement with Ralph's organization.

When he first met Ralph, they were both just launching into their own, and he had been impressed by Ralph's knack to locate very high-yield deals in unexpected industries and locations.

Ralph drained his glass, placed in neatly on the white napkin, and rose. He held out his manicured hand to Mark. They shook cordially, firmly, and flashed their thin business smiles. Ralph said warmly, "I hope to see you on the thirtieth. It should be a very pleasant and relaxing outing. Just a few close friends." He turned sharply and walked slowly away.

Mark sat down hard, very stunned by all this. He requested a house phone be brought to the side table. When it was provided and the waiter had disappeared, he decided to use his cell phone instead. He ordered another drink and attempted to sort it out. It was not that much money actually, just as Ralph had implied, but it would be a loss. Mark didn't even like to lose a penny down the sewer.

But why? He had never had any inkling Ralph even knew about his clients or his minor entertainment industry projects. All their dealings were with major international ventures and projects. Yet of all the business they did in the past, he could only think of one venture that went sour, and that was due to a small rebellion that turned into a bloody civil war that no one had factored into the project plan.

After the waiter placed his fresh drink on the napkin near to him and departed, he looked at the cold glass and the moisture accumulation on its side as if suddenly hypnotized by the magic process of condensation. Blinking hard, he took out his cell phone, flipped it open, and called Clayborn.

The phone rang three times before Clayborn answered, "Yes, Mark?"

The cell number was one only Mark had so each knew who was calling.

"Clayborn, sorry to call you tonight, but I need you to do something for me first thing in the morning."

This was the code again. What he was really saying was *now*!

"Certainly, what is it that you need?"

"I want you to do a quick cut at how much we can sell Sara's contract for and what the loss will be, both immediate and future."

"You want to dump Sara? We just set up the tour campaign, and we are closing several excellent sponsorship offers." Knowing he had reacted out of turn, his voice trailed off.

"I know," Mark replied tartly. "Do a quick workup at what we will lose and then send out a few feelers to see who might wish to buy her contract. Indicate that we are preparing to do a very big deal in Australia and do not have the time to continue with her relatively modest project."

Clayborn had already said too much, and he knew better than to ask more, so he merely replied, "Ok, will preliminaries by noon work for you?"

"Yes, that would be excellent." He didn't even bother to tell him to be discrete. Clayborn knew what he was paid to do and why. He was outside the corporation chain of command, and he worked as a "consultant" directly to Mark and Mark alone.

Seven days later, Mark's personal accountant from Bohs and Sons finished his report and seemed to be fidgeting. His name was Roger Swifton. He was a senior accountant who had worked with Mark's firm for over ten years before becoming Mark's personal accountant. He looked like an accountant and acted like an accountant, so Mark seldom spoke to him outside the office. Mark, who was finished, wanted to get on with it; so he abruptly pushed it, "Is there something else, Roger?"

Roger rolled his eyes and shifted his feet and planted them firmly in preparation.

"How did you know? How did you know what was going to happen?"

Mark, who was irritated but intrigued, replied, "Know what?"

"About Sara Francisco?"

"What about her? She is no longer this firm's asset."

"I know. You sold her contract to Luther Horn for three million, taking an estimated first-year 1.3 million loss with a projected four-year loss of over five million. But how did you know she was going to get into trouble?"

"Trouble? What trouble?"

"Why, the drugs and the shooting!"

Mark was now totally focused on Roger.

"What are you talking about?"

"Why, last night, she was picked up half naked in a Las Vegas hotel lobby with a recently fired gun. She had shot her new agent, Luther, over some artistic disagreement. Then they booked her, and she tested positive for several exotic drugs."

"Wow, first I have heard of this, Roger." Mark was not much for reading the front page of the newspapers, only the business sections of newspapers. He got most of his news in briefs prepared for him or via the big screen TV.

"Yes! She is now probably going to spend a lot of time in jail. How did you know to take the short-term loss? Why, this scandal will cost several million just for damage control and then another two to repair.

You dumped that asset in the knick of time. Overnight, she has gone from an invaluable property to a garbage dump PR disaster."

Mark, while stunned with the news, was intrigued. He was also surprised by the mixed metaphor and was looking at his accountant with renewed interest.

"What else do you know about this?"

"Why, that is about it I guess. Although I have heard that she was upset about his plans to put her back on the road for eight months."

"I see, well, it was just a fortuitous decision I guess. As our press release indicated, we were just shifting resources toward bigger efforts. Thankfully, for us all." He used his best good-guy-team buddy smile.

Roger rose to his feet slowly, juggling his folders and account information. After getting them all straightened out, he nodded to Mark. He still firmly believed his boss had a sixth sense about investments and had somehow known to drop her when he did. He slowly crossed to the office door and departed through it without another word.

Mark had watched his body diminish and then disappear through the large dark wooden door and was quick to react. As soon as he was out of hearing distance, Mark addressed his phone, "Contact Raymond!"

The phone answered, "Dialing Mr. Raymond Archer."

He said, "Thank you." Mark was more polite to his automatic phone than to most of his employees.

The phone rang three times, and a prim woman's voice answered, "Maston and Associates."

"Mark here. Give me Raymond."

There was a pause and then, "Why, yes, of course, as always for you, Mr. Harrison."

Then Raymond's voice boomed over the phone, "Hey, Mark, what's up?"

"You tell me. What do you know about the Sara Francisco shooting?"

"Nothing much but what I heard on the news this morning."

"Don't you keep up on the entertainment scene?"

"Well, yes, to some extent."

"Find out the inside scoop on this one."

"Sure, I'll get back to you shortly," Raymond said this without much enthusiasm and in general was confused as to why he had been approached; surely, Mark had a whole PR staff that could run this down for him. Raymond, like most good executives, had learned not to ask questions of powerful people when they asked for your assistance. The payoff for providing the assistance would be well worth any effort expended. He was just thankful Mark had called and asked.

Mark had a lot of business to clear out the rest of the morning, so he had forgotten about it until his executive assistant stuck her head into the office and announced Raymond was on the line. Mark hit the conference call button and vigorously waved the three staff people out of his office.

"Well?"

"Well, here it is. I spoke with Luther's attorney. Luther is in serious medical condition right now. He may die. Well, this is all confidential, right?"

"Right. Of course, Raymond," Mark replied sarcastically. After all, who was working for whom?

"It seems that Luther has a small drug problem and owes a big dealer a favor, so he set up the tour to meet that commitment, and Sara balked about delivering it for him. Luther, who was a little high when this happened, becomes unclear after mentioning the reason for the argument. He does say he had a gun in a table drawer, and when the police got there, she was wandering around the hotel lobby holding it while he was upstairs on the floor, bleeding into the luxurious carpet.

"Now the odd part is she was almost undressed. Luther said they both were fully dressed when they started to argue. He doesn't remember anything after she started to shout at him until he came to and was down and bleeding. That is when he sees her fantastic jugs in his face. She was topless at the time. She was screaming, and he blacked out again. He doesn't even remember going to the hospital."

"That's it?"

"Well, again off the record, Luther has been on the down-and-outs for sometime. He apparently borrowed the cash to buy Sara's contract and, in doing so, gained a new not-so-silent partner. The partner was supplying him with the goods he uses and was absolutely demanding he set up the tour."

"Sounds like a total screwup. Does anyone gain on this?"

"Good question. Not Luther who will not only have to spend a considerable time healing himself but will probably lose his agent's license and do some jail time since they found drugs all over his apartment. Not Sara since she is facing a lot of bad publicity and will see her music career go down the crapper. I am not sure on this however, but usually, there may be major tour insurance associated with her scheduled appearances. If that exists, then the holder would probably see several million in damages as the payoff for the tour being canceled. That would definitely be a tidy quick profit."

"Well, OK. If you find out about the tour insurance and anything else, let me know soon."

After hanging up, he thought for a few seconds and barked into the phone, "VP public affairs!"

The phone replied, "Dialing Ms. Marge Cartwell, VP of public affairs."

He waited very impatiently. There was something very odd about all this. It was such a small amount of money. However, what was Ralph's involvement if any? Why did he warn him, and how could he be involved if at all? It must just be an odd coincidence.

*Yes, that is it,* he thought.

The phone rang only twice when a syrupy voice said, "Ms. Cartwell's office, VP of public affairs of Harrison Venture Capital."

"Let me speak to Marge."

"Yes, sir! Immediately, sir!"

A pause and then, "Yes, Mark, how are you today?"

He ignored the greeting and went to the point. "I hear Sara had some personal problems in Vegas yesterday. I want a press release out now! It should clearly indicate that we have not handled her for over a month and we no longer handle her and that we always had a positive relationship with her and that we hope that it works out to the best for all concerned. You know the drill."

"Yes, sir, when would you like to review it?"

"No. I pay you to make it correct. Just have a copy here in the morning – no, by six tonight, and then you can release it the first thing in the morning."

"Yes yes, of course."

While Mark was used to deals that roared along fast and furiously, there was something very unpleasant and unnatural about this sequence of events. How did it happen? An argument ending in a shooting, drugs, and a half-nude, semiconscious singer – what in the hell kind of world do we live in anyway?

He read the release in his car on the way to a dinner meeting. It was acceptable and duly noted. Then Luther called back. Mark snapped the cell open. "Mark, Luther here. It took some tracking, but the tour insurance is rather a hefty sum over twenty-five million covering eighteen concerts. There are some strange aspects of it also. Instead of it being split by the local promoter based on the ticket-split percentages, which is the usual method, it all goes to the tour producers."

"How did they manage that?"

"Well, it appears they offered the local promoters an extra 15 percent of the ticket profits if they would forgo being in on the cancellation insurance. Of course, they do not have to pay their split for the insurance either, so they take a bigger risk for some considerable savings in up-front funds."

"Isn't that unusual?"

"Yes, in the States, it is. But international stuff is more creative, and this is not totally unheard of when you book European events."

"Who is the tour producer?"

"One Maximum Events Inc. A corporation that is in France and that is 50 percent owned by your partner in major projects, Ralph."

"Are you sure?"

"Sure, I am sure and also that the other partner is very silent but seems to have some roots in Sicily."

"Oh, OK. Luther, thanks for the help."

"Do you need anything else now?"

"No, that is enough for now."

Mark snapped his cell closed and wondered maybe Ralph is more into this than he thought. Would they go to such lengths for a paltry twenty-five million? Sure, he suspected they would. Ralph may be a little more devious and a lot more dangerous than Mark had thought. He would have to mull this over a bit. He was leaving for Spain late that night and would not return soon due to several days of meetings.

The next several busy weeks passed quickly for Mark. He had been very busy amassing ever more wealth. Occasionally, he wondered how much was enough and then realized no amount was enough especially when it was so easy to rake it in.

On the thirtieth of the month, after a relaxing flight on a small private jet, he arrived at Century Investments' private dock and Ralph's yacht on time and ready to enjoy some well-deserved rest. It had been an intense three weeks, hard but very profitable weeks.

When he boarded the large sparkling yacht, the steward arranged to get the luggage and install it in his cabin. He indicated that Mr. Tango was on the back deck entertaining his other guests.

When Mark appeared on the back deck, Ralph rose and walked toward him and greeting him most warmly.

"How good of you to join us, old man."

"How could I not?" Smile, smile, smile!

Smiles all around. The group included four others besides Mark and Ralph. Charles Merryweather, Ralph's personal assistant; Cheryl Lee, Ralph's "friend"; John Macon, Ralph's bodyguard; and Harry Renfrew, like Mark, a venture capitalist who had worked with both of them on various high-profile deals in the past. He worked mostly complex large real estate deals but was open for anything that made money.

Mark took the drink handed to him and dropped easily into a deck chair and tried to gather what they were up to. The group was just chatting about the pending trip. They were going out for a day, stopping at a private island for dinner and then returning the next day. He gathered someone important would be also joining them at the island. OK, he could handle that.

Mark became very relaxed after three large vodka drinks. He mostly had been watching the sun slowly descend into the sea and had not really actively engaged in conversation or much noted the drift of it. The ship had pulled slowly out into the harbor and anchored. It was rocking a bit.

Harry and Ralph were doing the talking with Charles and John agreeing and adding a little now and then. Cheryl Lee, a striking raven-haired beauty, was showing her age, about forty-six, but had a figure any woman would die for and any man would love to fondle. She seemed to be always touching Ralph and seldom did more than laugh at their jokes and drink her personal brand of champagne. She wore a beautiful pale blue dress that accented her breasts and showed a lot of tanned thigh as she moved around in her chair.

He was glad when they were finally called to dinner. He almost fell down the steep stairs but regained his composure. They selected their seats around a large glass table. However, Ralph motioned Mark to sit on his left with Cheryl Lee on his right. They were apparently the ones he was going to talk with this evening.

To Mark's surprise, the serving staff, all females, were nude. They were three blondes of various heights and statures ranging from petite to buxom. They moved professionally and correctly around the members of the dinner party, serving and assisting them to enjoy the meal. Mark was not unfamiliar with nude waitresses, but he found them a little distracting on the yacht. While it was large by any standard, it still seemed a little confining to him. These three especially since they all were apparently scrubbed, powdered, and perfumed. Their odor, while delectable, was very distracting when they moved past or behind him or bent over to serve him.

The meal was very Continental with a delicate crab salad followed by a rack of lamb surrounded by delicate matsutake mushrooms and tender spinach pasta in a cream cheese sauce. Large baskets of warm garlic rolls with ample butter or olive oil also held an aroma of interest. They all ate quietly at first then the glasses of wine began to empty with greater frequency, and conversation built but drifted toward business and the ever-present market.

All were drinking the fine wine of their choice, but these men were refined; while their faces flushed, they did not get boisterous nor rowdy. They were polite, educated, and restrained men who always controlled their lives, their world, and their subordinates. They did not have to act silly or roar to attain attention. They obviously admired the women that served them, but no one appeared to get out of line. There were no leers, off-color remarks, nor idle groping or pinching. Of course, it is easy to be a gentleman when you know that your host would supply any one of them to your cabin if you but asked.

Ralph, while friendly and very warm, didn't really talk about much, specifically with his immediate companions, but encouraged the others at the table to engage in boasting and gossip. Cheryl Lee, while very aloof, was full of smiles and laughter for all of Ralph's antics. She, however, assumed a disdained air while watching the others regale the group with their endless chatter.

While coffee was served, Mark strolled away from the group and leaned against the rail. He stared out to sea. It was a nice warm night, the food was excellent, Ralph seemed OK with him, and it would be a quiet couple of days. One of the party approached him from behind and, standing by his side, said, "It is really beautiful on the sea at night. I love to watch the moon hanging on the horizon." Without turning, he recognized her perfume and knew the gorgeous and titillating Cheryl Lee had joined him by the rail.

"Yes," Mark replied. "It is – "

"Well, I hope you enjoyed the dinner," she curtly interrupted him.

"It was excellent as always."

"We were not sure if you would be here."

"Oh, why?"

"Well, you took your time in dumping that bitch's contract." This cold comment startled him. It certainly shattered his feeling of tranquility.

"Oh, it was just a minor action that I took after dealing with some more pressing matters."

"You think so?"

"Well, yes. Why?" Now he turned and looked at her face in the moonlight. It was beautiful in a hard and angry way.

"Mark, in the future, when Ralph asks you for a favor, you better do it ASAP. He really doesn't ask twice you know."

He was surprised that she seemed to know so much, and he immediately became cautious.

"Well, some transactions take a little time."

"You are either very stupid or extremely daring. If you are daring, we may have more reasons to meet in the future."

"Why do you say that?"

"I have been with him for over three years, and you are the only person he has asked for a favor that took more than twenty-four hours to be done with it. Ralph is not an asker. He is a teller and a taker."

"Oh, he didn't seem to indicate that it was all that important when we discussed it."

"Well, you better learn that with Ralph, everything is equally important, and he doesn't like to wait for his requested actions to be taken."

He was looking at her intently now. Her face had softened, and she was smiling sweetly, almost seductively looking into his eyes. Stroking his arm lightly, she finished with, "Well, thank God you came through and were able to join us. Now that he has calmed down, the deal he will be offering you will be a major windfall. Just for my sake, if he ever asks you for a favor in the future, do it as fast as is humanly possible. Remember, you can always count on me if you need to." She turned on her heel and headed back to the babbling mix of people. He watched her seductive rear end swinging slowly back and forth finally disappearing into the semidarkness.

His evening was now less sublime. He thought, *Why should she warn me? Why was it all such big deal?* He had done what was asked out of friendship and had not expected it to turn into a windfall. Or had he? Oh well, it had all worked out OK. There will probably not be another favor requested for a long time.

After dinner concluded, while others were having some dessert, Mark went up on the top deck and relaxed in a large folding chair. He found a robe and pulled it around him and, although troubled, actually fell asleep. He was awakened several hours later by rough, heavy voices just below him. Two men were talking without much concern since everyone was supposed to be tucked snug in their cabins. The louder of the two said, "Well, I have to go back tonight. Damn it all! I was sure that little blonde would come to my cabin tonight!"

"Then wait till tomorrow and enjoy." This voice was less sure and lighter.

"Oh sure, the boss said tonight, and tonight it will be."

"What's the rush?"

"You know the boss. When he wants something, he wants it now!"

"No!" contradicted the other man. "He wants it yesterday!"

They both laughed at that remark. "I am sorry you won't make the brunch tomorrow. We have another group of waitresses coming on board for that. Redheads I think."

"No shit! Double damn and fucking shit to boot."

"When will you be back?"

"Not until Monday afternoon I am afraid. I have to get a flight out first thing this morning. Do the job and return on Monday's first flight back. There is nothing after four in the afternoon on Sunday! I will be staying at the corporation's suite. That should ease my pain. I really love that hot tub that lets you view the entire city while you get blasted."

"Yeah, remember New Year's in 2002?"

"Sure, who can forget? Old Jammy jumped off the damn penthouse patio and made a terrible bloody mess doing a belly flop on some old guy's Mercedes."

"No, not that! The dancers in the hot tub! Especially that black bitch who could hold her breath for sooo long."

"Oh yeah, you didn't care about her holding her breath. It was her tongue sucking your wrinkled old cock you liked."

They laughed again. Mark was a little embarrassed. He really didn't want to hear their macho crap, but it was too late to make his presence known. Surely, they would leave soon, and he could just sneak back to his cabin and go to bed.

"Well, Jerry, the boat will be here in a minute. I hear the motor now. Mac will be real happy he has to make another fucking trip back to the dock."

"Happy or not, that is the fucking order."

"What is it you are doing in Vegas? Getting married?"

"Oh, fuck you!" And Mark heard the sound of a heavy punch.

"Knock it off, you cunt ugly bastard! Or I will let you have a good one!"

"You little fart of a piss ant! You and who else?" the other one sneered.

"Me, myself, you shit-for-brains fuck!"

"Ok, right now, I have to finish the job the gangsters fucked up. Then I will be back, and we will see who is the best man, you worthless cock-sucking prick!"

"Sure, when you get back, asshole." Then more to himself than his crewmate he was going to beat up when he returned, "You know, I told him to get some of the regulars. But no, he wanted to use the spic gangsters to allow them to become part of our team."

"You mean the Latso Gang?

"Yeah, a bunch of loud-mouthed bling-bling punks."

"Yeah, what is the job anyways?"

"Well, you remember that real frisky, bitching babe the boss had on board several years ago? The one that did the striptease for the guests and crew when the boss was below on the ship-to-shore phone?"

"Oh yeah! How could I forget that one! What tits! And a nice voice too. Wasn't she a singer or something?"

"Yeah, it was that same dumb bitch that just got picked up for shooting her agent. That made a big ugly splash in all the newspapers this week."

"Oh, so what needs to be done? What's the fucking action?"

"Well, the agent was supposed to be dead, not flopping around in some hospital shooting off his sleazy mouth. Somehow, they shot up and killed a half-dozen pillows but only severely wounded him."

"So? So what's the dif? He got shot up?"

"Not good enough. Dead is what he needs to be. A cold dead fuck is what he will be. I will make fucking certain he has a fatal relapse in his intensive care room. That way, that Sara bitch will be sent away for murder, not just attempted murder."

"It's too bad! What a waste of a great pussy and tits."

"It's her own fucking fault!"

Mark was having some difficulty hearing all the conversation but was now alert and very interested. He even slowly sat up and leaned toward the stairwell to get a better listen.

"What the fuck did she do? What do you mean 'her fault'?"

"For Christ sake, Frankie! She was the boss's lady! The boss's ladies are not supposed to strip for his guests or anybody else. He dumped her ragged ass on shore after that cruise, and this is his get-even-time season."

"You mean he intended for her to be set up?"

"You know, Frankie, for a guy who has been around with the boss as long as you, you sure don't pick up on much. You're one super stupid cocksucker, man. Sure, he waits a couple of years and then makes it happen! I am warning you, man, don't cross the boss, ever!" Then he asked Frankie, "And do you know how she will find out about the setup?"

"No."

"After the trial is over, he will send her a card with some beautiful flowers when she is installed in her prison cell. The card will probably say something like, 'Sorry about your situation. Better keep your clothes on in the future. Love Ralph.' That is how she will know!"

"But offing a guy in the hospital, won't it be tough to pull off? I mean, with all those doctors and nurses around?"

"Are you kidding? Piece of cake. There is no lonelier place than a hospital. The staff is all so full of themselves, they do not notice the civilians or patients that come and go. How hard is it to kill a dumb fuck in the intensive care unit of a hospital? Actually, the way they run hospitals these days, they will probably kill him anyway before I get there. But the boss is in a fucking hurry, like always. The pot-headed agent jerk is there because he may die. I just make sure he does. It ain't the first time and won't be the last. Especially, if the boss uses those stupid spic gangsters again!"

"Well, here is the skiff, you dumb bastard. Don't fall in! You'll scare away the fishes!" The roar of the motor dropped back suddenly as the boat emerged from the darkness and pulled in close to the ship. Mark could hear it bump against the ship.

"Hey, Mac, you fucking gorilla! You gots to make another run."

"Fuck you, dork brain!" a high-pitched voice cut into the night.

They all laughed as the heavyset man descended the ship's ladder. He grunted at his effort while the ladder shrieked and shuddered under his massive weight. He landed on the deck of the small boat with a loud thump. The engine roared into action as the boat swung away. The remaining man below shouted out, "Maybe I can save you a redhead. You can have sloppy seconds, shit for brains! Hurry back."

The angry answer was lost in the engine's whine.

Mark felt suddenly cold, very cold. He was deeply shocked when he realized that his partner in business was apparently a criminal who had no scruples when crossed. He had heard rumors in the past of criminal connections, but since he had no evidence, he never worried much about them. Of course, as long as they were making money together, it was hard to really care. Now he knew that he may be in deep trouble.

Should he hide away or turn state's evidence?

*No, don't be silly,* he thought. He had overheard a conversation by some crew members who certainly may not be considered of the best source of reliable intelligence. It was all rather circumstantial. He really didn't know anything about his partner's other dealings, and they had always had solid commercial projects, projects that made them all considerable money! He reconciled with his conscious and thought he might do something later if he had more solid information.

Then a strange thought popped into his head. *Hey, maybe I could ask Ralph for a favor? He sure would be glad to be rid of his second wife who was killing him with an extremely heavy alimony. This new dimension of his partner's life could be a definite plus for him. Maybe just maybe?*

## The End

# The Final Excursion

Marvin looked at the temperature gauge. It looked all right. The small bathroom drinking glasses of water they poured endlessly into the radiator at the motel this morning must have slaked its thirst. The rental truck had given them trouble since they picked it up yesterday morning. The agent had seemed resentful that they could afford it or something. He kept asking them more questions. He seemed especially concerned that someone else besides Marvin might drive the truck. Marvin had assured him repeatedly it would be only him driving. When he had also agreed to all the added extra company insurance charges, the agent seemed to calm down. After his brand-new credit card had been swiped and the final papers had been signed, the three of them had all left with the truck as quickly as possible.

They had taken it directly to the storage company in San Jose as instructed. It was a major storage rental unit in the downtown area. They loaded the twelve heavy barrels from storage bin number 98 using the key provided in the envelope containing their instructions. They used ropes to tie them together so they would not move around in the enclosed truck bed when they drove. No one seemed to pay any attention to them loading the truck.

It was a large older rental storage facility with few people around. Those that were there all had things to do and little time to snoop into other client's business. The truck had already been acting up, but they did not want to make an issue of it since they were supposed to maintain a low profile. Anyway, after it was loaded, they didn't want to go back to the rental agency nor did they have any extra time to deal with this American company's obvious rip-off. They were on a tight schedule; for all of them, the clock seemed to be running faster every day.

Now it was another day. It was a bright morning. There were billowy white clouds in the pale blue sky. The air was crisp and clean. The

Monday morning San Francisco traffic was slow and dense at quarter to eight in the morning. Marvin was following the directions on the map he had printed from the Internet; he turned up a cross street and inched forward. He could just see the Golden Gate Bridge ahead of him every once in a while in the open slashes between the tall office buildings.

Marvin's real name was Omar Hefram Ellsinume. He was from a small village called Yarbea in the area known as Palestine by his people until it was partially occupied by Israel over thirty years ago. The village no longer existed and probably never existed on European maps but remained in his heart and the hearts of his people who had lived there for countless centuries.

He looked over at Jose and saw the young man, like a typical tourist, staring up at the office buildings and looking at the people on the sidewalks headed for work. He was so young, only twenty and so innocent.

His real name was Al Oran Maimed from the city of Yazd in Iran. His home was the center of the decadent Zoroastrian religion. There are about 150,000 Zoroastrians in the world, of which 65,000 live in Iran and 20,000 in Yazd. The Atashkadeh is their most important fire temple. Zoroastrians from all over the world come there to see the sacred fire that has been burning without interruption for over fifteen hundred years.

While Jose, as most of the people who lived in the city were well aware of this, himself was a devout Muslim, he looked down on these people in spite of their beautiful temples. He had to flee the city and go into hiding after the Americans invaded Iraq.

His father had become a prominent Baathist member of the Iraq government. He had obtained his post through another friend of an uncle who had convinced him to return to Iraq. Although Iraqis by birth, they had lived in Iran for over fifteen years when his father chose to take the position since it paid very handsomely. Over several years, he had provided for his family and was in the process of moving them all back to Baghdad. He had been murdered in the street close to his home three days after the American invasion in 2003.

Jose's four uncles had moved their families to Paris years ago and had begged Jose's father to go with them; but he chose to first stay in Iran, hoping to be able to return to Iraq, and then he did return. His father had told him they always would be Iraqis and that he should never ever forget that. Like his father, Jose did not abandon his homeland and chose to join the fight against the new infidel invasion.

*What was he thinking?* thought Omar. He glanced in the rearview mirror, looking for the second truck. There it was, about three cars behind. They had pasted a pale yellow moon shape on the top front, so he could spot it easy enough. They had rented the second truck from another rental agency, and it worked very well, or so they said. It was a white truck, and the moon shape on the front stood out. How could he miss it? They had been traveling about an hour from Palo Alto, California. They had left the modest motel after their morning prayers. They tossed their bags and prayer rugs behind the seats in the cabs of the trucks and left. There were two men in each truck. They were headed north on Highway 101, creeping slowly through San Francisco's heavy morning traffic as they approached the Golden Gate Bridge.

Omar looked at the cars all around him. He saw the knees of what he imagined to be a gorgeous woman in a red BMW next to him. He closed his eyes and tried to envision how she might look. A horn's cry snapped him back to the traffic. He started to think of his wife, dead now for over four years. She had been a gorgeous woman with beautiful legs and knees. She had starved to death during the evacuation of his village in one of the coldest Januarys in 2003.

When he thought of her, he wanted to cry. He could now control this emotion except sometimes at night when he was tired and alone. Then he cried long and hard for his wonderful wife. She did not deserve to die that way. He forced his thoughts back to the present, the now, the today. He had not even seen her for five months before she and his entire family had been evacuated! It was her mother who had sent the devastating message via a relative that his wife had died and for him to stay away. They were looking for him. It was dangerous times. But of course, Omar had never known any other times.

"Hey, Jose, are they still behind us?" Marvin felt the need to hear a voice, and Jose could answer anything, anything at all.

Jose pivoted in his seat, constrained by the seat belt; and then slightly twisting his neck backward, he said, "Yes."

Omar knew that, but he wanted to hear more words. "Jose, how long you been with the group?"

"Oh, in my heart, since 1990 right after the Soviets bombed my uncle's village. And that part of my family was all killed. I was not even born then, but my father's brothers always talked about it by the fires every night. I had to leave Iran after the Americans came, and my father was murdered in the street in 2003. That is when I joined the group officially. I then came to the states to live with my older brother, Asalah, but he died in a car accident in 2005. I hooked up with Ben one day when I drove him to our mosque. We were living in Circleville, Ohio, then." It all tumbled out. He spoke easily about it all.

Ben was their group leader. His real name was Offisma Madra Maharhani, and he was from the wild east coast of Yemen. He had trained with the Russians in Cuba and then had fought them in Afghanistan. He had been in Bosnia with Abu Jandal and his men. He was the oldest of the team of five; he was like a father to them all.

Omar ached with longing to turn back the clock. He missed his two daughters terribly. They were safe with his grandmother somewhere in Syria. He hadn't seen them in over two years. He had planned to see them next month. However, the group's plan was moved forward by six months, so that was no longer possible. Ben told him it was time to forget about himself and his personal life and think of the glory of Islam. Ben was always thinking of the glory of Islam – that was why Ben was the leader. It just seemed so natural for Ben. Ben was not a large man but heavyset and very strong. His eyes glowed all the time with either passion for Allah or anger for infidels. To look into his eyes was to be captured by his intensity. He repeatedly declared they were mujahedeen and soldiers of God.

Omar had heard rumors that Ben had been wounded several times in the war with the Russians. He had also seen some ugly scars on his shoulder and back when he was shaving that attested to that rumor. Ben would never talk about that war, even when asked directly by some fool who did not know any better.

He also had witnessed Ben, their loving father, kill a man with his dagger in an alley behind a bar in Oakland. The only reason was that the man, who was very drunk, had insulted their Muslim faith. He would never forget how the two, Ben and the stranger, had swaggered and shouted like two strutting roosters inside the dark smoky bar. However, the minute they went outside into the dark of night, Ben viciously pounded the man to his knees with his fists and then, within an instant, had cut his throat with a small dagger he carried in his belt in the small of his back.

Omar had seen a lot of death but not up close and delivered by the hand of someone he knew, someone you could see. He had never before seen the life fade out of a man's eyes. Mostly the death he had experienced was raining from the sky or buried in the earth and just exploding randomly. It was as if the people didn't matter, but the bombs' determination to explode took precedent over everything. If people happened to be around when they did, too bad for them! He had heard that Ben, like so many others, had lost his family and most of his village long ago in a now forgotten tribal war. He had been fighting infidels ever since, over twenty-five years perhaps. A long time to fight! A long time to hate!

Jose, bright eyed and alert, was looking admiringly at the girls walking briskly toward their office jobs. He whistled low when he saw a particularly attractive blonde. Jose really liked blonde women. There were no local blondes in the city where he grew up. He had seen them in the larger hotels and at some of the businesses of the European companies. He had, however, been able to date one while he was at Ohio State University for a semester. She was a real tiger. They made love all the time and smoked weed, listened to loud punk music, and together flunked out while embraced in their ecstasies of passion.

She promptly packed up her green Mustang convertible and drove home to her family in Chicago. He missed her. He also really missed her car; it was a beauty. He left the university and drifted into a taxi driver's job. That is how he had met Ben. He had been a fare in his taxi one day, and they got to talking. Although grinning, Jose was only sad that he had not loved more blondes. He was also very tired from the heavy drinking last night. He couldn't, however, mention that to Omar. Omar had gone to bed early like they all were supposed to according to their instructions. While the team rested last night, shadowy figures approached the two trucks and quickly did their work and padlocked the back doors. All was then ready. No one heard them. No one saw them, but they did their job as they had been instructed.

However, Jose and Kaster were far too excited to sleep. Kaster, whose real name was Ahmend Mar Aliumnee, was a child of the camps. He had been born in a refugee camp and had grown up in other refuge camps. When his sister died of cholera, he just slipped away one night into the mountains and eventual found an armed group that took him someplace in the desert for training. They had food, weapons, and trucks. What more could a refugee ask for?

The two of them had slipped out of their motel room and went down the street to the Bloody Hammer Bar. They were only going to have a couple of drinks. Well, they lingered to listen to the music and flirt with the women. The few drinks became many drinks he guessed from the size of his hangover. Kaster had indicated by a few signs that he was also feeling rocky this morning.

Anyway, it was a good going-away party for them, and they would get plenty of rest very soon. He remembered that last night, Kaster had been such a clown. He had both of them laughing and giggling all night. He did imitations of President Bush, Tony Blair, and Saddam Hussein that really made you laugh. They had almost enticed a couple of young women to go back to the motel room with them, but then they remembered they had to be at work early Monday. So they had left alone, laughing to themselves and looking back over their shoulders as they departed. They did slip each of the men their telephone numbers. Kaster gave his number to Jose.

Jose could feel the two pieces of paper that had their telephone numbers on them in his shirt pocket. He patted them with his left hand and smiled to himself. The girl he was interested in was named Lara, but she was not a blonde. She was very cute, however, and had huge grey eyes and wore the most pleasing perfume he had ever smelled. It was like a flower, a very delicate flower with only a hint of sweetness. It reminded him of nights he had spent in the deserted dark desert.

Jose saw a huge billboard advertising Cingular cell phones. Jose really liked cell phones. It was the one modern invention that he thought was really of value. He had a cell phone ever since he arrived in the States. His brother had provided it for him. America was so big and crowded, he believed you needed a cell phone to stay connected to the world. Without his cell phone, how would he know what was going on? He used it constantly. They had to turn them off during the trip however. He felt the small device press against his thigh in his jeans pocket.

"Hey, Omar, where is all this traffic coming from?" he asked nervously. He now also wanted to hear a human voice.

"You should know. You drove a cab over in Oakland."

"Yeah, but I drove the night shift using Hammond's cab after he went home. It is always easy traffic with only tired people and happy drunks who can't remember where they live."

They both laughed. In the past, they both had to rummage through a drunk's wallet to locate their address and haul them home before they puked up in the cab. When they performed this service, they strongly hoped the stinking alcoholic passenger had a wife, lover, or friend anxiously waiting for them who would give the driver a big tip for delivering their precious passenger home safely. He had once dragged a well-dressed heavy old man up several flights of stairs to his apartment. When he rung the doorbell, a stacked babe dressed only in dark blue underwear answered. She took one look at him and then one look at the drunken man he was holding up. She slammed the door in his face, screaming, "That worthless fuck don't live here no more!" He dropped the man next to the closed door and left. No big tip that night. He often wondered if she later forgave him and if they were still living together.

Omar nervously checked the rearview mirror. The other truck was now five vehicles behind him, but that was acceptable as long as he could see them. They were still about one hundred yards from the entrance to the soaring bridge. He saw the first tower. The towers that support the Golden Gate Bridge's suspension cables are smaller at the top than at the base, emphasizing the tower's height of five hundred feet above the roadway – a roadway that was almost two miles long, he remembered those few facts from their recent briefing.

The traffic going south into town was even heavier – full of trucks and SUVs, expensive BMWs and Mercedes-Benzes. Omar preferred a nice Cadillac himself since they seemed to be so elegant. Omar had never even ridden in one but had seen them on the TV and then frequently on the streets in America. He inched slowly forward, worrying about the temperature gauge, which was now swinging higher. It couldn't be much longer, but this slow traffic could really heat up the truck. He remembered clearly when he was a boy, his uncle Sinara told him to turn on the heater if a vehicle heated up. He was ready to do that. Overheated vehicles were frequent occurrences in his country. He then started getting mad since they had paid a lot of money for this rental truck, and it should have been in perfect condition. The rental salesperson had taken advantage of them since they were foreigners. "Some democracy, some equality!" he fumed to himself.

They were now past the buildings, entering the long row of vehicles paying the toll to creep across the bridge. This would be only the second time he had been on the bridge. Several weeks ago, Ben had borrowed his brother's Ford, and they drove across the bridge and stopped on the other side in a park. They had gotten out and stretched.

He found a pamphlet in the garbage can that proclaimed the park to be the Marin Headlands, part of the Golden Gate National Recreation Area – the largest urban park in the United States and one of the largest in the world. Point Bonita Lighthouse, several historic military sites, a Nike missile site, museums, campgrounds, beaches, and hiking trails can be visited and explored within the Marin Headlands. He shook his head in disgust when he read that. Only in America would they put missiles in such a beautiful park. He then wondered if they also planted land mines around the trees as the Russians had done in Afghanistan.

Then they had eaten some fresh hard bread with olive oil. They drank some warm tea and relaxed. They felt the warm sun on their faces and watched the huge San Francisco Bay full of shipping and luxurious sailing boats. *It must be so quiet and peaceful on the water although the traffic sounds must float down toward the water,* he thought.

He glanced at Jose again who was now looking more composed and somber. He then reviewed in his mind everything that had happened in the fleeting past several days. They had made their final videotapes, packed, and handed over their personal effects and had photographs taken for their newspapers and posters. He knew his family would be proud of him. He would not be the first martyr in his family, but he would be one with the greatest reputation. His daughters would always know that their father was a great martyr to Islam and his country, Iraq. They would always be very proud of him.

They would receive a small annual allowance from the group for the rest of their lives due to his bold actions today. He laughed to himself about the videos. He had just sat down and said what he had to and was done with it. Kaster had to retake his four times since he was so nervous and really unsure of what to say. They finally took him aside and scripted his statement for him, and he just read it from large hand written cards, just like politicians do. He quickly refocused on the present and asked, "Jose, you all set?"

"Yeah, sure," he said, smiling and holding up the end of a rope.

"Just say the word."

"I won't have to say anything. You will know when it is time to yank it and then yank it hard."

The gauge was arching higher, approaching the red-marked warning level. He flipped on the heater full blast and cranked down his window. Jose, feeling the heat, cried out, following his example. Omar silenced his complaining with the curt explanation, "I have to cool the truck!"

Jose had an arm out the window and was looking down into a convertible next to him on the right. They were in a center lane, creeping along very slowly.

The gauge dropped back and held down for the next few minutes. It was actually cold outside but hot in the center of the truck. He drove with his left hand and rubbed his right hand on his thigh. He actually stroked his thigh because he could feel the strange lump that was the remaining scar tissue from the steel scraps the doctors had removed from it when he was only seventeen. He remembered how surprised he was by the unexpected explosion while running home. Then the pain, the ceaseless pain, the pain he endured for over ten months. Even now, it hurt him on cold nights. Rubbing it always helped him to focus his mind on the task at hand.

It was hard to keep from thinking of his family. At one time, they had been so happy and hopeful when he was a youngster growing up. Then every year, something worse happened to them, and they all thought, *What else could happen?* But something else always did. His huge family was slowly destroyed by endless wars, tribal warlords, invasions, and random armed attacks. Every year, there were fewer and fewer family members left, with many of those remaining being injured or crippled.

He jumped! Jose had suddenly grabbed the hand he had on his thigh. He looked over quickly. Jose had tears in his eyes.

The young man blurted out, "I miss my father. Are we really doing the right thing? Are we?"

This shocked Omar for several reasons. He had never heard Jose speak of his love for his father nor question the plan before.

"Of course, this is our destiny!" He then added a little mechanically, "In the name of Allah, the compassionate, the merciful!" Thus having reassured them both, he checked for the other truck.

They now were both in position. He could see part of Kaster's face in his rearview mirror. He knew that Carl, with the long narrow nose, was next to him, holding his rope. He knew they all were ready. He did not know Carl's real name, but he had been at the Sabra refugee camp when the Israelis, under the orders of the devil, Defense Minister Ariel Sharon, had massacred thousands of innocent men, women, and children. Carl had managed to run into the desert during the terrible murderous raid and escaped into the opened warm embrace of the Al-Qaeda.

The traffic was very slow, and he was getting tired of hitting the brakes and then the gas so often. He was also afraid of hitting the car in front of him and left plenty of space between them, which allowed other drivers to quickly inch into his lane. This game of leapfrog further delayed their tortuous slow progress toward the center of the bridge.

All four of the young men were ready. He felt that they had been ready all their lives for this final moment. Although his heart was breaking for his daughters, he could not back out now. He was unable to stop the course of his fate. He and they were in the hands of Allah, and they could not change their destinies even if they tried. It had all seemed so correct when he started out, and he was committed to the cause. But as time wore on and his family suffered and dwindled, he certainly wavered. However, the organization was designed to direct young men into moving inexorably toward their commitment to Islam whether they still wished to or not. It was like swimming in the ocean when the tide starts to go out. You cannot swim back but must go where the tide of death takes you. They were now only flotsam being forced toward their destiny on a huge ocean of religious fervor without any other recourse.

The four had met only five days ago and had been introduced and instructed by Ben. They had been together ever since, and all knew only the code names of one another. However, Omar, who listened and kept his eyes open, knew more about each than the others. He also knew that they all were of one mind and one heart, which served Allah and their families. Their real names were no longer important since they were all pledged to Allah's will. It had not been a long enough time to learn anything about one another but long enough to become the warrior team to accomplish the mission.

He looked up and saw they were almost halfway across the bridge, and the pace of the traffic was finally starting to pick up.

He again looked reassuringly at Jose, smiling and nodding at the younger man. Jose had just wiped his perspiring face with his shirtsleeve and was now gripping the rope, staring grimly straight ahead, clutching the rope so tightly that his knuckles were going white. Jose was so innocent. He was not even aware that the rope was just a decoy. He was only along for the ride to keep Omar from having second thoughts and somehow subverting the plan. They were a team that ensured each stayed on course and did not flinch from their duty, from their destiny. The truck bomb would explode on impact, rope or no rope.

The needle was now back into the red area, but it made no difference now. He could see the second tower clearly as they were past the middle of the bridge, and traffic would open up, and the radiator could do what it damn well pleased.

He tried to envision his wife's face but could only remember odors and familiar actions and her little personal gestures. Her face was faded, unclear, and smoky. She seemed to be coming closer so he could discern her lips and her beautiful, adoring eyes. Then he heard the three long honks of the truck horn behind him – blasting, blasting, and blasting!

He slammed his eyes shut, thinking only of his wife. Angrily, with all his strength, he turned hard left into the oncoming traffic at almost a ninety-degree angle, crushing the pedal to the metal. The truck surged forward. Seconds before he crashed into an oncoming car, there was a loud explosion behind him. He was engulfed in a huge terrifying eruption of sound, pain, and smoke. He wondered if Jose had time to pull the rope. He wondered if Ben was watching their final action from a nearby location. The truck disintegrated around him.

The one behind him was already just a pillar of fire, smoke, and debris. He smelled heat. He smelled burning flesh. He saw only blackness and darkness. He tried to call out to his wife, but he no longer made any sounds. His body writhed in the anguish of his burning death. His soul leaped forward, frantically searching the oblivion for his beloved wife.

The bridge floor was blown wide open on both sides in the middle of the bridge. The entire bridge itself was swaying slowly sidewise. The roadbed crumbled and collapsed. It rained huge chunks of concrete, iron, and vehicles into the cold bay waters, hundreds of feet below. Several boats were swerving away from under the bridge. People, vehicles, and parts of vehicles were plummeting downward. People were yelling in terror and crying out in pain. Those cars behind surged forward, pushing more vehicles into the widening open breach. The edge of the breach was crumbling. It became larger and larger.

Omar, Jose, Kaster, and Carl disappeared along with their rental trucks. They were on their way to Allah's garden and the arms of the legendary seventy-two virgins. The democratic nations certainly would never mourn them. Their Muslim friends and brothers would mourn them and wish them well on their journey. In their Muslim world, they would be added to the list of martyrs and honored for their selfless devotion to Allah, the one and only god.

The supposed free world countries would however mourn the hundreds of innocents who died this day, who would die in the coming days, and/or who were injured on this fateful bright Monday morning. It would generate hundreds of repetitive hours of TV news programming – endless discussions of why they, the terrorists, did what they did. Why the CIA, FBI, or Homeland Security hadn't detected them. News specials would blossom and die before the next carnival of excitement came along to divert the public to watch another startling tragedy.

The distant wailing sirens of the approaching emergency vehicles were now filling the air. They were becoming louder and louder and louder. The bridge continued to disintegrate and fall apart. Cars continued to waver and then plunge off the opening's edge. Crowds of people who had abandoned their vehicles were being crushed in a frantic exodus off the bridge on both sides. Huge chunks of the structure continued to crash into the bay, shooting large water plumes upward in silent supplication.

That is why on the morning of July 30, 2007, the skies of San Francisco went dark, spreading another shadow of terror and despair across our land.

# The End

# The Night Visitor

F rank was tired. He had been a long grueling day, yet he felt like he had not accomplished a damn thing. He also noted that he had lost some money on the market, which was down and apparently dropping again. Anymore, he was not really a very happy person in general. However, as always, after work, he stopped in at the Do Drop Inn on the corner of Manchester and Smith. His office was located only a half block away. It was on his way home, and he liked to have a quick one before walking home to his large vacant and silent apartment.

It was October and not cold but not warm either. He pushed opened the heavy wooden door of the bar and was struck by waves of happy sounds. He entered with his head down and almost barged into a heavy blonde who was leaving in a big hurry. He quickly mumbled, "Excuse me."

She just pushed past him with a glare and went out the door, leaving an odor of strong perfume and talcum powder behind her.

He weaved his way slowly forward through the noise-pulsating crowd toward the wide bar area. He could see backs, shoulders, bare arms, and rich coat sleeves, and his ears were filling with a loud din of word bits and phrases and from the electronic gear sounds of music, sports announcers, and laughter. The huge TVs were on, and all the people seemed to have something to tell those with them as they drank and snacked the evening away. He had spotted a tiny slice of space at the bar and was trying to maneuver toward it when he heard a woman's voice calling his name.

"Frank, Frank, over here!"

He looked to his side and saw Margie with a big smile of recognition on her face waving frantically at him with both arms over her head. She sat at a table with several partially filled glasses and lots of used napkins. He took a deep breath and, changing direction, headed toward her gesticulating arms. He mechanically smiled and halfheartedly waved back at her. After slipping past several people and edging around several more, he arrived. Sitting down heavily, he spoke loudly. "Hi, Margie! Who else is here?" he inquired with a forced exuberance.

She rattled off the names, "Murray, Clancy, and Meg." They were all support staff-level people, which was good since they didn't know anything and bad since they had a tendency to gossip a lot in spite of not knowing anything. He nodded and silently approved and accepted his new society. Margie was half finished with her drink.

The waitress appeared at his elbow and asked him emotionlessly, "What will you have?"

She was one of the regular waitresses looking harassed and bored as usual. Her auburn hair was falling down on one side, and she had some dark stains on the left side of her white uniform blouse.

Then snapping him her "A" smile, she waited. He quickly ordered a lager beer and said he would pay now since he was going to leave after this one, handing her a ten. She smiled back mechanically, grasped the bill by the tip, and vanished in the crowd, which had briefly parted to let her through. The other office members drifted back to the table from different directions. They sullenly plunked down on their chairs. Murray looked plowed, and the other two just looked extremely tired.

*It had been a difficult day for everyone*, Frank thought.

They exchanged nods and mumbled inconsequential greetings. They resumed sipping at their drinks. Then he thought he heard his name mentioned again.

He turned to see Melvin standing there with his usual stupid grin plastered on his face. Melvin was in sales. He was, in fact, the sales manager. Frank nodded his hello, thinking, *Christ, this ass is all I need to make my day*. And then he took a big swig on his beer, which had just appeared magically with his change neatly piled next to it.

Melvin, totally uninvited, pulled up a chair, pushing closely to Margie, motioning wildly to the beleaguered waitress. She came over cautiously. He leered at her, saying, "I wish you were on the menu tonight, Bernice sweetie." Bernice was aloof and just gave him her standard customer smile. He ordered a scotch on the rocks and another round for everyone. They all protested, and Frank winced as he was ready to go. Melvin's presence only promised to be more of a pain. He tried to protest, but Melvin out shouted him with, "Look, I made a big sale today! I mean, a really b-i-g sale!" Doing a poor imitation of Ed Sullivan, he says, "And I want to share it with you all." He somehow partially bowed while still being seated.

Murray, like a fool he was, bit and asked, "Oh, what sale?"

That was good for another thirty minutes as Melvin elaborated in the smallest details his astute and astounding actions that closed a $1,400,000 sale. Bernice returned with a tray full of the refills and carefully but quickly sorted them out. She purposely approached from the other side of Melvin so the table was between them and, reaching out, passed his drink over to him.

He smiled and said gruffly, "Run a tab, honey."

Frank slipped her his usual five-dollar tip, preparing for a silent exit. He pulled on his new beer and didn't say much while tuning Melvin out. After another dull lengthy twenty minutes more, Frank had finished his third beer and half of the fourth one someone else had generously forced upon him when he stood to leave. The refills just seemed to keep coming. He was surprised to feel a little wobbly. Someone reached out a hand to steady him, but he waved it away. He simply said with feigned dignity, "I am very tired after today's events and not the least bit drunk." He dismissed their uttered false concerns and turned to leave with his parting statement tossed over his shoulder.

"I have to go now. All of you have a grand evening." He swept away through the thinning crowd toward the door. He focused hard on the door and almost tripped over someone's briefcase that had fallen onto the floor but caught himself in time and, deftly recovering his footing, continued undeterred. He reached the solid wooden door slipping gratefully outside into the crisp night air. Unfortunately, he was even more depressed now than when he had arrived. He walked slowly toward his large dark apartment.

That was the single advantage of his divorce; he now had an apartment only six blocks from his office and could walk it with little problem. No more large house in the suburbs – his wife now had that. Living there with her had required an endless mind-numbing morning and evening commute. Although now, he frequently hailed a cab when he was running late. Which seemed to be all the time anymore, to insure he got to work on time every morning. Since he had no one keeping track of him, he could always walk home after work no matter what the time. When he got there was only his concern.

Climbing the six shallow front steps of the large brick apartment building, he entered through the large polished glass door before the doorman could open it and waved as he passed him by.

"Hi, Harv."

Frank had lived there six years now since his divorce. He always said hi or goodbye to the doorman who was very heavyset and slow to respond both in actions and words. Yet Frank had no clue who this man was; he didn't know him at all.

He didn't really like the apartment itself since it was large, cold, and dark; but it was close to work and had a prestigious address. A former business associate who made it big-time sold it to him for a song right after Frank's divorce when he was a little thin on funds. He was one of the few employees of the company who never had to drive to work. The others complained constantly about their daily commutes both on the train, by bus, or in their cars.

Taking the elevator to the eighth floor, he fumbled for the door key and found it deep in his right-hand pocket. He inserted it into the lock and gratefully heard the acceptance click. He entered his apartment, flipping on the hall's light switch. The bright light surged through the narrow hall, reaching into the living room. Everything looked the same. Yes, it was the same, and the same was very boring. He hadn't done much to make the place his home. It was basically furnished in heavy pieces that his friend left, and he just sprinkled his personal stuff around like trimmings, and that was it. He went into the bedroom and took off his suit. He hung it in the closet after brushing it thoroughly. He slipped into some old torn jeans and a heavy very faded yellow sweatshirt.

He sniffed it as it went on past his nose and made a mental note to change into a clean one tomorrow. In his socks now, he padded into the kitchen and looked for something to eat. He ended his quest by making a ham and cheese sandwich and switched from beer to a Diet Pepsi. He seldom actually cooked but usually ate a sandwich or leftovers from a previous meal that he had at a restaurant earlier in the week. He always had a variety of cold meats to choose from courtesy of his local delicatessen where he stopped by on the way home every so often.

He went into the living room and sat in the big overstuffed chair. He slowly, with some effort, put his feet up on the hassock. Both pieces of furniture were of a faded grey color and still smelled a little of cleaning fluid after all these years. He balanced his sandwich on his knee and turned on the TV with the remote. Checking his watch, he switched to the movie channel. It had an old movie classic on, but he didn't care what it was. Whatever was fine with him.

He remembered the blonde actress he saw on the black-and-white screen in another mystery movie with Alan Ladd. He made a shift in his chair to be more comfortable. The movie was *I Married a Witch* with Veronica Lake. It had been made back in 1942. *My god, that is over sixty yeas ago!* he reminded himself.

He liked her, but the film was a little silly, especially by today's standards. Oh well, so was his life. He half finished his sandwich and started to fall asleep. His head slumped down, but he then snapped awake. Checking his wristwatch, he realized it was only quarter to ten in the evening. *My god, I'm getting old! How could I be tired so early?* he thought to himself. Well, he justified it by reminding himself of what a strenuous day it had been. He rubbed his eyes with the back of his fists and waited for the film to end at ten o'clock. It did. He flipped the TV off with a push of a button.

Sitting there in the dark, he thought about the day and the many mistakes he had made and that tomorrow would be much of the same. It seemed like the fire had gone out of the job or maybe out of him. In the past, he had enjoyed his work more. He laughed at himself and said in the dark, "Yeah, the good old days!"

He looked around the room and saw all the familiar items – books, magazines, some dirty socks on the floor, and the ugly matching couch. There were several days of newspapers on the floor scattered around the sofa.

He almost felt like dropping off to sleep on the couch but knew he would wake up in the middle of the night and have to get up to go to bed. Besides, the couch was lumpy. When he did fall asleep on it, he always ended up with a terrific backache.

He got up slowly and shuffled back into the kitchen. He put his plate in the sink with its dirty brothers and sisters and rinsed off the utensils he had used to make the sandwich. They dropped on the plate with a clatter, ending up in a pile with the others. Tomorrow, he would clean up the mess, filling and running the automatic dishwasher. He put the bread away into the old metal bread box. He thought, *Maybe I will go out for dinner tomorrow night. Nothing fancy, mind you. Maybe the place in the next block that had such good Italian food.* He was getting tired of sandwiches and really didn't enjoy the lunches in the office cafeteria anymore.

He no longer had the time nor the money to go out for lunch at one of the better-known business meeting watering holes. He was lucky to be able to grab a quick bite in the cafeteria. He turned off the kitchen light. He slowly went into the bathroom. Now the bathroom was the nicest place in the apartment. At least, that is what he thought. Everything was clean and neat, and there was a new sink and shower as well as deep built-in bathtub. He never took baths, but it was nice to know you could if you wished. It was bright and sterile and a little cold but at least extremely clean.

He had a maid come in every Friday to clean, but it seemed like only the bathroom benefited from it. He brushed his teeth without much energy and almost no enthusiasm. *Just another symbolic gesture in a life reduced to repeated senseless gestures and tasks*, he thought. He stared at the tired face that confronted him in the mirror. *Maybe I should go on vacation?*

The saliva dribbled out of the left side of his mouth as he spit the contents into the sink. The water gushed from the faucet for a few seconds, and everything swirled around, racing to go down the drain. He took a towel and wiped his face dry. He refolded it and hung it back up on the towel rack.

Turning, he saw the big framed poster of Marilyn with her skirt floating up. It was on the wall outside the bathroom in the hall. It was the famous scene from the movie *The Seven Year Itch*, a film he used to watch frequently in the past. It was his only art contribution to the apartment. Well, that and his twenty-year work award that was hung over his desk in the living room. As a teenager, he had grown up idolizing Marilyn, and it was only much later after her death that he realized she was a woman with a very checkered past and a zillion personal problems.

"But damn, she was hot!" he said out loud smiling broadly.

He slept in his shirt and jockey shorts. Climbing into his king-sized bed, he pushed the magazines to the other side. When he got in the bed, several magizines fell, one after another, plop, plop onto the floor, joining the others from previous nights. He swore softly and pulled the blanket up tight under his chin. Yawning loudly, he squirmed into a comfortable position and fell asleep faster than usual.

He was dreaming about something silly at work. All the managers had been shrunken to insect size, and the rest of the employees were trying to stomp on them like so many cockroaches. The managers were scurrying around in rapid circles as usual, and the employees were doing a hysterical foot-stomping dance to the sounds of "I Wanna Be Free."

He was just about to smash Melvin when he was startled wide awake. The room was dark. He heard nothing, but he felt like something was there. He was a little frightened. He smelled an extremely pleasing and exotic odor. It must be cooking from downstairs – no, it was not food; it was like roses and lilacs mixed together but with a dash of nutmeg. *Some new dope a kid is smoking in the next apartment?* he speculated.

"What the hell is that?" he wondered out loud. He pulled the cover up again and started to go back to sleep, and then he felt like someone was in the room. Someone was watching him! He started to get really frightened. He hoped this was just part of another dream. He closed his eyes hard and listened but heard nothing.

When he opened them again, he still felt like someone or something was watching him. He very slowly slid his hand out from under the cover toward the table light on the nightstand. He was shaking slightly but finally got control of his trembling fingers and switched it on! Rather than seeing the normal empty room he expected, he saw a shadow of a figure in the far left corner. Just standing there – just barely perceptible. It seemed to be behind or in the curtains. He didn't know what to do! He was gripped by fear and finally called out timidly, "Who is there?"

Expecting the shadow shape to immediately disappear, instead, a sultry low voice replied, "It's only me, Frank. Don't be scared. I just dropped by for a little visit."

The hair on his neck rose. *A practical joke? A hit woman? A burglar with a sense of humor? What in the hell!*

He managed to ask in a very weak, shaky voice. "Me . . . me . . . who?"

"Why me, Marilyn, Frank." And a very full-figured woman emerged from the shadows. She appeared to be Marilyn, Marilyn Monroe in the outfit she wore in *Some Like It Hot* when she was on the train.

"My god!" he exclaimed. He sat up abruptly and rubbed his eyes violently. *It couldn't be! It shouldn't be!* But as far as he could tell, there stood Marilyn Monroe in his dull dim bedroom.

*My god! This was the best dream I have ever had!* She looked so real and was slowly sinuously strolling closer to him in her sultry silky way just like in her movies. The intoxicating odor intensified as she moved closer to the bed. She walked so smoothly and seductively.

*What a goddess!* he thought to himself.

She smiled at him impishly and said in a low voice, "Why thank you, Frank. What a nice compliment. I think I am going to like you." Her smile grew wider and warmer as she settled onto the edge his bed by his side. She did her little adorable lip twists just like in her films and in interviews.

*This is not happening. This is dream,* he assured himself.

"Maybe, Frank, but let me tell you what your dream is going to be about. Sort of previews of coming attractions." She laughed at her little joke. "From now till dawn, you and I are going to be in bed together, and you can do whatever you want with me and to me. I am going to be the best dream you ever had, and tomorrow, you will remember every little tiny detail of it. In fact, you will never forget this dream, Frank. That is my job for the night, to please you and just you, Frank – owwee!"

He sat up abruptly, and the covers fell into his lap. She bent forward and slowly pulled them back, watching him. Then she dropped her gaze to his bulging crotch, saying, "Why, Frankie! Another great compliment. You do know how to welcome a lonely girl." And he felt her hand slightly stroke his upright penis under his underwear. He jumped and gasped and was filled with unbelievable joy. She seemed to float out of her dress and was wearing only a pale blue bra and panties. She stood up moved forward and pushed him over in the bed. Then she wiggled into the bed beside him. He had pulled the covers up to his chin and was paralyzed, frightened to even look at her. With her face so close to his ear, he felt her light breath dancing on it as she said, "Frank, this is going to be the best night you have ever had in your whole life!" Her hands touched him, and he relaxed and responded in kind, reaching out politely and stroking her shoulder and then her arm. She was not as warm as he expected but seemed to have an electricity about her. Her skin was smooth and supple. Her hair was cut short but was full and warm and smelled wonderful. He had a frightening thought, *My god, don't wake up, don't every wake up!*

She again replied, "Why, Frank, how nice of you."

*Is she reading my mind? My god! Who cares! What a vivid and wonderful dream!* The light faded out, and he felt her vibrancy creep around him wherever her electric body touched his. Her hair smelled wonderful as she pushed up against him. She was kissing him lightly on the shoulder. Marilyn Monroe was kissing him. Her lips were silky and tender. She was kissing him! He lay perfectly still, holding his breath. He was now afraid to breathe.

Pulling back a little, she said in a mock annoyed voice, "Well, Frank, I think maybe you could do something here. Wiggle a toe or something."

He gulped for air and weakly replied, "I am afraid if I do, you will disappear."

"Not tonight, Frank, this is an unconditional guaranteed six-hour dream. You can do anything you want, and you will not wake up. In fact, no one will hear either of us no matter how much noise we make."

"How do you know?"

"Oh, I know these things, Frank. Just like I know you want to grab little Sally Beth's ass every time she goes by your desk at work," she said accusingly.

"How did you know that? No one knows that!" he cried out.

"Frank, let's face it. I have passed on, and we know things. I am here because you deserve to have this dream, and I am here to see that it happens." Then sitting up and letting the sheet fall, displaying her gorgeous body, with a cute little pout she inquired, "Look, Frankie, you are in bed with a woman, and I believe a RATHER BEAUTIFUL ONE – how long has it been?"

"Well, let's see . . . Over three years, I guess."

"Frank, it has been six years! I bet you cannot even remember the big waitress you picked up on Twelfth Street at the all-night diner and slept with until she wet her bed. You snuck out to go home in the cold rain six years ago. Well, it is time to make up for all those lost years, Frank!"

She leaned forward and, slipping her hand under the covers, gently slid her fingers across his trembling chest. He turned toward her and tentatively reached out his trembling hand bumping her chin. He quickly moved his hand to her shoulder and ran it down her arm. It felt so wonderful! He ran it back up and slid it around to her back and pulled her slightly forward. She giggled in a delightful way and snuggled into him.

"You think it may be coming back, Frank?" she asked in a throaty, teasing whisper. He felt her neck and her cheek and slid his hand back to her ear. He gently circled her ear and then laid his hand open on her upper chest, and she sighed slightly as he tentatively moved it downward toward one of her full breasts. When it reached her breast, it naturally cupped it, and he felt the wonderful areola and her hardening nipple. Her underwear had disappeared. She squealed and rolled around against him in delight. She coyly pushed into his caressing hand.

This unleashed a surge of desire, and the rest of the time, he was all hands and lips and tongues and tastes and delights. And finally, after hours of exploring her body, he entered her! In a short time, he exploded like a firecracker! She relaxed stroking his old man's ample butt as they remained linked together.

"See, you haven't forgotten you really know how to please a woman." Her warm teasing voice broke the silence.

He replied shakily, "Are you sure? You are not just any woman! You are Marilyn! You are a goddess!"

"Yes, Frankie, you pleased me! Let's just relax a few minutes, and then we will see what comes up." And a deep throaty laugh erupted from her lips. Her hand played in his disheveled hair.

He was so excited but so tired he doubted if anything would; but to his amazement, there it was as she gently massaged his penis and then, to his astonishment, bent down quickly, taking it into her mouth.

And before he knew it she had given him the world's best blow job. What a wonderful dream! She lifted her head and was smiling at him. He couldn't see her well in the dark, but he felt the smile radiate at him. She said, "Did I please you, Frank?"

He was shaking with delight and very embarrassed and very much out of his depth. He never had a dream like this or a love affair anywhere near this level of sensual intensity.

She said, half teasingly, "Oh, Frankie, you taste so good." And she snuggled into his arms. He stroked her silky, electric body, and he felt so free and uninhibited. It was pitch-black, and he felt her warmth and smelled her odor and was overjoyed just holding her and thinking about her eyes, her lips, and her sensuous body.

He, to his surprise, started to kiss her lightly and then harder and finally, sliding down her body, lingered on her breasts, licking and nipping and mouthing them. He slowly moved down her stomach into her pleasure dome as she rolled over flat on her back. She spread her legs apart slowly, and his hands were fingering her breasts, and his tongue slid out and slipped into her lower lips and danced the circle of love. He felt her squirming in pleasure. She pushed into him and fell back repeatedly. Finally, she turned rigid, arching her back high. He felt her release as she shuddered and relaxed back, sinking into the bed.

He rose up, and she took his head in her hands and whispered, "Oh, you are such a dear, dear Frankie, such a lover. It has been a long time since that has happened to me."

He was a little surprised and stuttered, "You mean Joe and Arthur were not that type of men?

"Oh no, honey, they were just like you! No, since I have died I mean."

Then he asked in a serious tone, "Is this a dream for you too? Do you know what is going on?"

"What an odd man you are. I have slept with a different man every night for all these years in their dreams, and you are the first one to think about me and what I may be feeling."

Thunder struck by this admission Frank mumbled, "You mean you are in a different man's dream every night?"

"Well, yes and no, Frank. This may seem like a dream to you, but it is a reality to me, and it happens to me every night."

"Why?"

"You know, I am not sure," she giggled and shifted in his arms, making herself more comfortable. His long arms reached around her, and he gently stoked her majestic rear end and felt the flesh full and vibrant. He could feel her breasts pressing into his chest and his penis partially erect and growing on her stomach and, just barely, her vagina rubbing his leg.

"What is it? Could we be in a twilight zone?" he asked.

He wanted to think it through but was overwhelmed with waves of pleasure and surges of unexpected desire. His penis was erect again, and he wanted this woman, and he kissed her lovingly and long. She responded to him, and they were locked in the leap of love. He was panting and thrusting, and she was encouraging him and singing something in his ear. When it was over and the wave of lust washed away like a receding ocean wave, he felt love. He felt loved and loving. He felt wonderful and alive. He felt so warm and loved he could not image the feeling. It was overwhelming and engulfing. He had never felt this way before, and he was sure he would never feel it again.

*I must be dying!* he thought. *If this is death, bring it on, baby!*

"No, Frank," a tiny voice rose from his chest. "You are not dying. We are just making love. You are not fucking me like most men do. You are loving me like few men have." He felt damp tears on his chest. "I like you, Frank, and am sorry I have to go soon. But we still have lots of time. Love me, Frank. Oh god, love me, Frank. That is all I every wanted, for people to love me!" Her hands gripped him tight, and her nails dug into his flesh as she hugged him hard.

He was lost in a sea of love, and he was so tender. He wished to be so tender. He just couldn't get enough of her. He nuzzled her, he stroked her hair, and he hugged and gently massaged her in all the places he could think of. Like floating in an ocean of warm love, he was washed and immersed and buoyed by it all in wave after wave of ecstasy.

Over the next several hours, he possessed her. He touched, massaged, tasted, and licked every inch of her gorgeous body. All this was done by touch and sound with no sight in the darkness. He felt like he was beginning to slowly be tumbled dried in a huge cotton ball with their bodies always in contact at some point. He was dreaming within his dream when he heard the sad sounds of "Lara's Theme" playing in the background.

He finally stopped long enough to ask her, "What is it like being dead?"

She was a little slow in responding but said, "It is not much different except you no longer had to do anything to remain whole. I mean, you don't eat, fart, poop, or pee." She giggled. "You don't gain or lose weight, and you are always the same. There are no doctors, psychiatrists, drama coaches, secretaries, or movie producers or directors telling you what to do. There are no news conferences, no photographers jumping out at you. No pills or sessions. You never eat or sleep. You just are."

This was followed by a long pause, and then she concluded, "After a while, I missed being hurt and also being happy since everything was always the same. There is no time, and you just sort of slip along in a timeless manner, floating from one thing to the next without a reason or a plan. The best thing is that I will never be late again!"

He pulled her close and hugged her warmly; and she melted into his side and, like a cat, almost purred.

"Do you ever see anyone you knew?"

"Oh no, not really. Every once in a while, John floats by me in the passages, but I have never seen Joe or Arthur or Gable either."

"Do you miss the world?"

"No, not really. I just would like to sleep again. I like to sleep. You know, I always had trouble sleeping, and now I do not sleep at all."

"You don't sleep?"

"No, we just float through time and space and sort of perform our assigned tasks."

"What are yours?"

"Oh, Frank silly! Why, to make love every night of course."

"That must get old for you."

"Yes, frankly, it does until I run into someone like you. Most of them just hump me to death and then collapse in a state of satiated lust. They are a lot like most of my many unsatisfying affairs."

"Well, that is a shame. You are a wonderful woman. You had such a difficult life. Are you in heaven do you think?"

"No, I don't think so, but I am not really sure." Her voice was small and wavering a little now. He had made her become too serious.

"Well, I cannot tell you what a wonderful person you are and how much I enjoyed all your pictures. Making love to you is the best thing I will ever do in my whole life."

"Oh, Frank, you are going to turn my head," she said and giggled happily again. She put her hand in a very private place.

"I am sure other men have done a better job of loving you, but no one has tried harder than I have to make it special for you."

"Oh, you have, Frank, you have. I get very tired of the rough handling I usually get, and you were very affectionate. You remind of Joe. He was so respectful and loving, but then he had a jealous streak a mile long, and that made him get mean and angry with me."

"What about Arthur?"

"Oh, Arthur was fine. He just was so inhibited sometimes and usually wanted to talk and talk, and then he usually fell asleep in my arms. One night, he fell asleep, and I snuck out of the bed to go downstairs to sneak some chocolate ice cream. Well, he surprises me in the kitchen! I was bent over and only had my top on. He spotted the tattoo. My gosh, did he ever roar then."

"What tattoo?"

"Oh, I have a little rose one on the inside of my butt crack. You can only see it when I bend over. Or you, well, if you are up close and personal, if you know what I mean."

"Yeah, can I see IT?"

"Sure." The light came up. She turned her backside to him, and he bent over so he could inspect her butt crack. He politely pushed it open slightly, and there it was. The stem pointing in and the small pale red flower was sitting there all alone. His finger touched it lightly, and she wiggled and said, "That tickles." Then she turned around and put her arms around his neck.

"What did Joe think of that?

"Oh, he never knew about it. You are the only other person who knows about it." She didn't bother to mention that he would forget about it in the morning because he could not know. They allowed the living to know only what they already knew. He could remember his night with her as a dream but nothing she may mention to him that was not public knowledge. She was not to discuss secrets, and if she did by mistake, they were erased from the dream.

"Come on, who else knows?"

"I can't tell you that. It is another secret that only he could tell you, but he is also dead now."

"Who? The tattoo artist? Another of your boyfriends?"

She laughed at him and replied, "Why, Frank, you are sounding jealous. Are you jealous, Frank? Just a little bit?" She squirmed into his arms. He didn't reply, and she continued, "I was gong to tell Joe after we got remarried, but then, I was suddenly dead. You know, he gave me the money to buy my new house, and we were going to get back together again. Joe was so good to me. He really loved me and took care of me when I would let him."

He pulled her close and was talking into her hair and asked, "Did you commit suicide like they said?"

"I don't want to talk about it, Frank. I am not allowed to talk about that." He noticed that she now began to tremble.

"OK, but you were so young to die, that's all. You were only thirty-six years old and had so much to live for. I cried when I heard you were dead."

"Well, I can tell you I didn't want to be dead, but nothing else. I thought it would all come out if they found my green diary, but that didn't happen, now did it?"

"What diary?"

"I can't tell you about that either, Frank."

Pulling her into his arms, the light dimmed and went out. He asked, "Why did you get that tattoo?"

"It is a secret, Frank, and no one will ever know it now."

"Tell me," he said, moving her back into his arms.

"No, I can't tell you since you are not dead."

"I don't understand."

"I don't either entirely, and I don't think you are supposed to."

"Oh. Is it pleasant being dead? I mean, is it like being in heaven? Do you have a nice life? Ah, nice world?"

"Frank, I am not sure. I am really not sure. I have been dead for a long time now, but it never seems like time is passing. We just sort of do the same things over and over and then start over yet again. I am not happy nor unhappy, but I am not real sure what I am or what is going on, if anything."

"Oh." This made Frank sad. It sounded very boring and tedious to him. It sounded somehow like a low-level punishment, and he did not feel she really deserved that. Like making someone write the same thing over and over again.

She reached up and stroked his chest in consolation. She slid her fingers in tiny dancing swirls down, down toward his crotch, and he immediately had an erection, and they were diving once more into the raging love sea. The odors were strong and sweet, and the love was real and passionate. They were locked in the dance of love. He was engulfed in love and felt tremendous warmth and happiness pouring through him. Then he was suddenly aware of her voice, which seemed far away, saying "Goodbye, Frank, my lover" just as his passion exploded.

He sat up abruptly in bed and looked around in the pitch black and called plaintively, "Marilyn!"

*What a dumb thing to do*, he thought. *What a fantastic dream!* Too bad he will not remember it in the morning. He started to get up and realized his crotch was wet.

"Oh my god, a man my age having a wet dream!" he blurted out.

He turned the light on. The clock indicated it was six in the morning, and the alarm would go off at fifteen minutes after. Dawn was breaking outside, so he got up and went into the bathroom to clean himself up. Surprisingly, his face looked better after his long sleep. He had his hot morning shower. When he closed his eyes and the hot water streamed down his face and body, he could almost feel her. Amazingly, he vividly remembered the entire dream. *That was very unusual*, he thought.

He lingered in the shower, thinking about her with the hot water running down his back. He turned the water down to cool then cold then colder to give himself a sharp jolt of reality. He got out quickly. He dried himself off rapidly with a large yellow towel. He felt very happy. He was looking forward to the new day.

He could never tell anyone about his dream. How could he? It was his wonderful personal, private secret, a take-it-to-the-grave secret. He had spent a night with Marilyn Monroe. She had made love to him, and he to her. Him! Frank – Frank, the fifty-three-year-old wasted has-been sales supervisor. Frank, the lonely and worn-out salesperson. He was whistling as he finished dressing, something he had not done since he was in college.

He went into the bedroom to make the bed and straighten things up. The bed was more messed up than he had ever seen it. The sheets were all pulled out, and the blankets were on the floor, and the pillows were tossed around. Wow, he must have really acted out the dream in his sleep. He had to work almost ten minutes to get the bed into its old dumpy but neat condition. Looking down at the neat boring bed, he let out a long sigh. He closed his eyes and could not see anything, but he could feel the delight of the dream and almost reached out to touch her once more.

Out of the corner of his eye, he noticed something peeking out from under the bed. It was blue. He bent down and pulled out the pale blue item. Out from under the bed, it popped! He gasped in disbelief. Holding it up, he realized he was holding a pair of lacy blue silk woman's underpants. He stretched them and wrinkled them. He felt the cool softness as he rubbed them on his cheek.

He couldn't believe it. At that moment, he heard a small throaty voice whisper in his ear, "Goodbye, Frank. Love ya, baby!"

## The End

# Who Cares about Mildred Villars?

The exhausted desk sergeant stuck his head into the half-opened office door. The door had a large frosted glass front so you could see into the office, but you could only see ghostlike apparitions swimming around in the office with no pertinent details. The desk sergeant's head and part of his upper body were very clear, defined, and familiar while the rest of his body behind the frosted glass was an unnatural, dull, fuzzy form.

"Lieutenant, HE is here again."

"Who?"

"You know who – the old codger from Brigs Street." His head bobbed backward to indicate that a visitor was lurking somewhere right behind him.

"Oh Christ! Get him out of here."

"He won't go until you speak to him. I tried sending him off, but he will not leave until you talk to him. Look, it's the end of my double shift, and YOU really need to deal with him."

"OK OK, but let's make it fast. I have more important things to deal with today. Don't worry, Sergeant, I will get him gone ASAP. Give me a minute and then show him in." The lieutenant waved the desk sergeant off and, setting his jaw sternly, was mentally preparing to do a quick but firmly courteous brush-off of the intrusive old man.

The head disappeared. The door closed. A few minutes later, another patrolman opened the door and ushered Mr. John Jarvat into the office. The rumpled old man limped slightly on his left leg. He was wearing a faded sweatshirt with totally illegible printing, dirty jeans, and worn-down white tennis shoes without socks.

He looked old, haggard, and ready to die. But he moved with a vigor that said, "No, not just yet!" His face was deeply lined and his skin darkened from the sun. He had a full week's growth of scruffy white whiskers. His head full of white hair was uncombed and windswept into strange waves.

He strode in and fell into the chair directly in front of the lieutenant's desk without an offer from the lieutenant. He just settled in slowly. He then sat there, glaring at the lieutenant while scanning his bizarrely neat and empty desk.

The lieutenant was a twenty-year veteran of the police force and prided himself on his strong, dynamic leadership skills. He was neat. He was orderly. He was precise and particular in all his actions and behaviors. Behind his back, his men laughed at him since they thought of him as an obsessively orderly tight ass with no sense of humor or ounce of humanity. All their desks were piled high with the endless paperwork, memos, bulletins, and case file folders that were the bureaucratic measure of their profession. He, however, maintained a pristine desk; and he continually chastised them for lack of discipline and neatness.

With a sharp, commanding look, the lieutenant crisply asked, "Mr. Jarvat, what can I do for you today?"

"Find the sum bitch," a deep snarling voice spilled out of the rumpled pile of clothes.

The lieutenant, who was not used to such harsh language from civilians or his men, tried to remain calm and professional, replying, "Ahh, to whom are you referring, sir?"

"That worthless bastard that killed Mildred!"

"Mr. Jarvat, we are working on that case. But this is a large station, and we have many other cases. We cannot just do them one at a time, even if we would like to. Your neighbor Mildred Villars was murdered five weeks ago. And we have been conducting a precise, proper, and, might I add, intensive investigation."

"I don't give a fuck how many cases you have or will have. I want him fried! You find the sum bitch, or I will." The old man had very deep dark eyes that flared with an unexpected power of conviction. He spoke harshly, and he was powerful in his delivery. The lieutenant definitely did not like him or his tone. The fact that he seemed unimpressed with the lieutenant was also extremely unsettling. The lieutenant shifted uneasily in his chair, and the fine leather cried out at his movements. He was a little afraid of him and wanted to get on to his next item on his neatly prepared daily agenda, which lay in the exact center of his highly polished desk.

Lieutenant Sebastian Mc Fee looked at the old man with no compassion or interest and thought, *He is just an angry old man.* However, the detectives were all very confused by him. He had been to the station several times now after the murder and even had been briefly considered a suspect. His intense interest in the case, while not totally unusual in crimes of passion, seemed misplaced since he appeared, based upon all the interview information they had gathered, not to have been a friend of the deceased. In fact, he seemed to be possibly her archenemy.

Mildred Villars, eighty-eight years old, was a widow with no living children and only one grandchild who lived in Maine. The grandchild was so distant that she hadn't even bothered to attend her grandmother's funeral. Her neighbors who knew her all said they loved Mildred, but no one seemed to miss her once she was decently tucked into the ground. Jarvat was the one neighbor who had publicly fought with her on many occasions about their properties and different petty neighborly disputes. That is why they included him in the first suspect list, a list that was actually slim to none in terms of prime suspects.

They had quickly determined he had been out of town that day, visiting a sick friend at a VA hospital in the next state and had signed in and out at the hospital. He also had a verified credit card receipt from a motel where he stayed that night. In addition, the employee on the morning shift at the restaurant next to the motel remembered him coming in at about eight in the morning on the day after the murder and staying over an hour drinking several cups of coffee without ordering any food.

What confused the investigators was that of all the neighbors who they interviewed, he was the only one who had little good to say about her, yet he was the one that seemed to be most concerned about who killed her. Why? was the question that nagged at them all.

All her other elderly friends and neighbors had just dismissed her death as part of yet another example of a new twenty-first-century problem. The increase in occurrences of elderly attacks to rob them of their money and/or cars was now an established fact. It was now certainly a recurring crime news theme complete with grainy videos of the attackers bashing old women and men to the ground in submission. They all assumed that some crazed, tattooed gang member had killed her for her money to buy drugs. That explanation worked, and after all, they all had their own personal daily problems in staying alive to contend with. That explanation was also comfortable and reasonable to the police. *There must be something more to it*, thought the lieutenant while trying to study the old man before him for some clue.

He continued, "Well, Mr. Jarvat, I can assure you we will do everything in our power to bring the criminal to justice."

"You ain't got any power, or you would have nailed him by this time." The old man rose abruptly and, dismissing the lieutenant, turned his back on him. He began to limp out. The lieutenant was about to speak out in some protest of defense but shrugged his shoulders and let him leave without another word. The frosted glass door shivered and rattled when the old man slammed the door shut.

"What a strange old coot," he whispered to himself. *Why does he keep poking at this dead horse?* wondered the lieutenant. She was raped, murdered, and robbed; it was happening more and more to the elderly or infirm women living alone. It was probably some transient who saw her light late that night and just took a chance. He then panicked and whacked the old lady. They would never find anyone. My god, she was eighty-eight years old for god's sake! How long could she live anyway? It was just another unfortunate murder with minimal hard evidence to point them to the perp.

He dismissed the whole thing from his mind and returned his focus on what was really important. He began thinking about his luncheon later in the day with Mayor Tannebaum. They were getting along quite well these days. The lieutenant seemed to be making a good impression with him and the other council members. They liked his style and asked him for little favors ever now and then. He worked hard to cultivate them and be sure they were all behind him with his contract-renewal date rapidly approaching in seven months.

The old man strode out of the station house with less of a limp and looked at no one and yielded to no one. He was gone just like that. George Dartman, the young rookie police detective, noticed him going out the front station door however. George had been the lead investigating officer on the Mildred Villars case. He was still on it along with thirty or so others piled all around in bulky, overflowing file folders on his desk. As he watched the old man leave, he felt a little sad for him. He remembered how mad he had gotten when one of the other detectives suggested it was too bad about the old woman, but there really just were no clues in the case. The old man flared up and gave him several minutes of stand-down in scathing blue language seldom heard by them anymore.

He reminded George of his long-deceased grandfather. The detectives all sort of steered clear of John after that. After all, they had done the usual prescribed drill and had talked to all the neighbors. They had TV and newspaper interviews requesting anyone who had information to please step forward. There had been a small reward posted for a while by some women's group. Nothing happened after that. No valid information came in. Oh sure, the usual crackpot stuff but nothing of any practical use. In fact, now that he thought of it, they didn't even get very many crackpot calls on the case.

The murder happened late at night or, rather, early in the morning. The coroner estimated around two in the morning. No one had heard anything, no one had seen anything, and no one could remember anything unusual. Of course, they all were members of the "geriatric generation," with the youngest being sixty-seven. Their eyesight, hearing, and memory were not the sharpest in the world.

The woman had been struck several times with a blunt instrument and finally died from the last blow to the head. She had apparently struggled with the attacker, and she had been raped. The house was not that disturbed, but her purse was missing, and several dishes were broken in the kitchen including several covered bowls.

The body was discovered the next day by a meals-on-wheels driver who had brought her noon dinner. He did this every day but Sunday. He had a key to get into the house in the event she didn't hear him ringing the bell. The meal of the day was chicken potpie and stewed tomatoes with gingerbread and pudding for desert. He was startled to find her bloodstained body in the hall leading into the kitchen. He immediately called the police on his cell phone. Then he proceeded to throw up on the crime scene and went back out to the porch and sat there with his head between his knees until the police finally arrived. He was very pale and disappeared as soon as he could after they talked to him.

George reflected, "Elderly people were becoming victims more often now, and they were usually attacked because young punks thought they had money. In reality, most of them have less money than the punks. They have less food. And less attention is given to them as they slowly deteriorate, dehydrate, and die."

He had a grandmother Mildred's age who had died of cancer last year, so her murder touched him, but the other officers were as calloused as most veterans and just went through the motions of a typical investigation. They dismissed it for more promising cases after several weeks. Honestly, they had nothing really – no fingerprints, no shoe marks, no weapon, no car, no blood of the perp, no witnesses. They did have sperm but no DNA matches to any existing data bank.

Whoever got in to her home did what they wanted and left without much of a problem. There was no forced entry and no broken window, locks, or doors. The man who found her had to open the front door with his key, and all the other doors were also locked. George was going over all this in his head when he realized he had to be in court in ten minutes for yet another trial. He had better move his sorry ass. He grabbed his jacket from the back of his chair and hastily left the station, struggling to get it on as he headed for the courthouse down the street. The Mildred Villars case file remained on his desk but had descended to the bottom of his tottering case file pile.

Mr. Jarvat went several blocks toward his house and then decided to drop into the Late Night Diner for a quick coffee and maybe doughnut. While he sipped and dipped his doughnut, he talked to the owner, Ben Thompson. As always, they mostly discussed the old days in the neighborhood. Both men had grown up in the neighborhood and had gone to school together but didn't become friends until recently. John had not gone to the diner until after his wife, Jane, died several years ago. The two men were rapidly becoming the last remnants of their older generation in the neighborhood.

Ben was having a tough "letter battle" with the IRS about his waitresses' tips. He had five waitress working shifts at the diner during a day. While he ranted and raved about the issue of government invasion of privacy, John just looked sadder and sadder and finally burst out, "Goddamnit! She was a human being, and some asshole raped and killed her in her own home! In her own home, mind you! In our neighborhood! Goddamnit! That motherfucker needs to be brought to justice now!"

Ben knew John well enough by now not to argue with him on this point. There had been a lot of crime in the neighborhood lately. While younger couples were moving into the neighborhood, most of the people who still resided there were elderly citizens waiting out their remaining days. John was a big "justice man," and you did not want to cross swords with him on that point.

Ever since Mildred had been killed, John had been obsessed with seeing justice done for her. Ben could not figure out why since he had never heard John talk much about his neighbor other than to complain about something stupid she had done. Ben knew their talk was over now. Looking at the fire blazing in John's eyes, he just backed away from him to find something else to do. There is always something else to do in a restaurant.

John abruptly slapped down a five-dollar bill on the table and left. The waitresses all liked him since he tipped big and was not really much trouble to them. He was quiet, polite, and very respectful. He kept his hands to himself and had an easy smile and laughed with them a lot. Ben didn't like him lately because he was becoming so consumed with righteous rage, especially since Mildred had been killed.

He didn't really spend much money on food but mostly on tips. That was really no help to Ben's income. Actually, because he was a big tipper, all the waitresses fought to serve him. They then frequently ignored the other customers, which was certainly no great value added to his business either.

John left in a temper and walked the remaining six blocks to his home. No one noticed him, and if they did, he glowered at them so darkly they stayed their distance. John had been retired from a government position for over twenty years. He had lived there in the same house on Brigs Street for fifty years. His wife had passed away five years ago, and his children had moved away long ago, so he seldom saw or spoke to any of them. He kept busy in his yard, his home workshop, and volunteered several days at the local branch library. His life was settled and agreeable to him.

He had a good pension and had what he needed. His life was just fine. It was a little lonely without Jane, but he had learned to accept that. However, ever since that day he had returned from his visit to his friend in the VA hospital finding out the horrible news of Mildred's murder, he had become a very restless and angry man. It was like he had been hit in the face with cold water and suddenly recognized that perhaps he had let it happen in a way.

He should have had Mildred put in an alarm system. Someone should have been watching the neighborhood closer; they had all lived there so long in their own shrinking worlds that they had failed to notice the increase in crime looming about them. Their increasing personal physical problems drove them away from a sense of community, and they had neglected to check on one another.

He really didn't know what he could do either. He felt frustrated, angry, and confused. He had no training; he had no better ideas than the police. *However, by god, I would figure it out even if they couldn't,* he decided.

He entered his house with determination and went into his kitchen and poured a big cup of coffee and heated it up in the microwave. He slowly got out a pencil and some paper from the kitchen drawer. He sat down at the table with his coffee and began to write down what he knew about Mildred. *That would be a good place to start,* he thought. They had been neighbors not friends for over twenty years. They were certainly not good neighbors but they had each learned the other's patterns and habits.

She was an early riser, and he heard her taking a shower every morning about seven. She seldom left the house until noon when she went to the store or the Late Night Diner for lunch. She had two fussy friends who visited her every Thursday. She had a pizza delivered by Carl's Pizza on the first day of the month.

She no longer worked in her yard because of a bad back and had a boy come every three weeks and take care of it. She went to bed early but was frequently up in the middle of the night, perhaps having trouble sleeping. She would turn the TV on when that happened, and that usually woke him up. She was losing her hearing, and she turned it up loud. She went to church on Sunday morning at ten sharp and retuned in the afternoon about three.

She no longer cooked her meals. She fixed sandwiches and salads for her dinner. She liked watermelon and frequently ate it on the back porch with big glasses of iced tea in the summer. The Meals-on-Wheels group brought her lunch every day except for Sunday. In the past, some family members with their children would come every summer to visit and made a lot of racket. However, since 2002 when her remaining son died of a heart attack, they had no longer appeared.

She dressed in overalls every day but on Sunday when she would wear a dress and put on a small hat. If she went out in the afternoon, she would wear a dress and carry a large bag. She had an old Oldsmobile that belonged to her dead husband, Charlie. But she no longer drove, and it was collecting dust in her two-car garage. The postman delivered the mail at between four and five every afternoon, and she usually was there to greet him and take her mail from him. When she went to church, she was usually carrying something like a basket or box that probably had homemade food in it. She only put out two small half-sized trash cans every week, one for garbage and one for recyclables.

He stopped writing his notes and stared down at the pad. He wondered how little he knew about Mildred or perhaps, more frighteningly, how much he did know. What was Mildred thinking all these years? What did she like? What did she dream about? He certainly didn't know, but her friends would. There were two women who visited her every Thursday in the late morning and left in the middle of the afternoon. Who were they? He remembered a small woman who walked with a cane and a larger one with a slight humpback and a huge head of blonde hair. *Who might know them?* he wondered.

He reached for the phone after checking Jane's old phone directory and punched in his neighbor Stella's number. Stella and Paul Morgan lived on the other side of Mildred's house. They had been friendly with her for years. They had been friends with his dear Jane also, but after her death, he seldom bothered to visit them. Her phone rang several times; and then he heard her dry, thin voice answer, "Hello, the Morgan residence."

"Stella, this is John." He listened to her reply and continued, "Yes. I am fine, and you?"

"Yes, it has been a long time. Is Paul getting along OK with his new medicine? . . . That is good . . . Yes, I know, but time just flies by . . . You are right. We should get together for a long visit real soon."

"Stella" – trying to get her back on the trail of his interest – "do you remember the names of the two friends that always visited Mildred on Thursday?"

"Oh, you mean Julie Mark and Bertha Daonny?"

"Yes, I guess. Do you have a telephone number for them perhaps? . . . You do . . . Yes, I see you all used to play bridge until you had trouble with your fingers and dropped out . . . They were your friends too, but since Paul was bedridden, you no longer saw them very often . . . You say they didn't like Paul yelling at you for something all the time, so they stopped coming around to visit you? Oh, that is too bad . . . Yes, I got that. Julie is 990-8769, and Bertha is 997-0934. Thanks, Stella. Did Mildred have any other friends that you know of? . . . Oh, what church was that? . . . St. Martin's on the corners of Malther and Merriman? . . . Yes, the old gray Catholic church that has the large cemetery behind it. I know that one . . . Oh, you used to go there also but now don't get out anymore. I am sorry to hear that." John was now learning more than he really cared to.

"You say the priest was Father Granger . . . He was all that nice was he? . . . Well, I am working on the case for the police and am trying to get an idea of what might have happened . . . Yes, it was awful." John was now getting impatient to get on with other things.

"That is a good idea to keep your doors and windows locked tight . . . Sure, I will keep you posted. Thanks again. Give my regards to Paul."

He hung up, remembering all over again why he seldom talked to his neighbors, especially the females. They seemed to end up brattling on and on forever. Well, now rubbing his hands together in anticipation, he had something to work on. He reviewed his notes and figured that was enough for one day. He got a Pepsi out of the fridge, popped it open, and sat down heavily in his old chair and clicked on the TV to watch the early evening news.

There were more crimes and political foolishness along with lots of disasters, not to mention the constant arguing about the damn war in Iraq. He settled in to watch the news but within a few minutes was sound asleep. He awoke about nine in the evening. He was groggy, so he skipped dinner and went straight to bed. He fell right back to sleep.

The next day, he was up by seven sharp. He had coffee and the last of the stale coffee cake. It was a little hard, but he finished it off so he could get a fresh one later in the day. He went into the yard and checked the entire area and then returned with the newspaper. He turned on the TV morning news for background noise and read quickly through the newspaper. Not much exciting and certainly not much uplifting. After he finished the paper, he got out his tablet and reviewed his notes again. He cheeked his watch and saw it was just eight, plenty late to call the ladies.

He dialed Julie Mark's number. After five rings, he expected to get a voice message, but a sweet little voice finally answered, "Hello."

He gave her his name and explained that he was Mildred's neighbor and that he would like to talk to her about Mildred. John was surprised that she seemed to know him but remained a little cautious in talking to him. She finally agreed that he could come by at one today. She indicated that Bertha would be there also. They lived near each other and always had lunch together on Mondays.

He hung up the phone and was delighted. He could kill two birds with one stone. This detective stuff was a piece of cake. He went into the bathroom and quickly showered and brushed his teeth. He watched the mixture of toothpaste and blood he spit out in the sink slowly disappear, running down the dark drain.

He got dressed in clean clothes but nothing fancy. He put on dark socks and his good leather loafers. When he was finally ready, he headed out the door and then toward the church, which was several blocks to the west. The day was cool but not cold. There were only a few people waking but plenty of cars tearing recklessly up and down the street. He arrived at the church about nine thirty. He stood out in front for a few minutes. There were people pouring out or at least about a half-dozen patrons leaving all at once.

He waited patiently for them to depart and then went inside. It was a high-ceiling, cold, dark, and, he felt, unfriendly area inside the stone church. He avoided the worship service area and headed down a side hall. He tried to locate the priest's office but ended up in what seemed to him to be a gym. This puzzled him, *A gym in a church?*

He turned to retrace his steps when a relatively young man popped out of the corner and inquired, "May I be of some assistance?"

John, a little startled, asked, "Where is Father Granger's office?"

The man who was wearing a priest's white collar replied, "Oh my, he has been gone for several years now, I am afraid."

John was uncertain what that meant – he died, he moved on – but he knew it meant he was no longer running the church. "Well, then who is in charge these days?"

"That would be Father Malone, and that would be me!" he replied with a tight little perky smile.

"I see. I am John Jarvat, and I was wondering if I could speak with you about Mildred Villars."

"Of course, a terrible tragedy. She was such a nice woman, always helping with the Sunday school classes every week. She will be sorely missed." The priest pointed him down a hallway. John went in the direction indicated with Father Malone's footsteps trailing behind him. They quickly arrived at a small office at the end of hall. Entering the office, Father Malone moved past him and sat down behind his large cluttered desk and offered John a large dark stuffed chair. John sat down but was surprised at how low he sank in the chair. He struggled to sit up straight. Father Malone looked younger than he thought he should be and was all amicable smiles.

"Well, Father, I was a next-door neighbor to Mildred. And I am trying to help the police locate Mildred's killer. I wonder if you could tell me anything that might be of help."

The father shrugged, looking away and said, "I only saw her on Sundays. She helped with the Sunday school classes and usually brought the children homemade cake or cookies." His fleeting look of satisfaction regarding that activity indicated he probably shared in those treats every Sunday. He continued, "She was liked by all the children and their parents also. She was a fine, decent Catholic woman. May God have mercy on her dear departed soul."

"Well, did she have any close friends here at the church?"

"You know, I don't really know. With the church services going on, my sermon, and the congregation to be greeted after the service, and, of course, with the children scurrying about, it is hard for me to socialize with the volunteer staff much on Sundays. However, come to think of it, she seemed to spend time talking with the assistant Sunday school teacher, Mary Balkwith."

"Oh, and is she here today?"

"Oh, my heavens no! She is a volunteer like most of our dedicated church flock."

"Where does she work?"

"I don't know, but she lives on Carrigan Street with her father and older brother. She is always complaining about their bad behavior. They never attend church, you know." This last fact seemed to clinch Mary's complaint tight.

"Would you have her telephone number?"

"Well, let's have a look." After fumbling around for a few minutes in several desk drawers, he pulled out a scrap of paper and read a number slowly to John.

"That is her cell phone I believe. Yes, I am sure of it."

John wrote it down in his notepad.

"Has there been anyone hanging around the church recently? You know, just sort of loitering but not attending church or talking to any of those who were."

The father wrinkled his brow tenting his hands in front of his face. He remained that way for several minutes. John thought that he might have fallen into prayer for divine inspiration when he finally replied, "No no, not really." He shook his head in a negative motion to further emphasize this weighty pronouncement.

"Did you speak to the police about Mildred?"

"No, should I? They didn't come by actually."

"Oh, did she ever indicate to you she was worried about anything?"

"No. Only occasionally. She would begin to cry after the service was over and Sunday school had ended. Mary told me she mentioned her husband, whom she missed, and that was why she cried. Actually, I did not have the opportunity to talk with her much since we are always so busy on Sundays as I indicated."

He added casually, "On several occasions recently, she had fainting spells, so we always made sure she got some lunch before she went home. I don't think she was eating correctly. And Mary always insisted on driving her home to make sure she got there safely."

"That was kind of you and her. Did you perform the funeral service here for her?"

"Yes, she had requested that in a letter to Father Granger years ago. It was in the files when I took over. We had a wonderful service, and they buried her in our cemetery behind the church next to her dear departed husband." He said this with great pride of ownership.

*He was a collector of the dead apparently*, thought John.

Father Malone continued, "The junior choir sang their little hearts out. It was very impressive, a very impressive service."

"Were there many mourners at the service?"

"Well, not really. Only about three dozen including some of the Sunday school parents with their children. It was simple, dignified, and tasteful." After that final remark, he seemed to get fidgety. John presumed he had other more interesting things to do than talk about an old woman who happened to be recently inconveniently murdered.

"Well, thanks for your time. And if you think of anything else, let me know, will you?"

"Certainly! Oh, by the way, are you Catholic?"

"No."

"Well, maybe you would care to come by and visit or attend a service sometime?"

"I will think about that," he assured him. The father had thus technically done his recruiting duty for the church.

The father smiled widely in relief and waved at John as he departed, retreating back down the hall.

John left the church feeling a little lost. For some reason, he did not really like the father. He could not put his finger on it, but he didn't seem totally genuine somehow. He had also conveniently forgotten to get John's telephone number or address, as if he had any intention of calling him with more information. Mildred was dead and buried, and that meant the father and the church were finished with her. Well, that was OK. He certainly had no intention of ever attending the church, so they were even.

He walked back toward his house and checked his wristwatch. It was only ten thirty, so he had time to kill. Mildred's girlfriends only lived about twenty minutes away. He wandered back toward the Late Night Diner and slipped inside. There were only a few scattered people there now. He found a well-worn booth in the back. Ben was not there apparently, and the waitress who rushed over was Cathy. He seldom remembered their names, but his eyes were good enough, so he could always read their name badges. Occasionally, they forgot to wear their name badges, and then he had a few awkward moments. She gave him her million-dollar smile and inquired, "How are you today, John?"

"Fine, but I need some hot black coffee and ice water to make it all better."

She replied "Sure" and hurried off with the large tip floating in her head. He tried to review what had just happened. He found out that Mildred cried on occasion, had a few fainting spells, and that she was close to only one other person at the church. *A little odd considering how long she had attended that church*, he pondered.

Cathy arrived promptly with the coffee and glass of ice water. She placed them in front of John with precise care and provided him with a straight white paper-covered straw. He ignored the straw and took a big gulp of the ice water.

"Anything else?"

"No, that is fine." Then, as an afterthought, he added, "Cathy, did you know Mildred Villars?"

"That sweet old lady who was killed in her home several weeks ago?"

"Yes, that is the one."

"Well, I don't think so, but I haven't been here long. Did she have long gray hair and wear it up in a big bun?"

John was thrown by this counter question and had to think about the last time he saw her. She was so familiar to him that he forgot what she really did look like.

"Well, yes, I think she did. Yes, she certainly did."

"She was a tea drinker, right?"

"Yes." That trait John remembered easily since Mildred and his wife, Jane, frequently drank tea in their kitchen in the past.

"Well then, I think she used to come in here and wait for her boyfriend," she said with a little smile since to her, old people were not the dating type. "He would show up, and they would leave together holding hands. They were the cutest little couple."

"Boyfriend! Are you sure?"

"Yes, I am a woman, and we can tell these things. He was an older man with a cane and a very shiny bald head." She added with disdain. "He never ordered anything, and he always rushed her out of here even if she had just gotten her tea."

"Are you sure?" John was having trouble with the idea that Mildred was traipsing around town with some strange man.

"Yes, now that I think about it, she had a sweater with her name on it. Yes, it was dark brown and very full. The name Mildred was embroidered in fancy white letters."

"You are sure about all this?"

"Of course." Their continuing conversation was interrupted by the slight coughing of an impatient customer who had arrived at the counter and, up until now, had been waiting patiently for her to take his order. She rushed away to fulfill her duties.

This was a whole new area that John was at a loss about. He found a used newspaper at one of the other booths and read it while waiting. He finally finished it and his third cup of coffee. He tired to organize his thoughts around why he had never seen this man. He didn't recall seeing such a person around her house or on the street. Now he was sure he would have remembered if he had. A strange bald man with a cane would stick out in his neighborhood.

It was not that he spied on Mildred, but they did live in close proximity, and John was usually moving about his yard and inside his house – he generally noticed anything going on in the neighborhood, especially an unusual stranger.

He left a big tip for Cathy and hurried out toward Julie Mark's house. It was a short walk, and he was busy trying to sort out all this unexpected new information. He arrived promptly and walked up the short front walkway onto the old porch. It was full of pots and boxes that had a wide range of plants with an array of colors; and also, a lot of them, in no apparent pattern, had died among the ones that were vibrantly blooming. *Strange*, he thought. *It's like they didn't take care of them enough.* He rang the bell and waited.

Bertha, the larger woman, answered the door for Julie. She looked at him cautiously and then stepped back, no longer blocking his way, and ushered him toward the back of the house into the kitchen. This was all done with gestures without any welcoming words. The house in general was dark. The kitchen, however, was large, clean, and bright but very old-fashioned with a white stove and no microwave oven that he could see.

The table was set for three with two chairs on one side and one on the other. They had coffee in a metal pot for him and a large colorful ceramic pot of hot water for their tea.

They looked like they had dressed up a bit and were both crowded together, smiling at him sheepishly. They had on colorful dresses and some ribbons in their hair. As he sat down opposite the two chairs, John began talking immediately, "Thank you for allowing me to spend some time with you, and thanks especially in advance for the great coffee. It smells wonderful." This statement induced them to pour him a cup, and he smelled it and tasted it with an obvious pleasure.

"Mildred told us you were a big coffee drinker," Bertha said flatly. This revelation startled John. What else had Mildred said about him, and what in heaven's name did these ladies find to talk about all the time? He had forgotten how much women like to share things and how he may have been "shared" quite a bit.

They spent several minutes pouring hot water on tea bags and getting comfortable on their side of the heavy oak table. They both added sugar and cream. The table had little lacey place mats, but the power of the solid polished wood dominated them easily. John noticed the delicate smell of perfume and powder. It reminded him a little of his wife.

When they seemed to have their tea prepared, he asked, "What did the police ask you about Mildred?"

Their faces dropped; and they looked at each other in surprise then, shrugging, answered in unison, "Why, nothing. Why would they?"

"Well, I thought since you were Mildred's closest friends, they would call on you in regards to her murder investigation."

The two women looked at each other as if this was an odd idea but again shrugged and said in unison, "We weren't there, you know. I guess we are not important to her case."

This strange twin behavior unnerved him, and John stared down in his cup briefly and then said, "Well, being her good friends, did you know of any other friends that Mildred had?"

Little Julie now spoke for both of them, "No, not really. She had some friends at church, but they seldom came around to visit her anymore."

"How do you know?"

"Well, we always told one another anything that happened during the week. That was sort of the purpose of our weekly get-together. Mildred was getting up in years and didn't really get out much except for church anymore." A look passed between the two women, and then she continued. "We did talk on the phone every day, but Mildred was having trouble hearing, so our phone conversations got shorter and shorter."

"I see. What about her friends at the church?"

"Well, there was the Sunday school teacher, Ms. Littlet, and Mr. Remington, the organist, and the priest, of course, Father Malone. Oh, and Mrs. Potts, but she passed on last year. Yes, poor dear." They both then looked down in a brief moment of sadness.

"What about Mary Balkwith?" he inquired.

"Oh yes, I guess so," replied Bertha with an odd, reluctant acknowledgement of Mary's existence.

"Didn't she drive Mildred home from church on Sunday sometimes?"

"Well, yes, I guess she did."

"She also put strange ideas in Mildred's head!" they both blurted out.

"Like what?" John was intrigued. He had trouble imaging what strange thoughts an assistant Sunday school teacher would have to put into Mildred's eighty-year-old head or anyone's head for that matter.

"She got her all involved in computers and chat rooms, and then there was that man," Julie responded.

"A man? What man?"

"Mildred's boyfriend. She met him in a chat room," Julie said this with a depreciating sneer.

"Did Mildred have any other male friends that you know about?"

"No, only her precious mystery man." Both of them got all aflutter and agitated at the mention of him. John sat there looking at these two and was struck by an image of them sitting on a perch in a birdcage. They acted like birds with their heads bobbing slightly and even looked a little like birds.

"Oh, what was his name?"

"We don't know. Mildred was very secretive about him. We only found out about him several weeks ago by accident. He called her while we were there on Thursday. She only then confided in us that they had been dating for several months and that he lived across town. She said they went to the movies a lot, and he would then fix her dinner at his home. We tried to learn more, but she was trying not to jinx the relationship and did not want to talk more about it or him. We think she really liked him."

"Did you ever see him?"

"No."

"How often did she see him?"

"Oh, she indicated about once a week. Yes, every Friday I think."

He had finished his second cup of coffee, and after waiting for them to pour a third, he reached out and poured it for himself. They just sat there, blinking at him and waiting.

"Did you attend Mildred's funeral?" He changed directions.

"Well, of course, we were there. And so were all of Mildred's friends." This was said with an emphasis that indicated he hadn't been there and therefore was not one of her friends.

"Did you see her boyfriend at the funeral?"

They looked at each other and then, in unison, said, "No, he was not there."

"How do you know if you do not know him?"

"There was no strange man there. Just her dearest friends and some church people," snapped Bertha with finality.

"Did you see a man with a cane?"

"No," they responded slowly.

"A bald man perhaps?"

"No, no one – no strange man was there. We would have certainly noticed."

These last two questions seemed to get their attention, and they were about to ask him something when he rushed toward a fast conclusion.

"Is there anything else you can remember about Mildred that might help find her killer?"

They both looked away, and then both shook their heads sadly in a no fashion. He finished his third and final cup of coffee. He had emptied the pot into the cup and then had another big gulp and asked, "What happened the last time you saw her?"

"Well, nothing much. Just the usual."

"What is the usual?" he pushed them.

Julie started the explanation, "Well, we would go to her house and have tea, and she usually had doughnuts from the bakery down the street. You know, Marksman's Bakery, the one with the big red sign."

At this point, Bertha interrupted to describe in detail the bakery owner's family history, including all their children, and some intimate past family issues. John went glassy eyed and tuned out most of this unwanted gossip.

Then Julie, while nodding in agreement, regained the speaking role and continued, "We would talk about the old neighborhood and the days when we all went to school together. Oh, and the people that were no longer with us and what has happened to those that are still around. Sometimes, we would discuss our doctors and the medicines we were using."

"Did she ever mention any concerns about prowlers?"

"No, but she did complain that you were making a lot of racket that week fixing a fence or something." They both scowled at him after making this accusation.

"Oh." John turned a little red. "No, I mean someone coming around and perhaps bothering her?"

"No – Oh wait! There was some cat that got into her flower beds and made its business, and she had complained to the owner of the cat.

He was a neighbor across the street, and they had several harsh words about the animal's bathroom behavior. She had fixed the cat by waiting for it to get into her garden and squirting it with the hose, but then her neighbor came over and made a really big ruckus."

John recalled hearing the noise, but by the time he had checked out the window, he only saw someone marching back across the street and entering their house.

"Back to this boyfriend, did she have a picture of him or describe him to you?"

"No pictures, but she said he was wonderful cook and that they had great times going to see old movies and talking about the movie stars they remembered from the past. Mildred always liked the movies, you know. Even when we were little, she always wanted to go to the movies," said Bertha with a warm fondness in her voice.

"Oh my, yes, she was a real Hollywood fan. Always was reading the fan magazines," added Julie.

John really didn't know that. He recalled that Mildred and his wife, Jane, had gone out to the movies once a month; and they always left both of the husbands at home, which was fine with them. He was never very interested in the movies himself.

He finished off the last drop of coffee and could not think of anything else to say, so he got up and thanked them again. He moved toward the front of the house and the welcome escape of the front door. They looked a little disappointed. He could feel them hovering behind him at a slight distance as he progressed out of the house. He made his escape quickly with them fluttering at the door, imploring him to return.

"Come back another time. We love to talk to you about Mildred."

Once out of the house, he hurried home. He would add their information to the list he had been compiling. All this talking and thinking made him tired.

John was busy the next day and had to go out early on Wednesday to pick up some items for one of his friends. When he returned, he was surprised to find a big green dumpster container in front of Mildred's house and several people moving about with boxes, furniture, and garbage bags. He approached her house and saw that a crew of three men and two women were moving things out and also cleaning out items.

The dumpster was almost filled with a wide variety of items – papers, clothes, cookware, magazines, and the like. John peeked into the open front door and called out, "Hello!"

They all stopped working, and the older of the two women came to the door and asked, "Can I help you, Mister?" She wiped her head with a large dark handkerchief and smiled weakly. Her face was heavy and lined. Her hands were worn and wrinkled. She obviously worked hard for her money.

"I live next door and was wondering what is going on."

"Oh, that is easy. I am Maria." She stuck out a dirty hand and allowed him to shake it. "I run a cleanup company, and we are getting this house cleaned up for the sale."

"Sale? What sale?"

"Yes, the owner wants it ready by the end of the week, and there are lots of years to clean out and get rid of." She waved her arms wide to indicate the size of the project. John noticed several piles of boxes in the corner that were apparently material each of them was keeping from the haul for themselves. *The perks of the job*, he thought.

"Owner? You mean Mildred's granddaughter?"

"I don't know who she is, but we were hired to do the job by a nice man who is paying us a bonus to clean up fast and get rid of most of the old furniture in the house."

"Oh, what is his name?"

"I don't know. Is it important to you?" She was resting one arm on her hip, and he could tell she wanted to get back to work.

"Why, yes, I would like to find out how much he wants for the house. It might just be a good investment."

"Oh, sure then, just a minute." She held up a finger to emphasize the minute while walking backward into the living room to find something. She disappeared into the center of house. She returned slowly with her large purse while rummaging though it as she walked. She returned to the door and triumphantly handed him a business card. It said, Thomas Bento, Realtor.

"This is the man. I am sure he would be happy to discuss the price of the house, and here is my card if you ever need an outstanding cleaning service."

He looked at the second business card. It read, *Maria Carter: The Very Best Neighborhood Cleaning Service.* He looked up at the heavyset woman and smiled. He put both cards in his pocket and left with a quick thank you.

*My god, what is going on here?* he wondered as he went home.

He thought the granddaughter was not interested in her grandmother. *I guess when there is money to be made, she was.* He then realized that maybe he should talk to her. It was the police who had told him about her, and then they were the ones who said she never called them back.

It had been a very long day, and he was tired. He went home, kicked off his shoes, and had some thin canned chicken soup and white crackers and watched several news programs and then went to bed early. The next morning, he was up and ready to go after a quick shower and several large cups of coffee. He was all fired up and ready to investigate. He had decided while taking his shower to visit the Realtor and the police the first thing today.

He called the number on the Realtor's card and got a "friendly" long voice message. He left his number and indicated an interest in buying the house, giving its address. He cleaned up his kitchen and, within twenty minutes, got a callback. Mr. Bento informed him he would gladly talk about the house, but first, they needed to meet at his office and then perhaps look at it before they talked. John mentioned he lived next door to it and really only wanted to know the price.

Mr. Bento, who was obviously disappointed, tried to hedge a bit and then, in resignation, said flatly, "$325,000."

"Wow, that is steep!" responded John.

"Not really when you see the values in the neighborhood now that younger couples want to move into it since the schools are not crowded and have very seasoned and capable teachers," Mr. Bento raved.

"Yes, I guess you are right. I had not thought about that. Do you have the telephone number of the owner?"

"Why, I am representing the owner and can give you all the information you may need."

"Well, I would like to talk to Mildred's granddaughter. I missed the funeral and just wanted to pay my respects."

Mr. Bento interrupted him, "The owner is a Mr. Hafter, not a woman."

"Oh really, maybe he is Mildred's granddaughter's husband?"

"No, I don't think so. Mr. Hafter is the owner who is selling the house. He owned it jointly with Mrs. Villars. I am unaware of any granddaughter." His voice indicated some potential apprehension.

"Jointly you say?"

"Yes, they had some sort of agreement, and she recently transferred it to him in joint ownership for the loan of some considerable amount of money I believe."

"Do say, well, I guess I will have to locate the granddaughter some other way."

"Yes, I suppose so. Are you still interested in buying the house?"

"Do you have Mr. Hafter's number perhaps?" John was not giving up yet.

"Well, I will have to ask him if I can give it to you, you understand."

"Of course, please call me later whenever you can."

John put the phone back on its charging carriage and looked perplexed.

*What was Mildred up to? Why did she need money? What happened to the money? Who is Mr. Hafter, and how did he get Mildred's house?* This seemed like an additional mystery to be solved, but it was distracting him away from the murder – or was it?

John walked slowly down to the police station. This time, he cornered George Dartman finding him working on one of the many thick case files on his desk. When he looked up from it and saw John, he straightened up and said quickly, "Well, Mr. Jarvat, what a surprise."

John sat down in a hard, straight-backed wooden chair without being asked and looked the young man in the eyes. After a few moments, he said, "Did you know that Mildred had a boyfriend?"

George looked startled. "No, did she?"

"Did you talk to any of her friends?"

"Well, all of the neighbors were contacted of course," he responded defensively.

"What about her friends?" John badgered.

"Well, no one mentioned any."

"Well, she had several, and they knew about the boyfriend. Hell, even the new waitress at the Late Night Diner knows about her boyfriend. Now someone is selling her house for over $300,000!"

George looked surprised and a little amazed at this old man who had scooped him on these facts so easily.

"What about her granddaughter? What did she have to say?" asked John pointedly.

"Well, we never actually talked with her. We left several messages indicating her grandmother had passed on, but she never actually called back."

"She knows about her grandmother's death?"

"Well, yes, I suppose so." George wondered where this was going.

"Can I have her number?"

"Well, sure, why not? It is here someplace."

He spent several minutes rummaging through the file and several notebooks and then wrote it down for him and handed him the piece of paper. George then asked, "Who is selling the house?"

John glared at him and said, "Read the ad!" He then left abruptly, as usual leaving George a little unsettled.

George sat there and tapped the desk with a pencil. He wondered if he maybe should check it out, but then he had to be in court most of the day, and tomorrow was his day off – well, maybe next week.

John went home tired again and had some more coffee and read the mail and then reviewed the newspapers. He napped through the rest of the day and skipped dinner and had some Pepsi and peanuts and fell asleep with the TV on. He finally woke up at midnight, got up, turned it off, and went to bed.

The next day, he was up early and did the yard work. After that, he showered and had some breakfast. He spent some time watching the TV news and reviewing his notes on the case. When it was about twelve o'clock, he called Mildred's granddaughter. She was not very awake although it should be past nine there and acted a little abstracted in response to his questions. After lot of probing and follow-ups, he determined that she was not even aware her grandmother had a house and thought she had lived in a state home. She whined, "I had not seen her for over ten years and really am not interested in anything relative to her or her belongings. We really never got along."

*That made it convenient for others who did*, he thought. All the time she was talking, he heard someone in the background calling her to come back to bed again. He offered her the name and number of the police officer investigating the crime, but she was not interested. She really was not even willing to talk to him. Finally, she just hung up on him while he was in mid sentence. It appeared no one cared much about Mildred.

After the call, he contacted a retired attorney he knew, catching him just before he was leaving on a vacation to Germany. John outlined the problem and explained about the granddaughter. The attorney said to have her call him next week, and he would check it out. It certainly sounded like she had a case and should get the grandmother's share of the house sale at least.

He then tried to locate Mildred's boyfriend without much success. He visited all her other neighbors around her house and asked about him, but no one had seen or knew about such a person. He gave up and decided to call the "new" owner of Mildred's house. The real estate agent had called him back late yesterday and left the number on his message machine. He called Mr. Hafter and got a recording. He left a message that he was interested in the house and his telephone number.

He then called Ms. Balkwith on her cell phone, which turned out to be her office number. So much for the father's accurate knowledge. She answered the company phone politely, "Thanks for calling us. This is Mary Balkwith. How may I be of assistance to you today?" The voice was canned, crisp, and businesslike.

He explained who he was and then asked about the chat room and Mildred. Mary said she really shouldn't talk about it on the company phone and asked if he could meet her for a late lunch at the CoCo's on Fourth Street at three-thirty. The time would be a little tight for him, but he agreed. After hanging up, he got a sweater and jumped into his old Volvo and headed for his lunch date. He made it with five minutes to spare. He got a table near the door and waited for her to show up.

When she entered the restaurant, he noticed her right away. She was mousey and sort of walked on the fringes. She edged in and just stood there in a corner, looking lost. She had on a plain neat dress and shoes and clutched a large black purse. Her makeup was nonexistent, and her hair was combed straight. He approached her and asked politely, "Mary?"

She responded with a little yes.

He showed her to the table, and they sat down. She ordered a sandwich, and he ordered some coffee and ice water. She explained that she only had forty-five minutes for lunch, and it would take five minutes to get back. She had used eleven minutes to get there.

He jumped in and said, "Julie and Bertha told me that you had introduced Mildred to computers and chat rooms."

Mary looked a little frightened and replied cautiously, "Well, yes and no. She had a PC at home and used it for playing games and sending e-mail to her circle of friends. However, when she mentioned how lonely she was, I showed her how to get into a chat room for senior singles. And she later had me help her locate several others. She spent a good amount of time on them I guess. She had trouble sleeping late at night, you know. Then she found Bart."

"Bart?"

"Yes, he was a man about her age who she talked to every day for several months, and then they started dating. She really liked him and seemed to enjoy going to the movies with him. We always talked about the movie she had seen with Bart that week on Sunday after the kids were gone while we were cleaning up after them at the church." She spoke out of the side of her mouth while chewing on her sandwich in small bites. She nibbled like a little mouse.

"Did you ever meet Bart?"

"No, she was sort of secretive about him later on. She said he was not interested in being known, and she seldom discussed him but only what they did together. She was so happy after meeting him. It was wonderful. Really, wonderful!" She added this like someone talking about a dream come true.

She really didn't know much else except that he drove a big green Cadillac with wire wheels. Mildred had shared that much with her. She rushed through the remainder of her sandwich, leaving a third of it and, with a brief goodbye, left in a hurry. He watched her scurrying out of the restaurant and heading down the street, walking close to the buildings. He sat there nursing his second cup of coffee and wondering who this Bart character was. Then he had an idea and rushed home. He went next door, and it was very quiet. However, he found Maria packing up the last of the junked items.

She said, "Hi!"

He asked, out of breath, "Did you happen to see a PC in the house?"

She said, "No, well, yes. But the Realtor had taken that and several boxes of other things when he met Maria and her cleaning crew to let them in the house on the first day."

John was disappointed. This was a dead end he decided, so he went home. There was a message from Mr. Hafter indicating his interest in talking to him about selling the house. He would meet with John at his apartment that evening at six-forty-five.

John called the number and left a return message that he agreed to the meeting. He was tired, so he lay down for a quick nap. He was up at five-thirty and went over to Mr. Hafter's apartment house early. He would check things out before his meeting with Mr. Hafter.

The apartment building was in a shady neighborhood, and he felt a little uneasy. There was a general store across from it, so he hung out there and had a coffee in a paper cup. Most of the people he saw were elderly or young street punks. The working people had not started returning home yet after their hard day.

Finally, a man came up the street in a neat suit with a closed umbrella. He leaned on the umbrella as he walked. He stopped and checked his mailbox and then entered the apartment house. John, for some reason, felt that was Hafter. He checked his wristwatch, and it was 6:35. He waited another ten minutes and then crossed the street and rang the doorbell button next to Mr. Hafter's name but got no answer. The doorbell box only indicated names and not the apartment numbers.

A woman came along and was about to open the front door with her key, and he inquired about Mr. Hafter. She knew him and indicated he was in apartment 12 and let him enter the building with her. He located the apartment on the second floor and knocked. A gruff but small voice answered.

John explained through the door he was interested in the house that was for sale and had made an appointment to see him. The man opened the door slightly, checked him out, and then let him in. John was looking at a man of medium height with black hair and a tight, narrow face. The man, who was already in his shirtsleeves, led him into a room with a couch and pointed to it for him to sit. He said, "I am Mr. Hafter, and you are Mr. Jarvat whom I spoke with on the phone?"

"Yes, that is correct."

"You are interested in buying my house?" John looked him over and wondered how it had become his house. John nodded in assent. Mr. Hafter then apologized for the mess and offered him a glass of cold water, which was all he had right now.

John accepted. While Mr. Hafter was getting him the water, John peppered him with questions about the house, the price, and the potential for possible unexpected damage resulting in expensive repairs. Finally, Mr. Hafter, who couldn't really answer many of his questions, became impatient and asked him to leave, suggesting he contact Mr. Bento with all the detailed real estate questions. They agreed. They departed cordially.

As John was leaving the apartment, the same woman he entered with was also departing. She said, "Did you find Bart?"

"Who?"

"Why, Bart Hafter. That is who you said you wanted to find." She looked at him, puzzled.

"Yes, thank you."

She continued, "He is such a nice man. It is too bad about the accident."

"Accident?"

"Oh yes, he was a bus driver and had been in a big smashup last year and had taken a long time to recover. He was still using a cane you know and had to retire early from the bus company."

"I did not realize that."

She now looked at him strangely since she assumed he was a friend, which he apparently was not. She moved on faster and left him standing there on the sidewalk. John went back to the police station and found George missing, so he cornered another detective, giving him a note for George asking him to call him ASAP.

He then left. The next morning, George was surprised to see the note left by John, which the detective had placed on his desk half under a half-empty paper cup of cold coffee. Maybe John was onto something, or maybe he was just lonely. George had other things more pressing to do today and tossed the note.

A week went by, and the For Sale sign appeared on Mildred's home. John had tried calling the granddaughter again and found the phone had been disconnected. He called Julie and asked about Bart, but neither she nor Bertha knew the name. She invited him to come over for coffee soon.

John was getting tired of waiting, so he went down to the police station again. George was there and, after much hemming and hawing, admitted he had not done much more on the case. John explained the house issue and indicated that the man's name was Bart Hafter. George was a little surprised that John kept coming up with so much information. He took the time to run the name but only came up with the usual stuff; however, there was case file on him regarding a fraud situation several years ago.

When they checked the file, it was thin, and the charges had been dropped after only a few minor investigation attempts. He told John that it was not much to go on and shrugged his shoulders. John then asked if he could get his fingerprint from his driver's license and then run it. George said no. *If it were only that easy*, he thought.

John then asked, "What about his work record for the transit company?"

George looked at him and then realized that this was not an ordinary old man. He acknowledged it could be done and placed a call to someone who agreed to check it for them. He took John downstairs to get him some coffee. They sat at a battered old table and relaxed.

George got a personal call on his cell phone and, moving away, took it. Then they went upstairs, and he called the man who had done the check for him. George said, "You have his application records? . . . Yes, did they do fingerprints back then? . . . No? . . . Well, yes, would you please fax the file over to me? The number is 951-098-0078. Thanks."

George looked at John and said, "Close but no brass ring."

John was disappointed. They both sat there for a few minutes, and then John had another idea. "When you transfer deeds, you have a notary witness them? Don't they require a fingerprint now?"

"Why, yes, I guess so," admitted George.

"Well, call the lawyer who did the transfer."

George was taken aback slightly but followed the order. He located her lawyer's name in her address book they had taken from her house and called the number. Sure enough, after talking to several people, they had a copy of Hafter's thumbprint faxed to them by the notary within minutes.

George left John to retrieve the fax material down the hall. He retuned with it and fed the print into an office scanner and ran it through the state file, which was linked to the FBI files. Without much review, the computer quickly determined that Mr. Bart Hafter was really one Martin K. Bailey who had been dishonorably discharged from the U.S. Coast Guard in 1995. Previous to that, he had been arrested for several petty crimes including defrauding the elderly, but he had only one conviction, and that was for a minor drunk and disorderly conduct. He was not currently wanted for anything but was apparently a little dirty.

George looked at John, and John said, "I think he was Mildred's boyfriend, and he somehow duped her into transferring her house to him, and then he had her killed."

George replied, "That maybe, but it is stretch from what we know to that conclusion. We need far more evidence to even consider that accusation."

They then drove to John's house, and John spent the rest of that afternoon giving him all the details of the information he had collected. George was impressed. There were some problems with it all since Bart had hair and had been described as bald, and Bart was not walking with a cane.

George made a quick call to another detective and waited for him to run a DMV report. When he hung up, he looked at John and said, "He had several speeding tickets and drives a '99 green Cadillac." George then concluded by saying, "It is time to call him in and see what we can find out in a little friendly face to face."

John was happy but exhausted and went right to bed after George departed.

The next day after morning roll call, George and his partner drove to Mr. Hafter's apartment. It was only seven forty-five in the morning, so they caught him coming out of his apartment. They identified themselves and asked the usual introductory questions. The man had quick and easy answers for all of them. He also supplied, in addition, that he and Mildred had been planning to get married soon. He mentioned that he retired recently, and that he really could not understand how anyone could have killed her.

"She was so loving and kind." With that final statement, he started to cry.

They waited for the tears to ebb and asked him why he wasn't with her that night. He said she told him she was tied and would call him the next day. He also indicated that Mildred had mentioned the granddaughter but said they had been estranged for years. He himself had no immediate relatives, and they had cosigned on the house since he intended to pay 50 percent of the mortgage until they were married when he would assume full responsibility for it and let her take it easy. She had never liked doing her bills. He shifted his emotions easily and was too glib and too quick with information. He made the two detectives suspicious.

When George started to question him about his police record, he got a little darker and then refused to answer and said teasingly, "My goodness, perhaps I need a lawyer?"

They replied, "That is up to you, Mr. Hafter, but we need for you to come down to the station today. It is just routine stuff, of course, since we missed you on the first go-around in our investigation."

He begged off due to an appointment that morning and then agreed he would come in about four in the afternoon. They parted on amicable terms, but Hafter was obviously more than a little shaken and refused their offer to drop him off.

When they got into the car, his partner asked, "Aren't you afraid he will take off?"

"No, he has a $300,000 purse he wants to collect. He will be there. He may have a lawyer with him, but he will be there. Besides, I need to tie up a lot of loose ends, so I can use the extra time." His partner was used to George running things and didn't even bother to offer to help with anything. George liked to do it all himself. George spent the rest of the day making calls, receiving faxes, and checking and rechecking phone and bank records.

Sure enough, Bart showed up at the station about four fifteen with a well dressed man. He introduced him as Karl Malone, attorney-at-law. He handed them both his card. They all shook hands and moved to a conference room. It was not the type one sits in at a lawyer's office but the typical harshly lit run-down, bare-bones room with a worn table and few chairs that was what police all over the world use.

After they were all seated, George started off with, "I guess we all know the rules. Mr. Hafter, we asked you to come here to ask you some questions about Mildred Villars, who was murdered last month, to see if we can find some clues to catch her murderer. As I mentioned earlier, we were not even aware of her relationship with you until very recently."

Karl Malone said, "I want it noted that my client has come down on his own free will although he is still in considerable emotional distress to assist you, gentleman, in any way he can. He was engaged to Mildred. He loved her dearly and is still recovering from her untimely and brutal death." George looked at his partner wearily. They had heard this all before so many times.

George said, "This is routine stuff, but we need to fill in some blanks, and we respect Mr. Hafter's feelings and certainly appreciate his assistance." He was thinking, *Christ, just once, I would like to skip all this bullshit and go for the gold!*

George began, "Mr. Hafter, how did you meet Mildred Villars?"

"She and I met on a chat room, the Internet, you know. We both have a passion for old movies, those before 1960."

"You met, you exchanged messages, and the relationship grew, and you eventually asked her to marry you?"

"Yes, she was so wonderful and sweet. How could I not?" Bart smiled weakly, and the lawyer nodded in agreement.

"When was the last time you saw her?"

"Well, it was Thursday night. We always went to the movies and had dinner on Thursdays."

"Was she her usual self?"

"Oh yes, we had an early dinner at my place and then saw the great pirate movie."

"*Pirates of the Caribbean?*" the partner inquired.

"Oh no, none of that Disney hogwash. We saw *Captain Blood* with Errol Flynn.

"About what time was that?"

"Well, I always meet Mildred at the Late Night Diner at five thirty promptly, and then we drove to my apartment, and I fixed dinner. We would finish up in time for the seven o'clock movie showing at the old Strand Theater. After the movie, I would take her home. That was probably about nine forty-five or ten."

"Did you go into the house with her?"

"Oh no, she always made me drop her off at the end of the street, and she walked to her house, which was the third one up. I would wait and watch her until she got in and flashed her porch light three times to let me know everything was OK, and then I would go home. Neither of us liked to be up past ten thirty."

"So that evening was like all the others, and Mildred was feeling good?"

"Yes, I think so. Yes, I am sure of it. She had a crush on Errol, you know. She wouldn't admit it, but you could tell when she talked about him," he said with a little sheepish smile.

"Why all the secrecy? Why did she make you drop her off?

"Well, she could be a very secretive woman, and we were planning a party for the following month where we would announce our engagement, and she didn't want anyone to figure it out. She promised me she had not told a soul. I promised the same to her."

"Did you see anyone you knew that night?"

"Well, no. Oh, the ticket taker Billy Blarre knew both of us. And we talked to him about the film both before we went in and when we left."

"Anyone else?"

"No, but we don't know many people at our age, you know."

"Did you talk to her after that?"

"No, I usually called her every evening about nine. But the next night, I had to work late and didn't. I now work part-time as a warehouse guard at Markland Freight three days a week. The night shift supervisor asked me to cover that night for one of his patrolmen who was on vacation."

"That was Friday night, the night she was murdered?"

"Yes."

"Did you often cover the night shift duty?"

"Well, no, it was only the second time they asked me. I am new and sort of on probation, so when they asked, I assumed that it meant they trusted me and that I might get more opportunities to make some extra cash."

"How did you learn about Mildred's death?"

"On the early-morning radio news, the next morning. I couldn't believe it and called the radio station to verify her name. I was devastated. I got sick and just stayed in bed all that day."

"I can certainly understand your grief. Did you contact any of her friends?"

"Well, no, we hadn't shared our love with them. That was the purpose of the party. She had some friends she lunched with every week, and she had friends at church, but I hadn't met them yet. I only have two friends at work, and she never met them either."

"Did you attend her funeral?"

"No." The response was weak, and the tear pump began to work again. He started crying.

"Why?"

"Well, I didn't read about it until the evening it occurred, so I missed it. Poor Mildred." He was now weeping heavily and sobbing loudly. They all waited for him to dry his eyes with his handkerchief and regain some control.

"Now about the house."

"House? What house?" chimed in the lawyer.

"Mr. Hafter and Mrs. Villars own a house jointly," George added quickly.

The lawyer looked sharply at Bart but said no more.

"Yes, what about it?" asked Bart innocently.

"When did you two combine the deed, so to speak?"

"Why, only about two months ago, I think."

"And this was in preparation of the upcoming marriage?"

"Yes, we were going to get married next spring. I was going to move in with her after the party and help her with the mortgage and fix up the house."

"I see, and you never saw her again after you dropped her off? Nor spoke with her after that?"

"No, like I said." Bart's voice was now shaky, and he was getting more upset and looked like he was ready to cry again.

The lawyer, now getting impatient, asked, "How much more of this does Mr. Hafter have to endure? He is tired. Can't you see how hard this is for him?"

"Only a few more questions," George said with a narrow smile.

"Do you live with someone?"

"No." Bart looked puzzled at that question.

"Well, your phone records show that there were seven calls made from your home phone on the evening of her death starting at six o'clock in the evening and ending at four o'clock the next morning. Who do you suppose made them? I believe you said you were working late that night." George appeared to refer to the notes he had taken while Bart had been talking.

Bart was now getting a little concerned. He looked imploringly at his lawyer and replied, "I don't know. I don't know anything about them. What is this anyway?"

"I see. Well, just for your information, one was to a pizza parlor, three were to a Mr. Marvin Makworth's cell phone – more commonly know as the Cutter – and two were to Mildred's home phone."

Bart was looking extremely uncomfortable. He kept looking at his lawyer for support or intervention of some kind.

Finally, the lawyer said automatically, "I think that is enough for today. Mr. Hafter is tired. If you have any more questions, we will return another time."

George noted that no one asked about the seventh call and said casually, "Oh fine, just one more. Martin, why did you hire Cutter to kill Mildred?"

The stakes suddenly leaped high, and the room was full of emotional electricity. Hafter squirmed, Karl came unglued, the voices raised, the accusations flew, and no one was polite anymore. Karl, restraining Hafter from talking and shoving him toward the door, concluded with a loud, "That is it! We are out of here!"

George smiled and indicated the door and said simply, "A warrant is being issued for your client's arrest. We will be over to pick him at his apartment in an hour. Will you be with him?"

No answer, just an icy stare from the lawyer and a panicked look from Hafter and then their abrupt departure. Their voices in conversation could be heard when they were out the door but trailed off as they hurried away.

When there were no more voices and they were gone, his partner, who was as surprised as the man and his lawyer, said, "You take the cake, man. Do we have enough to make any of this stick?"

"Oh yes, I was just beginning on him. I did submit the request for the warrant. Let's grab a bite to eat and then come back to get it." They left to dine at the nearest local pub on some greasy and unhealthy food that tasted ever so good when washed down with a cold beer.

After eating and picking up the warrant, they arrested Bart. His lawyer followed them to the station and immediately went into a huddle with him. George's partner put out a wanted bulletin on Cutter and sent a patrol team in a car to check the last known address. The phone company records indicated that his cell phone that had been used earlier in the day was not responding to calls. Presumably, he had probably trashed it

The lawyer demanded to know the charges, and when he got the list, he seemed a little taken aback. He weakly argued for Bart's immediate release but was told it would be considered later in the week by the judge. A time was being set for the preliminary hearing as they spoke. Now the wheels of justice stared to roll slowly to collect all the pieces and players. The parts were starting to fall into place.

The next day, Mrs. Villars's lawyer, Jerry Hedges, informed them by phone that she and Mr. Hafter had come to his office three weeks prior to her death and executed the joint ownership deed. As it was explained to him, the agreement was that Mr. Hafter would give her $120,000 six weeks after the deed was signed. Mr. Hodges had all the documents; and they had been witnessed by a notary, Mrs. Gavern, who worked in the realty office next to the lawyer's office. She was the person who had provided the print for them.

He offered that he was surprised about the whole thing, which just came out of the blue as far as he was concerned. He also indicated that he had prepared a will for Mildred well over ten years ago and provided them with a copy. It left all her personal belongings and property to the Humane Society. While Cutter eluded them for several weeks, he made the mistake of getting drunk and ending up in a small-town slammer where he was finger printed and a mug shot was taken. He popped up as wanted, and the big city boys just had to go pick him up.

Cutter's lawyer, a lot more knowledgeable in the criminal case processes than Bart's, advised him strongly to plead guilty and name names. He cut a deal, so he only got life with a possible parole in ten years. He had listened to his attorney and accepted his sentence without a murmur. Bart had not selected his lawyer as well and had to change to several others later. Even after a long and exhausting trial, the best he could get was forty years for his part in hiring the killer. For a sixty-two-year-old man, that was as good as life. His trial was long and complicated, but the motive was painfully clear and the evidence was fairly direct and supportive of his jury's conviction.

Although his basic argument was that he had hired Cutter but later that night changed his mind and had called him to cancel the killing. It was a little too late, and this flimsy excuse didn't float. It was sunk with a verdict of guilty. Cutter's rather biased testimony was certainly a big part of why Bart was convicted.

It had been three and a half years since Mildred was killed. John stilled lived in his old house. His new neighbors were a 'young' newlywed couple of sixty-five. They were more active than many but still went to bed early and didn't have trouble sleeping. John thought that was because they usually had several glasses of wine with their dinner. He noticed their trash every week and saw the pile of inexpensive wine bottles.

That morning, John got his newspaper and opened it up. There was the headline about the trial finally ending. In the small print, it covered the details of the sentences for the two men. He had a big cup of coffee and read it slowly. He knew most of the story although George had stopped talking to him shortly after they arrested Bart.

He had followed the news of the trial closely for the past several months. The whole mess disgusted him – that anyone would kill someone for $300,000 infuriated him, that a sadistic rapist had been hired for the job since he offered a cut rate flabbergasted him. How could anyone know someone personally and still have them brutally murdered? That was beyond his imagination. His indignation burned deep and would remain smoldering within him forever.

He was surprised to see that George was mentioned. He was being cited for his hard and tireless investigative work on the case. There was no mention of John – now that was a big surprise! There was little mention of Mildred other than as the victim – another big surprise. The article was mostly about the judge and the lawyers' petty bickering and the defendant's civil rights. He finished the article about the trial and read the rest of the paper slowly. He folded it and laid it next to his empty blue coffee cup. He picked up the cup and rinsed it in the sink. He placed it in the bottom of the sink as he moved toward the back door. He went out into his familiar backyard.

It was a nice day, and the sun would be bright and strong. He felt at ease for a change now that it was over. He had never forgiven himself for what had happened to Mildred, but he at least felt he had somehow evened the score for her. Nobody should be murdered for money and especially not a helpless elderly woman. He thought about his wife and how peaceful she looked just before she died and how much he always missed her. "God, I loved that woman," he stated out loud.

*Well, looks like I need to cut the grass today,* he thought. He looked over at Mildred's house for a few minutes. The newlyweds were not stirring yet. He looked up into the clear sky, squinted in the sun, and said out loud, "Well, Mildred, I guess that fixed them sum bitches! Rest easy, neighbor!"

## The End

# Designated Driver

He was in the twelfth-floor restroom of the Amalgamated Securities building taking a leak. It was a familiar scene, something he did at least twice a day at the company. Like clockwork, once before lunch and once before going home, he relieved his sloshing bladder. He had worked for the company for over eighteen months now and was finally fitting in, he felt. The restroom was empty for a change, and he shook it out and tucked it away. He saw his lean but tired face staring at him from the huge wall mirror over the row of sinks. He felt it made him look intense. The look he was cultivating was that of a serious, driven potential executive. To his chagrin, he realized the last thing he wanted to do now was go to the weekly Thursday Risk Assessment Division happy hour held in the local ritzy bar around the corner.

He would like nothing better than to go home, have a beer, and fall asleep; watching TV while his wife finished her endless office work on the PC in their small den. She always had copious amounts of office work and spent every evening in the den working on it. However, he accepted the fact that as a newer member to the division team of accountants, he was expected to show up for the happy hour, smile, and make all kinds of team member – supporting noises and gestures. *Rah, rah, home team!* he thought.

He was really hoping that his recently submitted job application at the Morgan Company would get him out of this place and in over there. They were a more professional company, and they did not have time for weekly happy hours. During his time at the company, he had done reasonably well considering that his boss, who was little strange, seldom spoke to him. He was not considered a member of the in-group just yet but was working on it. Until he made the A team, his growth with the firm was limited to the slow track.

He slowly washed his hands under the warm automatic water faucet, playfully moving his hands in and out of the laser beam to get the water to jump on and then abruptly stop. He selected several paper towels and dried his hands off thoroughly. He turned back to the mirror and made sure his tie was straight, and that he was ready to play team games. Grimly, he steeled himself and turned to go to the "party."

He entered the bar and spotted the team over in one corner, the usual corner where they always met. There were about thirty people in his group, and at least twenty showed up for these occasions. He moved into the outer edge of the group, and those close to him were talking about a tragic multiple shooting that just occurred at a Virginia university. The TV news was full of the startling event. He had heard the initial news on the incident but didn't know the details, so he stood there. He was briefly acknowledged, and he assumed a look of interest. He didn't say much but easily followed what was being said and occasionally interjected a point. As he stood there, totally bored, the waitress who appeared took his drink order along with several others and then slipped away into a sea of bodies.

He quickly scanned the people present to see if there was anyone he might join up with and perhaps have a brief but lucid conversation. He was late. The happy hour started at four o'clock sharp, and it was now five fifteen. Many of the inside group were now very loose since they probably launched it at three forty-five. He noticed that Sheila, the office manager, was there with the two large account managers tossing them back as usual. She was a gorgeous blonde woman, but she was known to have balls bigger than most of the men at the firm.

She dressed with style and made the most of her stature, a good five feet eleven with her large and ample bosom. She was a legend in the office as a woman who could drink, swear, and hold her own with the big boys. As he understood it, she had been with the company for over fifteen years, moving up from a receptionist to an office manager position in that time. An excellent track record he felt.

He really never had any reason to speak to her much but was always acutely aware of her when she was around or within fifty feet of him. He had a vision of her as a Viking warrior princess if she had lived around 1100 AD. She had a huge open warm, welcoming smile, which hid the fangs of a big bad wolf that could and would chew you up and spit you out with the best of them. She was laughing with the two men, and they were freely mauling her with arms on her shoulder and around her waist.

The waitress discreetly moved her tray into his view, and he picked up his drink and then thanked her. The drinks were on the house for the two-hour happy hour, courtesy of the division manager who seldom bothered to come to the happy hour himself. The alcoholics, and there seemed to be quite a few in the group, made a killing during the happy hour by having doubles and then making sure at five forty-five, the witching time mark, that they ordered two more doubles for the road.

All in all, they were decent people, but they turned a little strange during happy hours. He noticed Ben Falkner over at a table with Kirk Rains, two of his more intelligent peers, and moved toward them. He sat with them, and they all greeted him as a teammate. They were discussing the new merger with Sloan and Magger and were trying to estimate the impact on their office if any. They all talked for a while about company matters, and he sneaked looks at his wristwatch repeatedly. He was finally pleased to see it was almost six. This was the point he set in his mind when he would be able to discreetly disengage and leave.

When the clock in the bar struck six, it triggered him to hurriedly say his goodbyes and start for the door. He reached it and was gone by three minutes after six. It was a clean escape into the warm evening. He hated to have to get his car from the company garage and drive home to the suburbs at this time of night. Due to the evening traffic, his normal fifteen-minute drive became a thirty-minute dive. On the way to the garage, he passed a large drugstore. On the spur of the moment, he went inside to look for some magazines and get some aspirin. He didn't need it, but his wife had mentioned that he might get some on the way home since they were almost out; so like a good husband, he would. She frequently got headaches from working on the computer for hours on end. She went through a bottle of aspirin a month.

He had lingered over the magazine rack more than he had intended so when he emerged, it was already six forty-five. He walked into the building's empty garage area and up the wide ramp for two floors. He noticed that only a dozen or so cars were left on the second level. His echoing footsteps made the only sound in the garage. His small blue Dodge was over in the corner, his usual spot. He reached it, unlocked it, and climbed in. After backing out, he started forward, slowly heading for the exit while snapping his seat belt in place.

Out of the corner of his eye to his left front, he saw Sheila with one hand on the wall, inching unsteadily forward toward her new red BMW. It was her car. He knew it from the license plate that declared MDEWOMN. She seemed to be moving slowly and was a little wobbly. He started to drive on past her, and then having second thoughts, he stopped. He backed up and, rolling down his window, called out, "Are you all right, Sheila?"

She didn't respond immediately nor look toward him but finally drawled out, "Yeah, sure. Just broke a heel and now needs to get homey." She waved in his direction in an offhand, random way. She then slipped and almost fell but held herself up with both hands on the wall and started sidestepping down it.

He could see she was a little plowed, so he parked next to her car and intercepted her path. She looked at him with vague eyes and said, "You're in my way, Huxley. Haul your bloody ass!"

It certainly surprised him that she knew his name, and then he said forcefully, "Sheila, you are in no condition to drive. I will take you home." He was a afraid he had stepped over the line this time since her response to his remark was to stand up straight and tall although swaying slightly and glaring down upon him. She seemed to be getting ready to let loose a tirade or even maybe punch his lights out.

The moment was pregnant with possibilities; and then she caved in, leaning over again, saying meekly, "Maybe you are right! Shouldn't had cocktails for lunch before a big happy whore, I mean happy hour." And she giggled shyly. "Thanks, Huxley old pal. You can be, may, I mean, my designated driver tonight." She dangled her keys in front of his face and jiggled them up and down at him.

He reached out and took them from her. He took her arm firmly and steered her toward his car. She limped on one good shoe and then stopped. She handed him the broken shoe. She then leaned heavily on him and bent forward to remove the other. Her motion was too rapid, and she almost tumbled over. Surprised, he grabbed for her and caught her with an arm across her breasts. She pulled herself up triumphantly, waving her good shoe and also handed it to Huxley. He had some difficulty holding her steady with the keys and the shoes while fumbling to open the passenger car door.

When he got it opened widely, he partially draped her over his shoulder. He then turned her with her back to the door and just let her large ass slump inward, and she sat down on the seat hard. She was half folded with her head forward, and her long blonde hair was falling all over her face. He grasped her knees firmly and swung them into the car and gently pushed her upright and tried to brush her hair back to some extent. He got her settled into the passenger seat.

She had inadvertently smacked him several times with her purse, which was big and very heavy, as she maneuvered it into the car. He had winced each time but finally got her to put it on the floor. He reached over her to belt her in. She was going rag doll limp on him, and he accidentally brushed her large boobs, but only he noticed. Her skirt was up to her crotch, and he saw the edge of lacy black panties peeking out at him. *No way in hell is going to try and straighten that out!* he thought to himself.

He got her buckled in and shut the door very carefully. He straightened his suit and got in on the driver side. When he was buckled in, he said loudly, "It will not be long. I remember where you live." He had attended Sheila and her husband's large open house last month. Her husband's name was Mike, and he was a salesman for a major sporting equipment company. He had been a pro football player several years ago. Huxley dropped her keys in the dash tray and tossed her shoes into the backseat.

She said absolutely nothing. Her head was slowly tilting forward at an odd angle. He headed out. When he reached the street he turned in the direction of her home. She lived in suburb closer to town than he did, and it was about a ten-minute drive but not really much out of his way. He kept glancing at her sideways, and although she was holding herself up stiffly and straight, her eyes were dropping closed. And she would squeak out a little snore every once in a while, waking herself up each time she did it. It was a very silent drive for him.

He thought about his wife and what she might think if she saw him now. He was a little depressed since he was sure she would not think much one way or another. They had not been very intimate lately, and she was always working on her case files at night. She was determined to get a promotion this year, and she really wanted it badly. She did deserve it after all.

*Well, soon that will happen. And we will go on a nice vacation to celebrate, and then things will go back to normal,* Huxley thought smugly to himself. While dealing with the heavy traffic, he frequently glanced sidewise at Sheila. She was now sitting bolt upright but was, apparently, sound asleep. The louder snores didn't seem to wake her anymore. He suddenly made a sharp right turn after almost missing her exit. She began to topple in his direction, and he held her with his right hand while steering with his left. That woke her slightly, so she sat erect on her own power, which was good since he was having trouble holding her up and also maneuvering the little car.

Finally, he drove up her long driveway between two stone pillars and parked in the drive close to the front door. She seemed frozen in place now. He got out quickly and closed his door. After releasing the handle, he realized just seconds too late that he had left his keys in the car, and both doors would now be locked! He was about to hit his panic button when he remembered that Sheila could open the door. *No problem*, he thought. He went around to her side of the car and knocked lightly on the window. She didn't move. He called out to her, "Sheila, Sheila, wake up!" She was in the land of the living dead. He went to the front of the car and, looking through the front window, jumped up and down and waved his arms wildly shouting, "Sheila, Sheila, open your door!"

Not a twitch, she remained motionless. In a wild fit of frustration, he threw himself on the car hood and shook the car bouncing it around. She started to fall over. This, however, woke her; and she sat up with a startled look. Her eyes were open, and he frantically gestured for her to open the door. After a long period, she seemed to figure out what was going on; and slowly, she raised her arm and moved it toward the door handle.

He heard a lot of fumbling sounds as she tried to grasp it and then it clicked open. He rushed to it and jerked it opened. She was holding on to it and almost fell out. He grabbed her in time and wrestled her back into an upright position. He carefully unbelted her, being extremely discreet so as not to touch her upper chest area again. He reached across her and got his keys from the ignition. She fell forward onto him, and he had to slide out from under her hair and body while holding her head so she would not smash into the dashboard. Her eyes were closed again; her breath was heavy and very stale. He grasped her by the shoulder and shook her a little, saying gently with pride of accomplishment, "Sheila, we are here."

Her large bleary blue eyes snapped open, and she looked right at him and then started to automatically pivot herself out of the seat. She planted both her stockinged feet firmly on the ground. She attempted to stand. Instead of rising, she lurched forward, and he grabbed her so she wouldn't fall on her face. As he did so, she emitted a loud eruptive sound as she dumped the contents of her stomach onto his shoes, socks, and pants.

He tried to jump back but could not go far since he was also still struggling to hold her up. She sat up with a stupid grin on her face. Her skirt was pulled high up on her thighs, and he saw a lot more of those delicate lacy black panties. She roughly whipped her mouth with her sleeve and demurely said, "Damn, I needed that! I feel a lot better now." Then looking down, she exclaimed in all innocence, "Christ! What mess! Huxley, how did you get your shoes so dirty? Huxley, you wuss! Did you upchuck?"

He was so stunned, he did could not reply. She again lurched forward in an attempt to stand erect. She was semiupright but weaving and unsteady even with all his help. She moved forward, elegant and determined. She suddenly slipped in her vomit and fell forward, fully into his arms. They swayed in an embrace of balance and imbalance. Then locked together, they slowly toppled over. They hit the driveway, and he was momentarily staggered. He regained consciousness within seconds but had trouble breathing. He was aware of her breasts partially wrapped around his neck and pushing up into his face. She had him pinned to the ground like an all-pro wrestler, and he felt the weight of her full body pressing down upon him. She apparently had gone to sleep again.

When he was able to wriggle free enough to breathe, he felt better. She was heavy but oh so pleasant to have on top of him. Holding her tight, he closed his eyes and wished for it to be a real embrace. He had to struggle, wiggle, and push hard to get out from under her dead weight. He was almost free when she woke up and began to thrash about in an effort to get up.

She clumsily kneed him in the groin several times, and her one high heel she somehow was now holding stabbed him in the arm repeatedly. He quickly rolled out of her way.

Then he raised her upper body up and grasped her around waist from behind. He was trying to encourage her flailing efforts and tried to haul her up. Finally, she was standing on two legs. She was leaning on the car door with both hands and pushing him away with her ass as he tried to hold her up.

She reached into the car and dragged her purse out. She swung it wildly over her shoulder, smashing him on the head. He finally got one arm under and around her waist and was sort of half supporting and half dragging her toward the front door. She could barely walk and seemed to get her legs out of sequence. When they climbed the three wide steps, he almost lost her again but managed by putting his hand under her arm while holding her waist. When they reached the door, she was leaning heavily on him, and her blonde hair was in his face.

He tried to blow it away from his eyes and shifted her weight, but she was very heavy, and he almost lost her again. They stood steady there in balance, finally after a few challenging minutes. He was huffing and puffing loudly. She was semiconscious. He caught his breath, and then he realized her keys were in his car on the dash console where he had placed them earlier. He didn't' know what to do! She just began to slowly collapse. He scrambled to hold her up and, in the process, was not only touching but gripping one of her ample breasts as she slipped slowly from his grasp and into to a semiseated position, leaning back against the door. She muttered "Boy, what a night." and snored loudly.

He propped her in place up against the door using her purse and then dashed for his car. He easily found her keys and turned while shutting the door. He started to run back and felt first one then his other foot slide in the wrong directions. He went down in a forward tumble on the vomit-smeared pavement, smashing his right knee hard into the cement. He staggered shakily to his feet and limped slowly toward the front door. Reaching the door, he struggled with the keys on her full ring. After ten tries and several frustrating minutes, he found the right key. When the door abruptly opened, her dead weight pushing against it threw it back hard, wrenching it out of his damp hand.

Sheila fell with a loud thud on the hall floor; she was now half in the house and half out of the house. He almost lost his balance and lunged for the door edge to steady himself. Sheila, snoring soundly, was comfortably passed out on the floor. He resigned himself to his task and stepped over her, so he now straddled her body and was looking down at her.

One of her hands suddenly grabbed his right knee causing him to wince in pain. She was struggling to grip at something and pull herself upright but almost immediately lost interest. She let both her arms flop back to the floor with a smack. Her action threw him off balance, and he crashed to the floor next to her, banging his head on the door. He struggled up into a four-point doggy position and, then using the door edge, pulled himself very slowly, hand over hand, into an upright position. Sheila seemed to be only barely conscious.

He moved behind her and, scooping her under the arms, raised her upper torso and, leaning backward with all his weight, dragged her backward with a series of tugs and twists. He fell hard on his behind after his one last desperate tug. She was however inside at last! He managed to close the door shut after swinging her feet and legs into a half-bent position. He sat down heavily on a chair next to door. They both smelled ripe, and she was passed out.

She looked so innocent although her clothes were a twisted, snarled mess. Her clothes were pulled loose and were partially unbuttoned. She certainly was a beautiful woman, he thought, and he even briefly envied her husband. He figured he needed to get her into bed, and that was a wrap for his designated driver responsibilities. Once again, he tried to get her to sit up and then stand. They rolled around half on the floor and half in midair. In the struggle, he had groped, grabbed, and touched every part of her body with absolutely no pleasure. Finally, by pushing her into a corner, he got her top over his shoulder and, in a squatting position, was able to push her partially upright.

Her clothes were now more twisted and tangled, and so were his. He had to use both hands firmly on her waist to keep her up while leaning his shoulders into her chest and under her chin. He slowly inched around her, so he was behind her. He now gripped her around the waist and had her upper body leaning back over his left shoulder. He tried using his legs behind and against hers, forcing them to move forward one step at a time.

At first, nothing happened, and then she started to move forward, but her upper body also swung forward and her weight was shifting rapidly. Then with a huge forward lunge, her body was slipping away from him, and he desperately tried to pull her back. She came back all right. All her weight suddenly was thrown onto him. She simultaneously twisted around so she was now half facing him. She crashed heavily into his arms. He was successfully holding her up for a brief moment, and then they both fell backward onto the carpeted floor.

She was on top of him again, and he could feel all of her womanhood pressed against him. His face was pressed between her breasts, and he was really gasping for a breath. He was startled for a brief moment. He felt a pleasure so intense that his loins seemed to warm with desire.

Then the sensual warmth was spreading across his stomach and sides, and he realized that she was pissing on him! His eyes bugged out in disgust, and he quickly rolled her off him and tried to get her out of her growing piddle puddle. Now, not only dead drunk, she was damp, wet, and slippery.

In desperation now, he got up and went into a downstairs bathroom and located a large bath towel. He tried to dry his pants and shirt and clean up the mess on his shoes. He then brought a second towel out and laid it next to her. He dropped the other towel on the piddle puddle and watched it slowly absorb the yellow liquid. He rolled her onto the other towel so she was face down and then using it like a sled, pulled and tugged her to the foot of the stairs. When he reached that point, he shifted her over so she was on her back with her head at the foot of the stairs. He sat down on the first step and pulled her up into his lap, holding her under her arms.

The stairs were to the right of the door and consisted of a section going straight up to a landing and then a section going to the right. He rested on the bottom step for several minutes, gathering his strength. Then when he felt ready, he, grasping her body from behind, pulled her around so her legs were to a ninety-degree angle to her body and then rocked her into a sitting position. He half stood and dragged her backward as her arms flopped about, and then he sat down heavily on the next step. Then he half stood and heaved her up to the next step, sitting down hard again. He lifted, sat, and dragged her up the stairs step by step. Twenty-six painful steps up straight and thirty steps to the right and he had her at the top of the stairs.

He stood up and was breathing so hard that he had to lean on the banister for several minutes, catching his breath. Sheila woke briefly and started to get up, and he reached out his hand to help her, but she pulled so hard on it that he fell over her and tumbled down the stairs. She was clinging to his hand and also tumbling down the stairs. She landed on top of him. He was back on the landing with his feet and legs in the air against the wall, and she was half sitting on his face. Her upper body was lying facedown on the stairs, and her legs were spread out to both sides. Her skirt covered him. His face now felt all the lace and bows on her underpants as they pressed in on him, not so sexy now. He frantically pushed with his hands and shifted his face sideways to get out from under her ample bottom when a long bubbly fart rolled like thunder out of her ass. The odor was a killer, and he was instantly motivated to break free. When he finally emerged from under her skirt, he gasped for breath. He sat there, gulping fresh air and resting. *Damn, how could such a foul odor be generated by such a beautiful woman?* he wondered. After a few minutes, he steeled himself for another round of stairs. By this time, he had perfected his stair-dragging strategy and hauled her back to the top faster.

He then used the towel again to drag her into the first bedroom he came to. He switched on the light and was shocked by how big a mess it was. Her clothes were everywhere and every place. He shook his head and said, "Wow, this must be her bedroom!" The bed was made, however, so he cleared off some of the clothes and pulled back the covers. By maneuvering her into a seated position facing the bed, he raised her arms and laid them on the top of the bed. Getting behind her, he slowly guided her upward toward the top. He had tossed her arms on the bed first and then, using her underarms, got her up a little at a time all the while leaning into her back to pin her in place so she didn't slide back. He struggled gaining and losing ground for several minutes

Finally, in desperate frustration, he just reached under her large ass, grasping her soft cheeks in both his hands, and heaved her upward with all his might. She rose into the air and fell onto the bed. That got her mostly onto the bed. He shifted her legs over onto the bed, and then he sat down heavily on the edge next to her. He was exhausted. He heard a loud snore from the drunken woman as she wriggled into a more comfortable position. He halfheartedly pulled the covers around her and then took off his jacket and tie. He laid them on top of the other clothes on a nearby chair.

His breath was heavy, and he was feeling a great deal of anxiety. Finally, after several minutes, he took one last look at the beautiful large woman with her face buried in a pillow and left the room, careful not to trip on the clothes. He turned off the light.

He passed a hall mirror and was shocked. His clothes were all wrinkled, stained, wet, and dirty. His one pants leg was torn at the knee. *Now how could I go home looking like this?* In addition, there was a pee stain on his shirt, and he smelled a little strange. The dry vomit on his shoes added to the problem. He slipped back into her darkened bedroom. He was trying to locate a robe or a man's shirt when he heard a noise from the bed. He froze. Then he slowly investigated. She was not moving or making a sound, and he leaned forward over her prone body to see if she was still breathing. Suddenly, Sheila reached up and grabbed him around the neck. She pulled his struggling body down and started kissing his head and neck.

Panicked, he pried her off, and she fell back into her alcoholic stupor. He found a heavy robe and slipped out. He retreated down the stairs and, after opening several doors, located the laundry room. He stripped down to the buff and loaded all his clothes into the washing machine and put it on a ten-minute cycle. He put on the robe. The size was just about right, but it was a bright tangerine color and had excessive lace trim.

The sleeves were also a little short. Although definitely not his style, he had to admit it felt soft, warm, and comfortable. He could smell her perfume that lingered on the robe. While he was waiting, he cleaned his shoes off with some paper towels. He got out the ironing board and put water in the steam iron. He was now all set. When the clothes were clean, he would be on his way in no time. He felt triumphant. He was sitting on a chair looking through a *Sunset* magazine he had found.

The bell rang, and he jumped up from the chair he was sitting on and quickly put his clothes in the dryer. He looked at his wristwatch and realized it was getting late. *What would Jean say?* She probably won't notice him missing since she would be deep in her work. He had some time to kill, so he went into the kitchen to get a glass of cold water. In looking around, he saw some cake, so he helped himself to a large slice. He had just finished it off when he noticed he had dropped crumbs on the floor.

He got the broom out and was cleaning them up when he heard a muffled voice in the other room. He went into the hall and then into the living room but didn't see anything. Just as he turned to go back to the laundry room, he heard a loud snore. He went into the dark living room and peeked over the edge of the couch. He was stunned by the sight of the most beautiful tits he had ever imagined staring up at him. He looked over quickly and right into the big blue eyes of Sheila who had a silly little smile on her face. He had not turned on the light, so he was shrouded in the darkness. She reached for him and said "Mike, you came home after all!" and tried to drag him over the edge. He struggled, but she was strong, and he tumbled on top of her. She whispered in his ear, "Sweetie, I am really hot. Remember Cabo? I am ready for that again!" And she hugged him hard, pushing his face into her left breast. He squirmed out of her headlock and struggled to get up. The robe was open, and his penis had heard the call to action. He covered himself quickly, wrapping the robe about this body. She had fortunately passed out again. He looked down at her and realized she had taken her top garments off and came downstairs in her lacy black panties for some reason.

Although he was fascinated by her naked breasts, he tiptoed backward out of the room and closed the door slowly. He turned to retreat to the laundry room. He was confronted by a huge dark shape rushing toward him.

"Honey, I am so glad you are home. Daddy needs some loving in the worst way!" He grabbed Huxley and planted a big wet one on his lips and drove his tongue into his mouth. Huxley shoved him away, pushed past him, and dashed down the hall, his robe flapping around him. The man fell to the floor and said in a slurred voice, "Aw, baby, don't be that way." Whoever he was, he also was very drunk and just sat on the floor and put his head back and started to snore heavily.

Huxley made it to the laundry room, shut the door, and locked it. He pulled his clothes out of the dryer and began ironing them frantically. The shirt was all right, the underwear damp, and the socks wet. His pants required several attempts to get them ironed reasonably dry. When he was finally done, he dressed fast! He carefully peeked out of the laundry room door. No noise, no sound, no stirring. He tiptoed into the hall and heard a dull snoring coming from the doorway. There were two levels of snores, so both Sheila and Mike were both in dreamland. He switched off the remaining lights and headed for the front door.

He tripped on something and realized it was the towel he had left in the piddle puddle. He picked it up gingerly and took it into the bathroom and dropped it into the sink. He returned to the front door and slipped out. He pulled the door closed behind him and hurried toward his car. He reached into his pants pocket for the keys, but the keys were not in his right-hand side pocket nor in his left-hand side. He then realized, *He didn't have his jacket! The keys were in the jacket! The jacket was where?* He danced around trying to think and blurted out, "In Sheila's room!"

"Oh my god!" he cried out loud. He returned stealthily to the front door. It was locked tight. No matter how hard he pulled, it was not going to budge. He looked around and slid past the front window and went into the backyard. He had to unlatch the gate to get to the rear of the house, and he soon found the back door. It was also locked tight. He now almost completely panicked. He hurriedly tried one of the patio doors. To his amazement, it slid open with ease! He entered the kitchen. There were no lights on, so he reached out with his hands and inched forward. He found the kitchen swinging door and pushed it open slightly.

*Bang!* The door came crashing into him and slammed him into the wall as someone rushed through it and dove for the sink. The large hulking shadow proceeded to vomit into the sink. Huxley held his tongue and his arm, which had been smashed. He slipped into the next room. He quickly fell behind a couch. He was trying to subdue the pain while straining to hear what would happen next. He heard the water running, some crashing sounds a few semi-identifiable swear words, then a chair falling over, and a loud grunt and crash.

All was silent after that. He waited, counting to two hundred. He then slowly raised himself up and tried to get his bearings. He thought the hall and the stairs were to his right, so he worked his way in that direction but then realized he was in the living room again, and he heard the heavy breathing of Sheila, still on the other couch. He retraced his steps and went in the opposite direction and found the foot of the stairs. Not wishing to take any more chances, he crawled slowly up the stairs on his hands and knees He stood up only when he was safely at the top.

He went down one door and into Sheila's room. He had turned out the lights when he left but remembered all the clothes everywhere, so he inched forward to the bed. He finally located the chair on the left where he had put his tie and coat. He felt all around, and they were not there. He was tired and angry now, so he took a chance and turned a light on. The small lamp flooded the room, and there were his tie and coat on the floor behind the chair. Sheila's blouse, stockings, and coat were now on the top of the chair.

He snatched them up and flipped off the light. He quickly found his keys and gripped them tight. He stood there for several minutes, listening to his heart pound and straining to hear any slight noise in the house. Not a sound! He put on the coat. He stuffed his tie in the other pocket. He shuffled toward the door and was about to slip out when he heard someone outside stumbling against the wall.

He froze and flattened himself against the wall to the right of the door. There was muttering and stumbling sounds getting closer and closer. Louder and louder! The door burst opened, and a small pleading voice said, "Sheila, are you in here? Sheila? Shelia honey? Please, baby." Then the person closed the door and stumbled down the hall toward the end bedroom. Huxley heard a door open and close and then no more sounds. He opened the door a crack and slipped around it, heading for the stairs.

He made it to the top of the stairs and then got tangled in some clothes and, twisting, felt a loss of balance. He clawed at the empty air as he was launched airborne and went tumbling down the stairs, head over heels. He hit the wall and lay there for several minutes, trying to regain his breath. There were no other sounds. Picking himself up gingerly, he inched down the second flight, holding tightly to the banister with both hands. When he reached the ground floor, he tiptoed toward the front door. He froze when he heard a voice boom in slurred words from the darkened upstairs, "Who's the hell down there? Sheila, is that ya, honey? Honey? If you're not Sheila, I am going to blow your fucking head off!" The hurried footsteps started down the stairs with a loud clatter and banging.

Huxley sprang for the door! Bursting out of it, he sprinted toward his car. He was in it, slamming the door. He had it started and was putting it in reverse when the porch lights arched on, slashing at him. A large figure lurched out of the front door. It fell off the porch, disappearing into the bushes. He threw his car into reverse. Looking behind him, he realized that Sheila's husband had parked directly behind him! Slamming on the brakes, he kissed the front end of the other car.

A loud shot rang out! He looked back over his shoulder toward the house, and a hulking dark figure wearing bush limbs was stumbling toward him. He slammed the car into drive and peeled out across the lawn. Swinging and sliding on the thick grass, he lurched back onto the driveway. He shot out of the driveway, missing all vehicles, obstacles, and the gate pillars on the side of the drive. Another shot rang out. Hitting the street, he accelerated hard and was long gone.

After a few minutes, he slowed down and snapped on his seat belt. He turned on the radio news. Glancing at his wristwatch, he realized he was really late.

He breathed a sigh of relief. "My god! What a mess!" He now knew Sheila and Mike far better than he ever wanted to. Although he had to admit that it was hard to forget Sheila's body, he would definitely never volunteer to be her designated driver again! No, sir, not again!

*At least, I got away clean,* he thought. *They were both so drunk, they will never remember what happened,* he began to rationalize. He settled into his normal drive home. He remembered he had put the bag with the aspirin in the trunk. He would get that out when he arrived home. He looked over into the backseat and saw the broken shoe on the seat. Reaching back and stretching, he almost swerved into traffic while retrieving it. He held it momentarily in his hand, looking at it. Rolling down the window, he tossed it out. He needed no strange shoes in his car.

Then he felt in his inside jacket pocket for his wallet. *It wasn't there. It must be at the office; he was always leaving it there since he took it out when charging a purchase by phone or Intenet and then putting it in his desk drawer.*

He was sure it must be there at the office, or was he?

## The End

# Adrift

I t was the end of September, but as it happens in California, it was still getting warmer. Karla was sitting on a stack of broken-down cardboard boxes behind the Nail Parlor. Feeling the heat, she stood up and peeled off one layer of clothing. She removed a sweatshirt and her long dirty overalls. She still had a heavy T-shirt on that once proclaimed "Love Me or Leave Me!" but was now so faded it appeared to say "ove Me or M." She also had on a tight pair of jeans that were only torn slightly at the knees. She wore old green flip-flops with heavy dingy gray athletic socks.

She felt a little easier without her outer layer. She carefully folded the two pieces of removed clothing and, with a considerable effort, stuffed them into her backpack. It was full, old, dirty, and worn. It was also fraying badly on one edge. It was all hers, and it been hers ever since she could remember. In it, she carried her possessions. She struggled with it to get the pocket zipped closed. It had been a bright pink originally, but now it was a pale pink going into gray in several spots. After she had it packed, she held on to the strap with one hand and sat back down on the collapsing cardboard boxes with her pack at her side. She leaned back against the cold concrete block back wall of the building, attempting to retreat from the sun's increasing glare.

The building was just one of several within the shopping strip mall. This shopping strip on the corner of Perris Avenue and Alexandra Boulevard was her favorite hangout since it was well lit at night on a busy intersection corner. It, therefore, seemed to have the fewest perverts skulking around. She guessed that was because it had an all-night AmPm store that the local police used to stock up on their late-night snacks – slurpees, slushies, malts, and coffee until the dawn broke.

Her high school classes had started, but Karla chose to not attend them right now. She had escaped from yet another foster care group home just last week and had been enjoying the free lifestyle of an emancipated person. She had emancipated herself rather than fool around with the lawyers and such. One day, in a fit of anger, she just stood up in the school's commons area and cried out to the pale blue sky for everyone to hear, "I am emancipated!"

The few students around her didn't even notice her or comment on her declaration. She was not totally aware of what emancipated people did or how they were different from non-emancipated people, but fucking straight, she was one now. So far this week, her first one of emancipation, she had been doing OK but was extremely hungry this morning.

One good thing about going to school was she usually could get someone to share their lunch with her. She was always standing around looking glum during lunch breaks, waiting for an invitation to share. The rich kids actually just tossed her their lunch. They preferred to buy a bunch of junk food from the school vending machines that stood tall and mute along the back wall of the school gym. Meals were no big deal for them; they had them all the time and never worried about not having enough to eat.

Her old physical ed teacher used to get mad at the kids for buying so much junk food. She even raised *Cain* with the school principal. Later that week, she was suddenly transferred to another school in Perris. When she saw Karla on her last day as she was packing up her things, she told her that that the school made considerable money on the junk food sold and were also given a annual payment by the vending machine and food companies. That is why they would always be there, and kids could always gorge themselves on the worthless calories easily available from them.

Mrs. Kent was her name. Karla saw her cry that day as she was leaving. Mrs. Kent had even hugged her goodbye and, absentmindedly rummaging through her large purse, had handed her a ten-dollar bill to get some food for the rest of the week. Karla had really liked Mrs. Kent because she wouldn't let the kids bully one another in her class, and she seemed to care about all of them. She really wanted them to do well in the phys ed classes.

She even tried to organize the students to do calisthenics before school each morning and was always encouraging the girls to eat a well-balanced diet. She was especially concerned about the thin ones, like Karla, since she thought they may be suffering from angora – no, antharax – no, but some word like that. Karla had come to her attention since she was a little thin, but when Mrs. Kent offered to buy her a dinner after school, Karla ate so much that Mrs. Kent realized her problem was not purging but the lack of available food. After that, Mrs. Kent always brought extra lunch items that she literally pushed into Karla's hands when she saw her. Karla liked her attention and always ate everything Mrs. Kent gave her.

While she sat there and was thinking of Mrs. Kent and her lunches, she was reminded again that she was very hungry. She hadn't had anything to eat now for over a day. *Maybe I could find Mrs. Kent and get something from her. No, that is not going to happen.* Thinking this, she smiled shyly at her own joke.

Old Mrs. Bender, who was always good for some coffee and stale rolls, had gone on vacation last week for a month. Mr. Henderson, the man in a wheelchair up the street from Mrs. Bender, had been recently moved by his son's wife into an old age home in Riverside. They both had been her prime sources of food recently. She drew her slender legs under her and reflected on her options. It was too early to check the garbage cans around the fast-food places. It was even early to go to the park and check on the tossed-away food.

*Maybe the doughnut shops? No, I just hit them two days ago.*

The grocery stores sometimes tossed out damaged food, but it was usually in beat-up cans and had to be cooked. She neither had a can opener nor a stove in her all-purpose backpack. Then she remembered Tommy. That may work!

He worked at the Union 76 gas station across the street. He was a tall skinny boy, a little older than her. He sometimes treated her to a taco when he wasn't busy. She picked up her backpack and slung it on her shoulder and worked her way across the wide street. She didn't bother about the lights. She just marched out and dared the cars to hit her. She got across with only two angry honks – one "Hey, baby!" and a one-finger salute from a little old white-haired lady.

At the front of the station, she skirted around the gas pumps and headed for the back garage bay and then approached it cautiously at an angle. The sun was bright, and she was getting warmer. She needed to see who was around. She lingered by the tire rack next to the air pump and squinted into the open garage. At first, she thought no one was there, and then she saw Tommy leaning over a fender of a blue car doing something. She waited a few minutes and determined that he must be alone. She quickly slid into the garage around the edge of the door and was standing next to him in a minute. His head popped up, and he said, "Karla, why aren't yo in school?"

And he looked at his watch. It was 8:35 a.m. She just shrugged her shoulders and smiled brightly at him. He said, "You know, Karla, it is important to go to school. Or you will end up like me, an auto mechanic. Just grease, dirt, and cuts."

She kept smiling, and he kept on yammering about going to school. Then he finally ended it. He resumed his work again but then stopped. Looking over his shoulder, he asked, "Yo hungry, kid?"

She vigorously nodded in the affirmative. He said, "I can't get yo a taco right now, but here's a couple of bucks. Go on over to the sandwich store and get yourself something." He shoved his greasy hand into his pants pocket and pulled out the crumpled bills. He handed them to her. He dipped in again, deeper, and followed up with some change. She took the three bills, which felt cool and damp. The change was three quarters. She just smiled and said thanks and ran off toward the sandwich store.

When she got there, she fished in her jeans and found another seventy-five cents, two quarters, two dimes, and a nickel. She ordered a half sandwich with everything on it, and it cost her $3.99 with tax. She sat in the back of the store in a corner booth. She placed the large sandwich on the table on top of a large white paper napkin. She got a warm cup of water, and that was her breakfast feast. She liked to take her time eating. She ate with very small bites, chewed long, and drank lots of water to wash it down. The store manager glared at her, but there were not many customers, so he said nothing to her. It took her a full hour to eat three-fourths of her sandwich. The remainder she carefully wrapped in napkins and hid in one the smaller zipper pockets of her backpack. One of her homeless friends had advised her to always save something for rainy-day emergencies.

When she was done, she cleaned up all the trash she had made and brushed off the seat. Her third foster mother had been very strict on making sure one cleaned up after themselves. She had been good at that. Karla was a quick learner, but it took her five missed dinners before she was able to clean up to Mrs. Macelwane's standards. After that, she didn't miss her dinner, but frequently, it was not that much to eat. Mrs. Macelwane said little girls should be slender and quiet. Karla was slender enough but had a lot of trouble with quiet. She liked to talk, and Mr. Macelwane liked to talk. So he would, and she would listen to him. That would not last long since Mrs. Macelwane always had yet another job for both her husband and Karla to do. Mrs. Macelwane was a believer in keeping busy and minimizing frivolous talk.

Mr. Macelwane died in an automobile accident on the way to work shortly after Karla had been sent to stay with them. Mrs. Macelwane descended deep into her grief and suddenly decided to move away. She just deposited Karla back at the county office, like an unwanted shirt she decided to return to Wal Mart. She didn't even have to produce a receipt!

As she pulled the backpack higher on her shoulder, she realized that she now had to pee after drinking all that water. She felt she no longer could linger in the sandwich shop, so she walked out briskly and gave the manager a big goodbye smile. He only briefly looked disgustedly at her with an unchanging face and no hint of a smile. She walked down the line of stores to the small Chinese restaurant. It was not open of course. She checked for anyone watching her and determined it was safe, so she moved behind the restaurant after walking to the end of the row of small stores.

She located the dumpster that was directly behind the store, pushed up to the back wall of the restaurant. She looked all around again, listened for any noise, and quickly climbed up onto it. As she stood unsteadily and moved about on the lid, it groaned and shifted slightly. She had learned that they didn't lock the back window of the store because it was so small. It was only about eighteen by twelve inches. The waitresses opened it when they were sneaking a smoke and didn't bother to lock it again when they closed it.

She could just squeeze through it and spend all the time she needed doing her morning toilet. She pushed it open, dropped her backpack on the floor, and snaked herself through it. She had a little trouble with her boobs but made it into the restroom. Sometimes, women left or forgot toilet items on the shelf above the sink that she could use. She frowned because today it was clean. At least, it was a clean restroom that had nice soft toilet paper.

She pulled open her jeans, and her pink underwear showed. Her underwear, which was her favorite pair, was a pink color that was getting very thin in many places. She liked the color and had been trying to make them last. She touched the little pale purple flowers that covered the cotton fabric. She had stolen them from a Wal-Mart months ago. That had been a phase she and several of her friends went through. When they found out that another student in their class, Addie Hill, got caught and was sent to the county jail for six months, they decided that they would not do that again. They took an oath to never steal anything again – from a store. Maybe she would talk her granny into buying her some new ones, maybe several pairs of them so she wouldn't have to wash them so often.

She dropped them to her ankles and squirmed into a comfortable position on the cold toilet seat. She proceeded to stain and strain. Finally, a few small turds dropped into the big porcelain toilet bowl with little plopping sounds.

Then she peed to her great relief. She used extra toilet paper to wipe her butt clean and dry between her legs. Now that the seat was warm, she just sat there and relaxed.

She got tired of that quickly and, jumping up, pulled up her panties and jeans. She had to do a little wiggle dance to get the jeans up over her hips. She zipped them up and turned and flushed it all away. *If only life were like that!* she thought. *When you are tired of it, just flush it away.* She reflected on that idea for a moment and then washed her hands at the sink using a nice liquid soap provided by the store management that smelled like oranges.

She dried them on some scratchy paper towels she pulled from the wall container. Then she turned the cold water on hard and waited a few minutes and then scooped several handfuls into her mouth. It was cold and good. She ran her damp hands though her long blonde hair and tried to finger brush it into some sort of style. It was now just shoulder length. She had worn it short and long over the years, mostly dependent upon the whim of her current foster parents. She kind of liked it the way it was now.

She would really like to get it washed and trimmed at a beauty parlor like all the other girls were always talking about doing. She had never had that done to her hair. Once Mrs. Wizer, an old lady neighbor, had washed her hair in her backyard and put some large old-fashioned curlers in it. Karla was ashamed of them and was very glad that none of the girls from school came by and spotted her. When she was done, she had to admit that it did look nice and shiny and rather stylish.

Mrs. Wizer got sick later in the week and passed away from too much smoking, the neighbors said. Another time, when she was just fifteen, a girl she was best friends with, Jenny-Sue, got some hair dye from another girl; and they both dyed their hair purple. That got everyone's attention and, unfortunately, a lot of days grounded as well as an endless harangue about the mess they made in the girl's bathroom. Jenny-Sue's mother had her head shaved and sent her to a "special camp" for the remainder of the year. She never saw her again. Karla just let the hair color wear itself out and returned to being a blonde.

She used a wet paper towel to clean her armpits and wipe her face. Then she pulled out several more to dry herself. Watching her image closely in the mirror, she critically assessed it and was finally satisfied with her look. She liked to look in mirrors at herself. She had a small mirror in her pack, but it was not nearly big enough. She briefly thought of putting on some makeup but passed on that. She had only a little left, a few scraps of odds and ends she scrounged up somehow. Anyhow, she didn't need to look glamorous today. She had a special lip gloss she really liked called Pouty Pink, and she had used most of it up. Her friend Gladys had given her some of her old extra makeup, and that was in it.

She slowly turned from side to side and then looked at herself over first her left shoulder then her right shoulder. She struck several poses similar to the models she saw in the TV news coverage about fashion events. She felt she would be really beautiful one day, even if old Mrs. Natact told her she was ugly inside and added that she was ugly both inside and out. Of course, in addition, just for good measure, she added that unless she found Jesus, she would always be so. Mrs. Natact made outstanding scrambled eggs but was always bugging you when you ate with wild stories about God and Jesus and eternal damnation. It was hard to put up with it even if you got a second egg.

She pulled the loose sweatshirt tight in the back, and her rather ample breasts emerged like an evil twin curse. She thought they were nice at first when they budded on her rather thin chest, but they had been nothing but trouble since they first appeared.

"My god! It had been only eight months when they were big enough for the boys to come sniffing around," she exclaimed to herself. Thanks to them, she got her arm broken and several teeth kicked out.

It all happened last fall when Marco Decaro started to hang around her locker talking to her. He was cute and nice. He kept asking her to go for ride with him in his brother Tony's car. She was shy and afraid of him, so she put him off. Her few school friends envied her and told her to go out with him. They said he was a great catch, and his brother's car was really 'stone cold'. She had decided to agree the next time he asked. Then she daydreamed about what it would be like if he kissed her. Daydreaming was an important part of her life. But before she talked to him again, she was attacked.

Marco's current girlfriend and five of her heavyweight Chicano sisters caught her in the school crapper. Immediately, when they walked in on her, they screamed curses down while pounding her to the ground. They continued screaming at her and kicking her until she passed out. Someone had danced on her left arm and had broken it in two places. She bet it was Glory. That bitch weighed in at two hundred pounds at least.

A substitute teacher found her and took her to the school nurse who patched her up until the emergency ambulance arrived. The ride with the siren blaring was exciting. She had to spend several days in the St. Margret's Mercy hospital since one of her eyes was so badly damaged they thought she might lose her vision in that eye. Her foster parents showed up and were angry about the cost and inconvenience of the incident. They complained that now the caseworker was asking them lots of questions about her care and that of the other three children whom they also took care of for the state. One of them had been run over when a neighbor had backed out of their drive and was almost killed three months ago.

She liked the hospital once the pain was gone. She had a nice bed, clean sheets, and no chores to do. She could watch TV and drink soft drinks all day. She had always loved Dr. Pepper and got a ton of them there. She could daydream and enjoy all her fantasies about being a doctor someday. Marcy, one of her passing friends, came by and filled her in on what happed at the school since her beating. Someone saw who did it and reported it to the principal. The police got involved, and later, two of the girls were expelled but not the one who instigated it. She was still there, waiting for another go at Karla and bragging how she was going to cut her next time.

Karla then used all her acting skills gained over her brief life of survival. She feigned abject horror going back to "that school" and convinced her caseworker to move her to another family that would put her in a different school district. When she was released, she was relocated. She started to go to the new high school, but as soon as she did, the boys were really hanging around.

She met an older girl named Mary Beth in her history class who smoked and did drugs. She invited Karla and several other girls over to her house, and they had some pizza and smoked weed. Karla had not really smoked much and thought it was little strange but tried it. Unfortunately, Mary Beth's parents had gone to the movies and left them to their own devices. Then she regaled them with tales of all her sexual adventures. Mary Beth also bragged about how many boys she had sucked off and when and with whom. They were excited and couldn't believe their ears.

She even said she had done the junior track coach last year. Mary Beth then taught them all how to do blow jobs using bananas. Karla found it a little awkward but not hard to learn. One of the girls decided to give it up and just ate her banana. They all had a good laugh at that. Mary Beth congratulated Karla on her technique. Since then, this one skill probably saved her poor, ragged ass more than anything else she knew.

Now when some guy got too hard to handle, she would offer to suck him off or give him a hand job, and he would not only let her but thanked her afterward. She had learned how to do hand jobs when she was only ten, and one of her many foster fathers taught her in the garage. She thought it was a little stupid but was fascinated with how excited they got when she did it, the big squirt as she thought of it. The foster parent who taught her allowed her to do it to him quite frequently, giving her plenty of on-the-job training. Unfortunately, her foster mother caught them one afternoon, and Karla went back to the county that night.

Giving blow jobs was also an easy way to make some fast money. After her first one with a sixteen-year-old in his bedroom, it became easy since she never thought about what she was doing but always daydreamed about being a doctor. She somehow equated it with being a doctor, helping patients feel better. She actually thought that boys were idiots who just needed to be relieved. She only did it as the last resort to make money or, certainly, to escape being raped again.

Finally finished, she checked her backpack to make sure everything was in the right place and, standing on the back of the toilet, hoisted it and herself out the window. She turned and carefully let it close behind her. She dropped off the dumpster. Absentmindedly, she dusted off her clothes as she walked toward the front of the shopping center. She found an old chair by the side of the Stater Bros. store and sat down briefly. Then she got a great idea when she saw an old man toss an empty soda can into the trash barrel.

She was up and on it. It was right on top. She had to pick it out and then shook it dry. Looking around more, she located a large plastic bag. She dropped the can inside. She also found a short stick to poke around in the trash barrel and located three more cans and two large plastic bottles. She fished them out and moved on. Karla spent a good two hours moving from trash barrel to trash barrel, ferreting out more aluminum cans and plastic bottles. At about eleven thirty, she had over thirty empties.

She now had her large bag of empty cans and bottles and her backpack. It was time to find Crazy Old Mary for her big payoff. Crazy Old Mary was a homeless woman who pushed a cart all around Moreno Valley, collecting things no one else wanted. She also would buy aluminum cans and plastic bottles from Karla at the rate of four cents for cans and eight cents for bottles. Karla sort of liked Crazy Old Mary but was afraid of her. Every once in while, she would get very angry and shout and threaten everyone. She had been known to even pull out a scissor, waving them over her head as she yelled at you. This was enough to send people on their way.

No one had every seen her hurt anyone. But who knows with old homeless people? Karla counted her trove three times and finally was coming up with about the same number each time. Karla was not really good at math or reading or any other school skill for that matter. She could play volleyball well, and all the kids wanted her on their team usually. Anyway, she guessed she had a good two dollars' worth of empties and needed to get the cash.

She looked around the shopping center but did not spot Mary shuffling about on the fringes. In front of the doughnut shop, she ran into Bill and Binder. They were a couple of dropouts she knew slightly. They had their skateboards and were eating some doughnuts. She asked them, "You seen Crazy Mary today?"

Bill just kept eating, and Binder stopped and wiped his mouth and said, "Nah. Whatcha want the old loon for?"

He spewed doughnut particles out of his mouth since he was missing some teeth. He, however, also held out the bag of doughnuts to her, offering her one. She gave him a slight smile and pulled one out quick and started to nibble at it. They were jelly filled, and she liked to take her time in reaching the sweet jelly heart. They all walked along for a few minutes, not speaking. Then Karla said, "I have to find Mary."

"Whatever," came their reply. They were not interested in her or Mary, and she just turned and went in another direction. At the gas station, she hung out for a few minutes, but there was no sign of Mary. She crossed the street and headed over to a field just behind the fancy new drugstore. There were some high bushes in the far corner were Mary camped. She approached them, and she heard some dogs growling, but they ran off when she appeared.

She pushed under the front bush and saw Mary's home full of junk, clothes, and some pillows – but no Mary. She looked around a few minutes but didn't see anything worthwhile. She sat down on a pillow and waited. She found a torn magazine with some pictures of woman doctors talking about breast cancer. That set her mind off on her lifelong dream.

She closed her eyes and saw herself in a white smock with a shiny stethoscope. She was going to be a doctor. She had seen *Dr. Quinn, Medicine Woman* at Mrs. Moses's home when she lived with her for a while. Mrs. Moses smelled like a dog and had several around she slept with. She loved watching TV and didn't do much about cleaning her house. Mrs. Moses was supposed to take care of Karla and Steven, who was about seven; and after a meager dinner, the three of them always watched her fading old TV until bedtime. Karla loved Dr. Mike and wanted to be just like her.

Her plan was to become a nurse first and then work her way up to being a doctor. Then she would save people and be loved by all the townsfolk. She sometimes got tired of repeating the dream but knew in her heart it would happen. She departed the camp to continue on her search.

It was almost one thirty, so she walked down the street toward the Moreno Valley Library. It was closed due to some problem, but a lot of her friends hung out in the back sometimes. She got near it in time to see a group of boys leaving in a hurry and figured it was not the time to go back there and returned back up the street. In the dentist's building, she got some water from a drinking fountain before one of the clerks noticed her and chased her off. She cut through a yard and found Mary upended, her head half inside a garbage barrel. She was going through someone's garbage with her bare hands. Karla called out, "Hey, Mary!"

Mary didn't respond, not really, but finished her search and emerged triumphant with several aluminum cans. She quickly dropped them into her black trash bag and squinted hard at Karla.

"Wha you wan, child?"

"I have empties for you."

"Why?"

"You say you will pay for them."

"Yeah, how many ya got?"

"Dozens."

Mary snatched the bag from Karla's grasp. She opened it wide and poked her head and then hand into it, checking the goods. Mary squinted at her again, turned her back to Karla, and seemed to be digging around in her clothes. She finished and triumphantly faced Karla. She held out a crumbled dollar bill and some change. Karla grabbed it all, and Mary grabbed the empties.

Her business was done, and Mary moved away in a not-too-friendly way. Karla jammed the money in her pocket, waved goodbye, and backed out of the yard.

Mary was on her quest and could not be bothered with small talk. Karla now had the afternoon to herself but had nowhere to go. She had hoped to run into a few of her friends, but they were not around today. She hung out at a park for a while and then headed back toward the shopping mall. She could tell from the clock in the service station that it was now almost four.

She went into the dry cleaners and got four quarters for her dollar. She searched around for a pay phone. She located the only working pay phone in the area, which was by the service station. As she dialed the number, she saw many people in the mall with cell phones talking easily to heir friends. She never had a cell phone in her life.

She listen to the money rhythmically cling into the pay phone and dialed for her grandmother who lived in Apple Valley. She had put in enough change to make a collect call. It went through, and her grandmother's voice said, "Hello. Karla honey, is that you sweetie?"

"Yes, Granny."

"Why aren't you in school, honey?"

"School is over now, Granny. It gets out at three o'clock."

"Oh well, how you doing then?"

"Not real good, Granny. I ran away again."

"Oh sister, what is the matter with you? You gots to stay in one palace and get an education. How you ever going to be able to get a good job?"

"I can't live there. It is too much hassle. They bug me, and the man looks at me strangely all the time. He's real creepy." This always got Granny's sympathy running. Granny didn't trust mens – as she called them – no way, no how.

"Well, where are you living then?"

"Nowhere actually."

"Oh land, Karla, when will you get some sense?"

"Don't know, Granny. Can I came and live with you again?" There was a long dead period.

"Well, honey, that is a little hard, you know, with Clive being sick and Henry losing his job again. We ain't got much room nor food anymore."

"Oh, Granny, I will help you garden. And I will not eat much food. I can be real good, Granny. You know I can!" she pleaded for another chance.

"Oh, I don't know. You always seem to get people all riled up, honey."

"I know, but I can be good. Remember last year? I was real, real good."

"Yes, child, you were. Can you get yourself up here?"

"No, Granny, I need some money to buy the bus ticket."

"Wilma and Shorty went to Vegas and won't be back until tomorrow morning. Can you go by their house tomorrow and get money from Wilma?"

"Oh yes, Granny, sure can!" She was very pleased with that idea.

"Well, I will call them on their cell phone and tell them to give you enough for the bus ride and a little lunch. Now you ask Wilma to drop you off at the bus station. If you get the ten o'clock bus, it would get you here by early afternoon, and we will see what we can work out."

"Oh, Granny, thanks! I am tired of this dump of Moreno Valley. I can't wait to see you, Granny!"

"Love you, Karla. Be good and careful now."

The phone clicked off at the other end.

Karla fished out the returned coins from the call and put them carefully in her pocket. Now Karla was really happy. She liked her granny. It was just all the riffraff she allowed to hang around that she got in fights with. Her granny had a strong religious leaning and brought all types of strangers home to minister to them. They came, and they went, but seldom did they do much to help Granny. While she was very happy with the agreed-upon plan, Karla now had another eighteen hours to kill before being on her way to Apple Valley to stay with Granny.

She headed out toward the mall area across the street. She went behind the buildings and checked out the action. There were several stray cats slinking about but no garbage cans with any tempting food falling out. She was walking behind the SUBWAY sandwich store when someone came out of the back door. He leaned against the wall and lit up a cigarette. He was an older man who looked tired and dirty. He pulled off the plastic gloves he wore when he made sandwiches and, leaning with his head back, blew smoke out into the air and sucked hard on the cigarette. He was so busy enjoying his break, he didn't even notice her until she moved a little. He squinted at her and said, "Hey, kid, whach you do here?"

"Nothing."

"Yeah, sure."

He inhaled and exhaled more smoke and seemed to relax.

"You looking for some food maybe?"

"Well, suppose I am."

"None of my business," he continued to enjoy his cigarette. He had on an apron covering his white shirt and jeans. The apron was stained and dirty. His shoes were old and scuffed. She watched him for few moments more and started to move past him toward the next business. He asked her, "You hungry, kid?"

"What if am?"

He finished his cigarette, and tossing the butt on the ground, he looked at her for few long minutes and then said, "You wait here, and I make you sandwich." And he disappeared into building. She froze in place and prepared to run. In less than three minutes, he was back with a white bag. He just waved it at her from the door, and when she approached cautiously and took it, her thanks was cut off by the door slamming. She went down the back of the building until she located a low retaining wall, and she sat on it and explored the contents of the heavy bag. It was a hoagie sandwich with all the trimmings and several bags of chips and even a big chocolate chip cookie wrapped in cellophane. To top it off was a cold can of Dr. Pepper!

"Wow! This is really my lucky day!"

She first ate the cookie slowly while daydreaming of the last time she had stayed with Granny. Her visit went well enough until one her church friends started to go after her about finding Jesus. Then she freaked out and started screaming. They called the emergency room, and they came and got her.

After much time wasted in tests, they determined she was not taking her medicine. They knew her from previous visits over the years. She had a slight split personality or something and had some heavy meds that she was supposed to take every day. She didn't like them and sold them to some guy, telling him they were painkillers.

She had spent the money on ice cream and a movie. Her granny had a fit when she got her home. She scolded Karla and told her if she didn't take the medicine they gave her, then she would end up in the nuthouse, and she wouldn't like that much. Karla didn't like that idea, so she took them but decided to leave that night and return to find her mother in Moreno Valley.

As long as she could remember, they had always been pushing pills in her, and they really didn't seem to do anything to help her. Sure, every once in the while, she got really scared and started to scream bloody murder. If they just let her be, she would eventually just fall down and cry herself out of it. They were the ones who made a big deal out of it. It was nothing as far as she was concerned.

Unfortunately, when she got back to Moreno Valley, her mother had moved. No one seemed do know where. She had just disappeared. No one had a trace of her whereabouts. The police picked Karla up several days later, identifying her from her past records, and she ended up in another county foster home.

She nibbled ever slowly on the sandwich and reflected on all her foster homes and parents. There had been so many now that she couldn't remember them all. She certainly remembered the bad ones and could remember two good ones, but the rest were just a blur of angry voices, strange faces, and demanding people. Most of the foster parents just wanted the money paid by the county and were seldom interested in the kids other than to have someone fetch and clean for them.

After a full hour, she finished two-thirds of the sandwich and carefully wrapped the remainder in the paper bag and stuffed it in a side pocket of her backpack. She could eat it later or first thing in the morning. She now had two backup meals! As she sat there, a dark mangy dog came moseying down the alley. She watched it sniff and shuffle down toward her. She called it, but it only snarled and scurried away.

The sun was going down gradually, and it was a little cooler. She hopped off the wall and headed toward the park on JFK. It was early, but that was all right. She just needed to hang out now only until morning. It would take her some time to get there anyway. It was blocks away.

When she got there, she sat at a picnic table and watched a family nearby having a real picnic. The father – a heavyset, bearded man – was busy cooking on a small grill. The mother – a well-stuffed, dark-haired woman – was warning the two kids every other minute to keep them safe.

Karla tried to remember having a picnic with her family or anybody for that matter but could not. She had some good birthday parties at her friend's homes when she was in grade school and had some friends but never a picnic. She waited for the family to finish, pack up, and leave.

She noticed an older couple walking their dog, and then when they moved on down the street, she went to the back of the park and slipped under a heavy bush and crawled into the hiding place, dragging her backpack behind her.

I was like a little cave under several bushes, and there were a lot of dirty newspapers and worn blankets all strewn about. The bushes backed up against a retaining wall, so it was private and cozy with only one way in. She had spent lots of time there in the past. Only a few kids ever knew about it. Now many of them had moved on, gone to juvie, or disappeared, she guessed.

She lay on her backpack and looked up into the dark green leaves. It was getting a little darker, but she could still see bits of the blue sky way above her. She wondered if it went all the way to heaven. Granny talked a lot about heaven, and it seemed like a good place to be. She would like to be in a good place for a change. She would definitely be after she became a doctor. She would be a doctor, take care of Granny, and help people. They would all love her for her good works and healing love. That was her dream to be doctor. Her backpack was crammed with all her possessions, and she a had picture of a group of women doctors at a meeting she had torn from a *Time* magazine in the school library years ago. She liked that picture and almost dug it out but was too comfortable just daydreaming.

She rolled over and unzipped a compartment. She pulled out an old stuffed blue dog. It was worn bare in many spots, and its eyes and nose were long gone. You could still see its mouth lines though. His name was Wallace. Her mother had given it to her when she was very little before she disappeared. She had only seen her three times since then, and she always missed her. Granny told her that her mother, Caroline – that is what Granny called her – was not right in the head and ran around with a tough crowd, so she couldn't keep her daughter with her, or so she said. Karla put the dog on her cheek and rubbed herself slowly with it, closing her eyes and trying to remember what her mother looked like.

It was hard for her. There was only a vague outline of a shape and a slight smile. She never even heard anyone talk about her dad. She hadn't even known that there were dads until she was in the third grade when the other girls kept asking her what her dad did. She finally got mad and had hit one in the head, and that made her even more of an outcast at the school. It was a thing that often happened to her over the years. She was used to it, but others were definitely not. When she got real mad at being harassed or bullied by someone, she just hit them hard. She didn't like hitting other people, but that at least shut them up.

Anyway, that is how she learned that normal families had both mothers and fathers and that she had neither – then or now. She fell asleep and later was awakened by some rustling of the bushes. Suddenly, a head popped into the cave. It was Arty. Arty was a punker who hung around the same areas she did. He was rather slow and really harmless, but sometimes, he smelled since washing was not a priority with him or his crowd. Most of the kids laughed at him and would not talk to him. He had been nice to her several times, sharing food and money, so she tolerated him for short periods. She was not happy he was there, but she couldn't do much about it now.

"Hey."

"Arty, what's happening?"

"Just chilling."

"Oh, you in school?"

"Nah, I ran away and am looking for a job. Then I am going to get a killer skateboard and head to LA."

"Doing what?"

"Whatever."

"Well, how is your mom doing?"

"She left for Vegas with some neighbors. I'm free for the weekend."

"Shut up! Whatcha doing here then? Go home and veg out on that big leather couch of your mom's and watch the tube."

"Can't."

"Why?"

His face looked rather silly and he answered,

"Lost the key and can't get in any of the windows."

"No way! You're kidding me! You are locked out of your fucking house?"

"Yeah, so I thought I could hang out on the street."

"Well, that isn't much fun." She inhaled deeply, and he smelled OK, which was definitely a good sign.

"Well, I have a house to stay at tonight, but I thought you might want to go with me," he defensively bragged.

"Me? Why?"

"Well, a couple of guys have a rad pad in a vacant house on Cactus. They are having a party with pizza, beer, and everything. And they said I could crash there if I brought along some chicks."

"I am only one chick, Arty."

"I now. But that should work, don't you think?"

"Who are these guys?"

"Just some guys. One of them works at the Pizza Kitchen. They both hang out there and have seen you hanging around."

"Oh, pizza. Are you sure?"

"Straight on."

"Arty, I am fixed for the night. I'm staying right here." She pounded the ground next to her for emphasis.

"C'mon, Karla, I need you to do this for me, huh," he whined.

She felt a little sorry for him. He was so stupid and took so much shit from everyone, and now he had locked himself out of his own house. What a total loser!

"Look, let's go to your house and smash a window, and you will be home free," she suggested.

"Oh no, can't. Can't do that. Mom put in alarm system." He seemed truly frightened by her idea. "Look, Karla, all you have to do is go with me, get me in, and have some pizza and then cut out."

"Come on, Arty, give it a rest. Besides, it is fine here. No one will bother you but the ants."

"Ants!" He jumped up and looked around. His pants were falling down, and she saw ugly green-and-blue boxer shorts. She definitely said the wrong word.

"Karla, I wont ever ask you to do anything again. Please. I am not designed for the outdoors."

"Well, where is this place?"

"Only a couple of blocks from here, on the corner of Cactus and Perris."

"You sure these guys are OK? You hang with them?"

"Sure, they're golden. They give me pizza and stuff all the time."

"Well, I am comfortable here and will be going away in the morning, so I will just have to pass this time."

"Nah, come on. I don't like the grass, and this park at night. Let's just go over, and at least, we will be inside and get some good pizza."

"Pass, Arty, you go ahead."

"They won't let me in without you or some girl."

"Wow, do I feel honored. No way, Arty! Go home and break a window."

"Way."

"What's these guys names?"

"Frank and Rex."

"Where you met them?"

"At school last year. They both dropped out this year and got jobs. They used to have an old car, but it got stolen or something."

"Something? They wreaked the fucker!" she laughed at him. Kids were always wreaking their cars.

"Don't know."

"Well, you have fun with the guys, Arty. I will send you a postcard when I get to my grandma's."

"C'mon, go over with me. You got nothing else happening. We can have some warm pizza. and then you can split. They won't let me in without bringing you."

"Arty, that's shit! That is just plain old shit!"

"No no. I know these guys. They like girls, and they want to have a party. So tonight, they need some girls."

"When you see them last?"

"Yesterday."

"Why tonight? What is so special about tonight?"

"I don't know. Look, I lost the key this morning, so I need a place to hang tonight. I am really afraid outside." She felt his wave of fear and realized he was only a poor, stupid kid who had lost his door key.

Karla looked at the pitiful boy. He had on low-riding shorts too big for his narrow ass and a wrinkled tee shirt that looked like shit. He wore a strange hat that he had with the brim in the back and his face was full of old purple pimples. She felt a little sad that he had no place to go although it was his own stupid fault as usual. What a stupid shit he was!

"Lots of pizza?" she asked to give him some hope.

"Oh yeah, they work at Papa John's and make three to go when they close up at night. They are loaded with other stuff too!"

"I thought you said Pizza Kitchen?"

"Pizza Kitchen, Papa Johns, dono – its one of those. They always have pizza is all I know for sure, for sure!" She had had such a great day. She was going home to Granny tomorrow, and she really just wanted to wait it out. However, he was so stupid that she had to help him out one last time. Besides, she really did like pizza.

She finally said, "Well, OK, but I won't stay long – just to get you in, and then I am long gone. That clear to you?"

She had hurriedly put her dog away when he entered the cave. She double-checked, finding it was in a zippered pouch. She grabbed the backpack strap, and they both crawled out from the safe hiding place. Arty followed her. Once out, they stood and dusted themselves. Arty was all smiles, and he waved her down the street. They headed down the street; they cut over a few blocks and finally approached the corner of Perris and Cactus.

Arty was very animated and talkative and was telling her about the time last year he lost his mother's car keys when she was in bed with the man from next door. He was so mad at his mom that he had intended to drive off to Florida to visit his dad. He got a good licking from her after that.

It was little darker than normal for seven or eight at night since there were clouds in the sky. She saw several boarded-up houses off to the side. They went over to them but stood under a tree nearby for some cover. The sun was dropping but fast; however, the clouds darkened the area even more. She sat down on her backpack, and he just sort of wandered around, looking for something. He had trouble staying still.

"Well, some party! Where are they?" she asked sarcastically.

"They be here. Just wait." Arty was dancing about, his eyes darting in every direction.

They waited a full thirty minutes more, and she was tired of it. Arty was very nervous. She rose suddenly and announced, "Arty, you got the wrong night. I am going back now."

"No, don't! They will be here – honest."

Just then, he spotted two boys ambling toward them.

"There they are!" he exclaimed and pointed them out.

She was disappointed and not impressed by what she saw approaching. They didn't seem to have anything in their hands. They both waited for them under the tree. They were dressed in old dirty clothes. Like Arty, their pants hung down, and their ugly boxer shorts showed. As they neared, the taller one said, "Arty, my man. What's happening?"

She watched as they did a silly hand-slapping routine.

"Nothing, bro, just looking for a place to crash. Where's the party?"

"Yeah, what bout her?"

"She just came along to get some pizza."

"They be her soon. The Hook went to get some beer for us."

"Watcha your name, honey?"

"Karla. Who is Hook?"

"Who? You the Karla from Canyon Springs High School?"

"Used to be there, but I have been to all of them."

"I heard some dark stories 'bout you." He was leering at her too as the other smaller boy acted like a puppy, jumping around at his feet.

"Well, don't believe everything you hear." She didn't care for these two. They were definitely not nice people. *Arty better go home and break a window rather than hang out here*, she thought to herself.

Then an old pale pink Ford pulled into the dirt driveway. It was stained and tired and blowing a lot of exhaust. She did like pink however. The driver stopped and turned it off, but it keep sputtering for a few last moments.

He emerged. He was a tall thin man with dark tattoos all over his left arm. He had a sad narrow mouth. He asked, "What's this?"

"We here for the party," Arty blurted out with a little party-dancing shuffle.

"Oh great! Help me with the food," he said to the two other boys. They jumped too and got out several pizza boxes while the driver pulled out a six-pack and then a second one.

He went up to the nearest boarded house and pushed opened the door. The car was parked near the tree closer to the other houses. They all filed into the house behind the Hook. Karla, who began to feel uneasy about this, was pushed in by Arty who was the last to enter. She immediately didn't like the house. It smelled and was dark and dirty. They lighted some big old candles sitting on the floor, and then ugly shadows danced on the mess of junk and broken things. Someone turned on a boom box, and it cried out some noise that was incomprehensible to understand but had a strong underlying beat.

They opened the beer and passed it around. Karla sat close to the door on a broken chair and took the can offered her but didn't drink any beer. After about ten minutes, they started on the pizza. It smelled great when they lifted the box lids. Karla had one with pepperoni, and it was warm and tasted great. The three boys were mumbling and laughing to one another in the back corner. Arty was just sloshing down beer, looking goofy. When Karla got up to get another piece, Hook said, "I have a better piece than that for you, Karla." And then they all laughed nastily.

She froze but managed to say, "Sure, you do, but I prefer plain cheese right now."

This got a little laughter. Hook got mad. He downed his second beer in a huge gulp, crushed the can, and bounced it off a wall. He approached her. She turned away from him, but he spun her around. She instantly knew this was going to get bad, real bad.

She saw from his eyes that he was big trouble. She held him off with her hands as she was trying to gauge the distance to the open front door. She shoved him back hard darting quickly for the open door, grabbing and dragging her backpack along. For a split second, she thought she was going to make it! Someone tripped her, and she was down on one knee, holding her backpack in her left hand. She jumped up fast, but someone grabbed her from behind, partially lifting her off the ground. She screamed and yelled, "Arty, help me! Arty! Damn it!" He was frozen in place. She smacked someone in front of her with her backpack. He cried out in pain.

Arty just stood there. His eyes were intently studying the floor. The arms holding her partially released her. Hook rushed in, grabbing her tight and trying to kiss her hard. She lashed out and kicked him in the thigh, missing his groin. He cried out and smacked her hard with his open hand. She spun to the side and tasted a trickle of blood, *Damn!* she thought. *Damn that fucking stupid Arty! Damn that fucking pizza! Now what am I into?* She was scared shitless and thought briefly about Granny and tomorrow. She realized she just had ten hours to get through, and she would be home with Granny.

She squirmed away when several hands groped her ass. She was able to twist free and again bolted for the door, but a small shadow stepped in front of it and smacked her in the stomach with a hard fist. It was over now, she knew. She yelled out, "You mother fuckers! Let me out of here! Oh damn!" Then she started to cry while continuing to yell at them all.

"Fuckers! Son bitches! Let me out of here. You shit head bastards and pricks are all alike!" It then all happened almost at once. Arty was grabbed by Rex and Frank and shoved out of the house. The door of doom slammed shut behind him, blowing out several candles, making it suddenly darker. Then six hard hands were pushing and passing her around in a circle. She struck at them, and they laughed back. Hands were ripping at her clothes. She had lost her backpack. They roughly groped her body. She screamed, "Owww! Let me alone!"

She pushed them away, squirming and twisting in horror, trying to get out. Each time she pushed one of them away, they slammed her with their fists. She jumped at the smaller boy, knocking him down. With all her might, she raked her nails across his face, scratched it, and tore his ear with her teeth. He shrieked in pain, and the others laughed. Someone hit her in the side of the head from behind, and she dropped down. She was very groggy and tried to leap up but could only stagger.

They all took hold of her and pulled her into a lying position on the floor. She couldn't see them but felt them, oh she felt them. She was fighting them hard – bucking, kicking, and squirming with all her strength on the floor. They managed to tie her hands and feet to something heavy although she strained and struggled to escape. When she was firmly bound, they stood back, and she heard the popping of cans. She was breathing heavily, exhausted, and then she erupted in ear-shattering yells, "Arrgh!"

They all fell on her and attacked her remaining clothes, ripping and tearing them off. She felt her panties stripped away. She strained to escape in desperation, but the bindings cut, and she was trapped. She was still aware of them but was trying to forget the rape that she knew was coming up fast. She tried to think of Granny's warm smile.

She suddenly tore loose one foot and took one last kick at someone's leg. She heard a cry, "You fucking bitch!" Then she felt a sharp pain in her side as she was viciously kicked – then again and again. She felt dizzy and was losing consciousness from the pain shooting through her body from the vicious kicks.

She passed out briefly. When she came to, a fleshy, smelly, wriggling body was on top of her; and she felt a jabbing sensation between her legs. Hook was raping her, and the others were laughing and groping at her naked available parts. He finished quickly and was off her. She could finally breathe but felt light-headed. Her side really hurt now. The pain was stabbing deep. She cried out "Arty, Arty! Help me for Christ's sake!" forgetting they had tossed him out of the house.

The three of them took turns with her. She bit one who tried to kiss her, and he stuffed a dirty rag into her mouth. She was struggling and moaning in anger but had a lot of trouble breathing because of the terrific pain in her side and the rag. She was frightened now that she couldn't breathe! They were suffocating her!

Much later, she came to and was lying there alone and cold. She vaguely heard the sounds of their drunken voices as they finished the rest of the beer. She had one thought. *I have to get out of there!* There was her bus to catch. Then someone came over and started to piss on her face. This infuriated her, and she got an arm lose, grabbing his prick; she twisted it, attempting to rip it off. He got away easily and swore, "You fucking whore! Goddamn you to hell!"

He fell on her stomach hard with both knees, knocking all the air out of her. Then he punched her hard in the side and face until he was too tired to hit her anymore. The pain shot into her head. Her body decided enough was enough. It was time to shut down. She passed out into the latter stages of shock. While she lay there in their piss, they got drunker and drunker. They continued mistreating her body, hitting and slapping her. She no longer was that aware of there vicious, depraved activity. When they repeatedly burned her tits with a cigarette, then matches and then heated beer cans, she moaned a little reflexively. But those violations were not much pain compared to her side, which was burning and aching so much she could only gasp to breathe.

They were so sodden they no longer could effectively get it up. In frustration, they penetrated her body with other objects. They drunkenly amused themselves by stuffing things into her vagina and ass to see how big an item they could get in. Blood was trickling from both locations. However, they quickly lost interest especially since she was no longer playing the game. After a while, all the beer was gone. The smaller one called Frank was amusing himself, cutting his name on her stomach when they all realized they had gone too far. Way too far. Hook snarled, "What the hell you doing, man? She ain't making a sound, and you are carving her up? Is she dead?"

Rex got down on the floor and put his ear up to her mouth. He was so drunk that he didn't notice the cold piss soaking into his pants. He heard short gulping sounds as she desperately sucked in the putrid air.

"Nah, bitch, she is breathing. She is good for another hundred fucks."

This brought a wild laughter from their three throats. However, they now sobered up enough to realize they had done something really bad. They looked down on the beaten, bruised, bleeding, and torn body.

Even in the deep shadows, they saw the ugly burns all over her chest and the partially carved words on her arms, legs, and belly.

They moved away form her and huddled for a quick discussion. It ended abruptly when Hook decided what to do. He sent Frank to the car. The boy returned, lugging a sloshing, half-full, beat-up gas can. They quickly splashed it around the house's trash piles, her body, and themselves. Without a signal, they left the house without looking at her. Hook struck a match and lit the trail of gasoline leading back into the house. They went running and stumbling away from the building toward the car.

Karla's soul, which had already left her physical pain behind, soared to a brighter new place. It didn't even bother to look back at the smoldering shell of a dead body that had once been hers. She barely heard the flames below. She felt no heat nor breathed any smoke nor smelled her roasting flesh. She was going to be a doctor very soon, that she was certain.

She had died at approximately three forty-five in the morning, about six and half hours after entering house and just seven hours before the ten o'clock morning bus departing for Apple Valley.

The three boys didn't turn back. They crawled in the car and pulled out fast. Only Arty saw them leave. He was afraid to go into the building because of the flames. He hid behind the bush and cried silently. He had wet his pants. The fire burned loud, long, and bright. The smoke billowed high and dark in the morning sky. The firemen arrived within ten minutes after a sleepy passing motorist had reported it on his cell phone. It still took them another fifty minutes of hard work to extinguish it.

It was much later in the early morning hours when they were cleaning up, putting away their equipment and studying the cause of the fire, that they discovered her charred body. It was burned partially but had the general shape of a person. They thought it might be a woman since it was small. They notified the policeman at the site, and he called the coroner. She was later photographed. They bagged her and took the remains to Riverside's morgue.

It wasn't until the autopsy two days later that it was determined the extent of the sadistic brutality visited on the young girl. They identified her from two fingerprints taken from her partially burned left hand. Like all foster children who are protected by the county, they had her complete fingerprint record.

## The End

Note: Kalya Lorrain Wood was found dead in a burned building on the corner of Cactus and Perris avenues in Moreno Valley on September 9, 2006. An autopsy revealed she had been tortured, raped, and murdered before the fire had been set. Three young men were later arrested for her murder. The house was demolished and the area cleared one week after her death supposedly because the owner had not previously brought it up to code. The murder scene is now a vacant lot with a lone tree standing vigil. The defendants still await their day in court.

# Index